SAN CAFÉ

ALSO BY DAVID PERLSTEIN

Fiction

Slick!

* * *

Non-fiction

God's Others: Non-Israelites' Encounters With God in the Hebrew Bible

Solo Success: 100 Tips for Becoming a $100,000-a-Year Freelancer

SAN CAFÉ

DAVID PERLSTEIN

iUniverse, Inc.
Bloomington

SAN CAFÉ

iUniverse books may be ordered through booksellers or by contacting:

iUniverse
1663 Liberty Drive
Bloomington, IN 47403
www.iuniverse.com
1-800-Authors (1-800-288-4677)

ISBN: 978-1-4759-4170-8 (sc)
ISBN: 978-1-4759-4171-5 (ebk)

Library of Congress Control Number: 2012913556

Printed in the United States of America

iUniverse rev. date: 07/28/2012

To Tom

"What's good for General Motors is good for the country."
Charles E. Wilson, president of General Motors
and Secretary of Defense designee for the Eisenhower
Administration

* * *

"Hell, I never vote for anybody. I always vote against."
W. C. Fields

* * *

"He's mad that trusts in the tameness of a wolf, a horse's health,
a boy's love, or a whore's oath."
Fool, King Lear, III, iv, 19-21

ACKNOWLEDGEMENTS

WRITING A NOVEL ESSENTIALLY REPRESENTS a solitary task. However, such an undertaking becomes much more effective with the involvement of others. I must thank my loving wife Carolyn, along with good friends Jane Cutler and Jim Shay for their comments on my work in progress and continual encouragement. Doug Kipping provided me with a magician's special knowledge of card tricks, which enabled one of my characters to conduct himself appropriately at least once as the story unfolded. Ron Eaton proofed the manuscript and also offered valuable insights into Latin American culture and the Christian Bible, which I gratefully incorporated. Tom Gehrig leant his considerable talents to designing the front cover. Finally, I cannot adequately express my appreciation to Tom Parker, an incredibly perceptive and supportive writing coach/editor/teacher. What is best about *San Café* is due greatly to Tom and in no small measure to all the others I have mentioned.

SEMILLAS

| Seeds |

1 | UNO | 1

THE SHOTS SEEMED BOTH NEAR AND DISTANT, *Capitán* Enrique Hauptmann-Hall reflected. Like voices cackling in a far corner of the house while a man tried to sleep off a night of drinking with important clients in the company of elegant whores. Assuming he actually had heard shots. Could not the late afternoon rain pelting the highlands and the unnerving jungle gloom have distorted his senses? For five months rain had fallen. Now October—presaging the end of the rainy season—had begun, but the skies offered no hint of relief. How noble yet awful the sacrifices one made in a country like San Cristo—his country and that of his fathers—where wet and dry seasons marked the passage of time, and nature stubbornly maintained its power to disrupt and destroy.

Hauptmann-Hall signaled the *sargento* to halt the patrol, stilled his breathing and listened intently to the rain splattering the jungle canopy of oak and laurel. He had only to remain calm and observant. But how was a civilized man to make sense of such wild terrain even if it provided one of the finest coffee growing environments in the world and thus the lifeblood of the nation? Thirsting for oxygen at such a high altitude, he took a deep breath to clear his head. He had only to use his reason. What then did he know? He had heard—or thought he had heard—sharp noises. Suspicious noises. And he had seen—or thought he had seen—the *sargento* just steps ahead of him cock his head.

Seeking confirmation of his suspicions—or delusions—Hauptmann-Hall glanced at his distinguished American guest.

Bobby Gatling, a retired U.S. Army lieutenant colonel who had spent most of his thirty-year career in Special Forces, stood motionless. Taking his cue from Hauptmann-Hall, he held his Beretta in his right hand, his index finger poised along the gun's barrel. Something had attracted the *capitán*'s attention. Had he missed it? True, this kind of work was a young man's game, but given his experience tracking terrorists and enemy soldiers in jungles, deserts and mountainous terrain all over the world, there was no excuse for anything to get by him. On the other hand, the highlands, as he understood it, had experienced only small, random acts of violence over the past months. If anything should have drawn attention in this jungle, it was Bobby Gatling. At six-foot-five, he towered above the patrol's soldiers, all *indígenas*—native Indians dark, short and stocky.

Hauptmann-Hall forced a smile. Perhaps he had acted in haste.

Bobby held his position a moment longer, swiveled his head then holstered his Beretta. Removing his green baseball cap, he brushed his right hand across his close-cropped, graying hair. Reflexively, he lowered his hand to his right ankle to which, as always, he'd strapped his KA-BAR fighting knife.

Hauptmann-Hall attempted to blink the moisture out of his eyes. He could not let the colonel's presence unnerve him. General Gomez had called regarding the colonel's visit the previous evening as Hauptmann-Hall prepared for bed in a village several kilometers from the brigade's base. The *sargento* had procured a house for him—hardly worthy of a man of his stature but suitable given the conditions. The men would shelter in the local school grateful to have a roof—no matter how leaky—over their heads.

Bobby nodded at Hauptmann-Hall. This was the *capitán*'s show. He was only an observer doing a favor in return for a favor he might extract from General Gomez sometime in the future. He had contacted Gomez before arriving in San Cristo the day before and agreed to the general's request that he accompany the patrol on its last day of a modest three-day field exercise—little more than a walk in the woods. As commander of San Cristo's Highlands Brigade, Gomez could prove a valuable resource given the nature of Bobby's mission. Regrettably, the task was taking its toll on his bad right knee, but the patrol would soon reach the *finca*—the coffee plantation where he and Hauptmann-Hall would spend the night.

The next morning Bobby would compliment the general on what a formidable obstacle the Highlands Brigade posed to the budding but incompetent revolutionary movement seeking to turn nearby Azcalatl National Park into an autonomous political entity. The alliance having been firmed, Bobby would return to the capital, Ciudad San Cristo, to coordinate additional security arrangements for the major American corporation that had contracted with his employer, Crimmins-Idyll Associates, global provider of paramilitary and security services.

Hauptmann-Hall, despite the colonel's seeming reassurance, raised his hand to his chest. An unknown malevolence seemed intent on sucking the air from his lungs. True, this was only a training exercise. Still, the risk of danger remained ever present in places such as this, even if the previous two days had proved uneventful.

Bobby gazed back at Hauptmann-Hall. "*¿Hay problema?*" he asked softly. Is there a problem?

Drawing upon his resolve, discipline and God-given station, which placed him above the men of the patrol—racial and social inferiors—Hauptmann-Hall willed his breathing to return to normal. He could not—would not—permit the jungle to light a fuse in the dark places of his imagination. *Sín duda*—without doubt—he had not heard shots at all. Most likely a tree—possibly several—had fallen elsewhere in or above the ravine. In the dank highlands all things rotted and became corrupt.

Hauptmann-Hall put aside his fear only to yield to exhaustion. His legs ached. His usual physical pursuits focused on golf with clients and horseback riding in the capital's wooded park on Sunday afternoons. Surely the men also would be weary. "*¡Sargento!*" he called.

The *sargento* approached. "*¿Señor?*"

"The men. We should give them a rest."

The *sargento* spread the patrol out in a circular defensive perimeter, each man within sight of the man to his left and to his right.

Hauptmann-Hall pulled down on his poncho to keep his backside dry and lowered himself to the ground. How long should the men remain here? *Finca Jiménez* with its large and welcoming main house stood somewhere on the ridge just above them. Twenty minutes pause seemed appropriate. Surely the colonel, who limped now and then, would welcome a short respite.

He set his unfamiliar M16 rifle—General Gomez declined to make newer M4s available—against a tree and reached into his small daypack. It contained his laptop and a satellite modem with which he hoped to follow the *fútbol* friendly in Montevideo between the Azcalatls, San Cristo's national team, and Uruguay. A man who did not love *fútbol*—who did not appreciate the effort, discipline and teamwork required of any successful enterprise—was not a real man. As to the rest of his equipment, one of the men carried it. The *sargento* maintained possession of the patrol's radio, rendered useless whenever they descended into a ravine.

Bobby withdrew a water bottle from the side of his own green daypack. *"¿Está bien?"* he called. Are you all right?

Hauptmann-Hall waved. All was now well indeed. What could possibly have alarmed him? Workers from the nearby *finca* tending the coffee trees? Perhaps. The spirits of the highlands so feared by the *indígenas*? Such nonsense! *Sín duda,* this altitude played cruel tricks on the minds of the savage and uneducated. Granted, the air was not as thin as atop Azcalatl, the nation's last active volcano and holy to the *indígenas*. But here a man of refined blood—German, English, Italian and Spanish forebears all affirming his pedigree—might easily mistake the clamor and din of nature—red in tooth and claw as Tennyson, if he remembered correctly, described it—for a threat.

Enrique Hauptmann-Hall was, after all, an urban sophisticate. The scion of a prominent banking family, he maintained a web of business and social connections, which included General Gomez. Understandably, he knew little of the rainforest—a dripping sea of green in which a man's boots drew sucking sounds from a drenched earth that fiercely contested his every step. What he did know—what he held as an article of faith—was that coffee, like the holy blood of *Jesús*, sustained San Cristo as a civilized nation. Cristanos, and the rest of the world for that matter, referred to their country as San Café for good reason.

He glanced again at the colonel, vigilant and yet at peace, then retreated into his poncho like a turtle into its shell. Closing his eyes, he directed his thoughts to the finca and the grand welcome that awaited him. *Sín duda*, the foreman and his workers were nearby, probably hunting deer or wild pigs. That would explain the shots—if he had heard shots. By the time the patrol deposited him at the *finca*, his hosts would have gutted their kill and placed it atop a roaring fire to provide Colonel Gatling and him with a hearty country dinner.

He deserved to celebrate. He had come through this field exercise quite well. Even heroically, given the weather. He ran a hand beneath him to make sure his poncho covered his backside, gently rocked back on his heels and sat.

A sudden chill sliced down Hauptmann-Hall's spine. With darkness approaching, would it not be wiser to leave for the *finca* now? But no, he'd promised the men their rest. If he suffered in the wet, chilled to the bone, he would bear his affliction with grace as did *Jesús*, who had died for his sins and, evidencing the magnitude of the Lord's love, for theirs. Leading a patrol of ten common soldiers represented his penance.

Enrique Hauptmann-Hall, after all, was not a professional military man. A court had perverted the law and sentenced him to a year of army service.

What offense had he committed? Why had his inquisitors dismissed the truth? In earlier, more stable times, the matter would never have gone before the court at all. But in recent years, undercurrents of discontent had arisen in San Cristo. Radical political winds whispered of treason across the nation. The Ministry of Justice lacked the courage to properly dismiss such an insignificant case. Really, no case at all. Thus three judges publicly mocked their allegiance to the fatherland by trying a member of the nation's elite as if he were some worker in a processing plant or *campesino* in the fields, the kind of men who would welcome prison for its higher standard of living.

In this, the judges proved as spineless as San Cristo's elderly president and as traitorous as the fractious National Assembly that played to the malevolent mob and flouted the interests of the upper class—patriots devoted to the nation's wellbeing.

And all because a young *indígena* girl claimed that *Señor* Enrique Hauptmann-Hall had raped her. Raped! *¡Ultrajante!* Outrageous!

Hauptmann-Hall's lawyer presented the simple facts. The girl was young—fifteen—and a recent arrival from the countryside. Yes, she possessed a sweet nature. That was why *Señor* and *Señora* Hauptmann-Hall hired her as an au pair for their three-year-old daughter. Their priest had recommended her—a favor to the girl's priest. How could they say no? And yes, she was capable with their daughter, although they had to teach her many things, such as how to cook something besides tortillas, rice and beans, and pupusas.

The girl, however, was not the innocent she seemed. She was pretty—very pretty—in a primitive sort of way. Dark skin. Long, black hair. Big, brown eyes. An almost slender nose that belied her Indian blood. And *tetas*! She practically forced him to stare at her breasts. What the judges refused to acknowledge was that the girl knew—yes, *knew*—how she stirred men's blood. No man who was a man could help but desire such a beauty.

More to the point, the girl wanted *him*. Clearly! And why would she not? *Señor* Hauptmann-Hall was a handsome man with straw-colored hair and blue eyes, a sophisticated man, a virile man of wealth and power, a man who represented everything her people could never be. He had employed her for no more than a week before he discovered that her desire matched his own. And on that Sunday afternoon when she told her mistress that she felt ill and could not take their daughter to her little friend's birthday party at the zoo while *Señora* Hauptmann-Hall would be visiting a dear friend . . .

Sín duda leftists exerted obscene pressure. They sought to sacrifice one of their betters to their primitive demigods. The judges convicted him. Yet they knew he had done nothing wrong. Thus his lawyer negotiated a yearlong interlude in the army to restore his honor. He would serve as a captain—a humble rank, but still sufficient for a man of his breeding and position. In doing so, he would endure a posting to the army base in the highlands near

Lago Azcalatl, the ice-blue lake whose waters reflected the volcano towering above it. He would live apart from wife and daughter, dedicated to safeguarding the nation in a time of brewing turmoil.

And so the *capitán* rented a lakeside house in the town of Pueblo Azcalatl with a cook, a maid plagued by warts and too fat to draw his interest, and a gardener. He had a car, of course, but no chauffer as befitted a man leading a rugged life in the hinterlands.

Each day he put on his smartly tailored uniform and then telephoned business associates and friends from his patio. Evenings, he dined in restaurants filled with Americans—a community of blonde, tanned, sleek Californians drawn to the lake and volcano on journeys of a spiritual nature. Like him, those with resources favored the restaurant at the Hotel Lago Azcalatl for its upscale fusion of Cristano, French and Lebanese dishes. Truly, *Jesús* had taken pity on him.

God was merciful in other ways. Women flocked to him—a man of the world, who knew good wine and the ways of love. Of course, he received his wife and child for one weekend each month as permitted by the court. He had always been an exemplary husband and father. And he watched *fútbol* via satellite—all the *fútbol* he wished.

General Gomez understood, taking Hauptmann-Hall under his protective wing. They spent many evenings discussing politics, business, art and women.

Then Hauptmann-Hall grew troubled. What if some people—ignorant and mean-spirited—questioned his service to the fatherland? What if they protested to the newspapers or the television or the radio, all of which evaded government controls to spew out a steady stream of falsehoods? What if they blogged on the Internet? Would it not be prudent for the general to send him on a mission? A patrol? Just one so that *Capitán* Enrique Hauptmann-Hall could clearly display his courage?

The general balked. As a matter of conscience, he could not put Enrique at risk. Incidents took place in the highlands. Not often, but every now and then.

Hauptmann-Hall insisted. As a man of honor, he refused to cower in the face of potential danger.

General Gomez demurred.

Then a gang of *indígenas* robbed the Banco Colón in nearby Maquepaque. The local police and regional *Seguridad Nacional* investigated, but the thieves disappeared into the jungle. Adding insult to injury, one of the bank's owners happened to be Hauptmann-Hall's uncle. Worse, President Quijano compromised San Cristo's sovereignty by permitting a heavily armed American paramilitary force employed by the same company for whom Colonel Gatling worked and paid for by Mobys Inc. to establish a camp near Maquepaque. They would threaten terrible violence to pacify the region as if the Highlands Brigade was nonexistent.

Several uneventful weeks after Hauptmann-Hall first broached the matter, he and the general chatted over beers on the landscaped patio at the Hotel Lago Azcalatl.

"It is time," said Hauptmann-Hall.

"Time?" General Gomez asked quizzically.

"To go into the highlands. To search for the criminals."

The general sipped from his *Cerveza* Azcalatl. "The police and *Seguridad* have not found them. The Americans have not found them. The Highlands Brigade . . . This is not our task."

Hauptmann-Hall persisted, bombarding the general with a daily barrage of pleadings. A matter of honor, he insisted, could not be ignored.

The general devised the patrol.

Hauptmann-Hall embraced the opportunity.

"So there you have it," Gomez concluded. "Two days in the field . . ."

"Three," Hauptmann-Hall countered.

"Three days in the field," Gomez assented. "But not nights. I am sure you will agree that no purpose can be served by camping in the mud like a savage."

A rustling startled Hauptmann-Hall.

The *sargento* approached. "*Señor*, it is time."

Hauptmann-Hall emitted a sigh akin to the soft hiss of a leaking tire.

The *sargento* roused the men.

Bobby stood and winced. The damp and chill had left his right knee stiff.

Hauptmann-Hall grabbed his M16.

The *sargento* led the patrol up the ravine. The trail rose steeply.

Hauptmann-Hall's feet dragged against the undergrowth. He shuddered. The rain had ceased, but vapor rose from the ground like steam from a pan filled with overheated cooking oil. The stillness unnerved him. In this green hell of canopies and thickets, a man easily could get lost forever. Or be hidden away and never found. He slowed to let several of the men pass.

Bobby stayed respectfully in the rear.

The top of the ridge appeared. It revealed the road with its welcome macadam buckling but still serviceable.

"*A la derecha*," said the *sargento*.

Hauptmann-Hall filled his lungs with the cleaner, purer air of the road. Mission accomplished. To the right—almost due west in the direction of the sun's quickening retreat—a half-kilometer stroll would take them to the finca.

"*¡Adelante!*" the *sargento* bellowed.

The patrol trudged forward.

Hauptmann-Hall hummed softly, although he could not identify the tune—perhaps something from his childhood. Soon he and the colonel would enjoy several beers followed by a hot dinner with hopefully a decent wine and most certainly excellent Cristano coffee. After retreating to his room, he would sit by the window and go online to review the highlights of the Azcalatls' friendly with Uruguay. Then he would drift off into a good night's sleep. A car would come in the morning while a truck picked up the men spending the night in the nearby workers' quarters, which would be mostly empty until a horde of *campesinos* arrived for the January harvest.

In four more weeks he would return to the capital, his reputation and honor restored. The next day, the Pope would say mass at the

National Cathedral on a stop unexpectedly added to his tour of Latin America. Hauptmann-Hall and his family would receive communion from the Holy Father as befitted their deep devotion to Holy Mother Church.

His spirit renewed, Hauptmann-Hall caught up to the *sargento* and matched him stride for stride. It would be most improper for anyone but an officer—the commanding officer—to be seen leading the patrol through the *finca*'s entryway.

The *sargento* dropped back.

Hauptmann-Hall passed through an entryway marked by piles of volcanic rocks. Iron posts supported an ironwork arc six feet above his head. Welded iron letters read, *Bienvenidos a Finca Jiménez.*

The patrol crossed a well-kept lawn in front of the main house with its pale-salmon stucco walls and red-tiled roof. When not in Ciudad San Cristo as he unfortunately was now, the owner lived there and entertained family and friends on holiday. The foreman occupied a small apartment in a semi-detached wing behind.

Hauptmann-Hall stopped and looked expectantly towards the front door.

A pronounced silence greeted him.

He shook his head, his tongue making a soft tsk-tsk. Had not General Gomez telephoned the foreman? How much was being asked of him? At a wedding in Cana, *Jesús* had fed an enormous crowd on just a few loaves of bread and two fishes. Or was he thinking of the feeding of the multitude after the death of one of his disciples? Or was it following the death of John the Baptist? Regardless, was it too much to expect that hungry patriots be welcomed with beer and pupusas?

Bobby laid his hand on Hauptmann-Hall's shoulder. *"El silencio,"* he said. The silence. He nodded towards the *sargento.*

The *sargento* sent a *cabo*—a corporal—and three men to the rear of the house.

Bobby withdrew his Beretta.

Hauptmann-Hall held his breath. Was there no end to his trials? Had General Gomez conspired with Colonel Gatling to put him through one last ordeal in order to prove his mettle?

The *sargento* led Hauptmann-Hall to the front door.

Bobby remained in the front yard with the rest of the men.

Hauptmann-Hall gripped a large iron knocker and rapped it against the door.

The silence continued.

What would General Gomez or Colonel Gatling expect him to do now? Break the door down? Have the patrol storm the house? Empty their weapons only to destroy precious private property?

He started to knock again then withdrew his hand. Clearly, the foreman and his men had gone somewhere—to the workers village or more likely to Maquepaque to buy beer and fresh bread and perhaps sweets for dessert.

Overhead, dark clouds fused together. The last vestiges of daylight hovered on the border of night.

Very well, thought Hauptmann-Hall. A man—an officer—had to take the initiative. He turned the large iron doorknob, nudged open the heavy wooden door and stepped inside. He found a lamp and turned it on. The burst of electricity heartened him. The civilized comforts of a shower, a hot meal and a good night's sleep would soon follow.

"*¡Sargento!*" cried a voice from behind the house.

Hauptmann-Hall recognized it as that of the *cabo* and stepped outside.

"*¡Sargento!*" the *cabo* called again.

The *sargento* and the men who had accompanied him jogged to the back of the house.

Bobby followed, his Beretta cocked.

Hauptmann-Hall, playing along with this unexpected but hardly intimidating piece of theater, approached. He stumbled to a halt.

Against a wall of what must have been the foreman's apartment, three bodies lay crumpled like partially emptied sacks of coffee beans.

Hauptmann-Hall's throat constricted as if gripped by a corpse's hand.

The *sargento* squatted over one of the bodies and looked up at Colonel Gatling. "Perhaps an hour, *señor*. Maybe more. I am not sure."

"Spread out!" Bobby ordered in Spanish.

The response constituted a sharp sound, like the cracking of a tree branch.

Bobby dropped to one knee. "Down!" he shouted.

The men dropped to knees and stomachs, their weapons aimed at the jungle that concealed anything or anyone from their vision.

Only Hauptmann-Hall, speechless and disoriented, remained standing. Then he raised his hand. Something warm and wet trickled down the right side of his neck. He glanced up to see if the rain had resumed.

The silence of the dead amplified the unseemly tranquility that enveloped the *finca*.

The *sargento* warily regained his feet.

The men did likewise.

"Stay down!" Bobby called.

The *sargento* looked towards his *capitán* and startled.

Hauptmann-Hall withdrew his hand. Blood covered his fingers and palm.

As he collapsed to his knees, strange, unfamiliar sounds assaulted his ears as if all the birds of the rainforest had burst into song. A crescendo rose, displaying a gusto and power he never imagined such fragile creatures to possess.

And was that Colonel Gatling leading the *cabo* and two of the men in a slow, deliberate advance towards the rainforest, their weapons firing into the shadows of night? But too late. Too late.

The *sargento* lay sprawled on the moist earth alongside four of the men as if the strange music had cast a spell upon them. But this spell took the form of bloody wounds—wounds like those of the men they had discovered. Wounds suggesting those born by *Jesús* himself on the cross.

Only as Hauptmann-Hall toppled forward did he realize that the roar that threatened to burst his eardrums had not been that of tanagers and buntings, orioles and warblers—the first arrivals from the States establishing their winter home.

Silence returned.

Now Hauptmann-Hall felt oddly detached from his body. Surely he was dead. But just as surely in just a moment—however a moment might be measured in celestial time—heaven would welcome him. There was, of course, the matter of last rites, but combat often made that impossible. *Jesús* understood this. *Jesús* understood all.

Hovering between death and everlasting life, Hauptmann-Hall found himself burdened with questions. Would his wife and daughter remember him? Would his family commission a statue to honor his heroism? Would *Jesús* truly forgive his sins—those sins, at least, of which all mortal men stand guilty in the eyes of God?

But if he was dead, why did he feel himself being turned onto his back? Why was he looking up into the face of the colonel? Or was he really looking into the eyes of *Jesús*? The sun having plunged into the distant sea, he could not be sure. He blinked twice, three times, and in doing so reasoned that he must still be alive.

He felt the pressure of the colonel's hand on his neck. "Stay down," the colonel urged. "You were lucky."

The voice of the *cabo* rose then yielded to the squawk of a radio.

Yes, he was still alive.

A chorus of birdsong—true song—burst forth from among the trees.

In that moment, as if nature sought to provide the uplifting musical score in the defining scene of a film, Enrique Hauptmann-Hall underwent an epiphany as revealing as that experienced by Paul on the road to Damascus. Luck played no role here. *Sín duda* he had been touched by the hand of God.

In spite of protests by the colonel, who seemed to be tying off a bandage, and the large, wet stain that covered the front of his trousers, Hauptmann-Hall struggled to his feet. And why should he not? *Jesús* had performed a miracle, had saved him from death.

"Half an inch," said Bobby. He shook his head. "Jesus Christ, I'm just trying to pay off my condo and my truck. I thought I was through with this."

Hauptmann-Hall spat. Had the colonel seen too much of death? Nonsense. Enrique Hauptmann-Hall scorned death. God's grace shielded him. Clearly, his entire life, including the episode with the harlot au pair, had led towards this moment. *Jesús*, through the intercession of the Virgin, had guided him towards danger then spared him. But the Lord did not simply will that he bring the bandits who had decimated the patrol and the men of the *finca* to justice, a task to which he would devote all his energy. His was a higher calling—a vocation—to defend the homeland against the greater evil that sought to destroy all that was good and pure. From this moment on Enrique Hauptmann-Hall would wage war against the enemies of San Cristo. None would find respite. Not even Satan.

2 | DOS | 2

THE STRETCH PRIUS, its dollar-bill-green exterior matched to the spouting whale logo of the Mobys Foundation, pulled into the driveway of Whitman Scharq's stucco-walled home painted the color of an enticing latte. Like all the multi-million-dollar residences perched on the hillside above China Beach in San Francisco's Sea Cliff neighborhood, it offered expansive vistas stretching from the Golden Gate Bridge—its orange-vermilion paint suggesting California's setting sun—westward along the golden headlands of Marin County, the tidal waters of the Golden Gate flowing into San Francisco Bay and the endless blue Pacific flecked by wind-whipped whitecaps.

The driver—tall, lanky and tanned with blonde hair spilling over the collar of his green blazer—sprang out and opened the rear door.

Scharq, chair of Mobys Inc., the world's largest purveyor of coffee, and head of the foundation, stepped forward.

His dinner guest, U.S. Representative Gusher Wells, a black Stetson perched on his head, emerged from the vehicle. Wells' ruddy, lined face featured the long, straight nose and prominent jaw of the rodeo star he might have been had he not been raised in the wealthy San Antonio quasi-suburb of Terrell Hills, summered on Padre Island, starred on the golf team at Texas A&M and gone directly from law school to a prestigious Houston firm before the Republican party found him a congressional seat he could occupy until Judgment Day. He removed his sunglasses to reveal the penetrating bluebonnet-blue eyes of a man who revered straight talk and detested play-actors who were all hat and no cattle.

The driver smiled.

Ever the politician, Wells nodded in return. "We got some sick surfin' on the Texas coast, you know." He withdrew a business card from his pocket. "Call me whenever."

The driver slipped behind the wheel and drove off.

Scharq extended his hand and studied his guest from head to toe. From the American-flag pin proudly displayed in the lapel of his dark blue suit coat to his black caiman-tail cowboy boots, Travis Bowie "Gusher" Wells fit every Hollywood casting director's image of a powerful, twelve-term congressman from Texas. And those were the kind of public servants Whitman Scharq appreciated. "Gusher," he said, "let me introduce you to our dinner companions."

María Skavronsky, Mobys' senior vice president for Latin America, accepted Wells' hand. Short and petite—her figure aroused envy in women half her age—she flaunted an exotic beauty combining the heritage of her Cristano mother and Russian father.

Scharq gestured to a tall, dark man of military bearing. "And this is I.A. Khan."

"*Major* I.A. Khan, sir," said the dark man. "Ph.D. Please do not confuse me with I.*Q*. Khan, father of the Pakistani bomb, because mine, sir, is a doctorate in biochemistry!"

Scharq led his guests to an expansive redwood deck and extended his right arm towards the ocean where two container ships dotted the horizon. "You have not seen the sun set until you've seen it set here where the magnificent waters of the Pacific flow beneath these majestic, untamed cliffs into the Golden Gate and beneath the glorious bridge that bears its name." He winked. "What do you think, Gusher? Should I appoint myself chief of corporate communications and give myself a raise? Our shareholders haven't been in a very generous mood of late."

"Myself," said Wells, "I'm partial to the sun settin' over a Texas oilfield. It's so . . . so goddam American. And now that we got that out of the way, how 'bout rustlin' up some drinks before dinner?"

"Jolly well spoken," commented Khan.

Wells searched María's espresso-brown eyes. "Y'all ever seen a Texas sunset, Miss Skavronsky?"

"Well, I'm a California girl," María offered. She rose up on her toes, hinting at the extensive training that had led to two seasons with a small modern-dance company between her undergrad years at Stanford and Harvard Law. "I was barely three when we came here from San Cristo."

Scharq imagined himself lifting María like one of those well-muscled dancers she'd performed with. He was, after all, a big man—six-feet-one and two hundred thirty pounds. Like many big men, he despised smallness. Whitman Scharq dreamed big. Spent big. Ate and drank big. He also had very big things in mind, which with help from Gusher Wells would reverse some of the bad luck that had dogged him of late.

"I appreciate the invite," said Wells. He slipped his sunglasses back on.

"I heard you were in town," Scharq replied. "Although I can't imagine what would bring a man like you to San Francisco."

"I'd rather be back in Houston. Got us a golf tournament at the country club. But there's lots on my plate. And talkin' 'bout plates, I don't suppose y'all invited me to dinner just to be sociable, Whit. Not that I don't count Mobys as a real friend."

Scharq threw his right arm around the congressman's shoulders. He considered offering a gentle hug. Down deep, he was an affectionate man belying the nickname jealous competitors and the vindictive media gave him—the Great Whit Scharq. But not wishing to be misunderstood by Wells, whose voting record reflected an unswerving devotion to family values, he lowered his arm. "Just thought you'd like to know I'm flying down to San Cristo in the morning. María and I.A. are coming with me. Important business."

"As it happens, I'm headin' down to Rio in a couple weeks," said Wells. "Wish I could take the missus, but this is gov'mint business."

"Rio's quite a town," said Scharq.

"Beats Ciudad San Cristo any day. The way I understand it, things seem to be a little dicey down in San Café."

"Not to worry. María's got people in place . . . Americans . . . to see that things go our way."

Wells glanced at María. "So I hear."

Scharq raised his face towards the sun hovering above the edge of the sea like a hang glider. Wells' key role on the Energy and Commerce committee and heavy involvement in Latin American policy on the Foreign Affairs committee made him a valuable friend. Or foe. "And of course, Gusher, our business in San Cristo involves *your* business."

Wells scratched the underside of his chin. "I was under the impression that y'all's trip had somethin' to do with a certain national park."

Scharq's shoulders bunched towards his neck. How had Wells found out? María wouldn't have said anything. He glanced at Khan but dismissed him as a source. I.A. Khan knew which side his bread was buttered on.

Wells ran his right hand along his hat brim. "Y'all're gonna score some points with our pal, President Quijano, and that's fine as far as it goes. But let's get down to the nut cuttin'. What's y'all's little jaunt down to San Cristo got to do with me? Bidness-wise."

Scharq's shoulders relaxed. Obviously Wells hadn't gotten the full picture of what the trip was about. Quijano, of course, was part of the equation. In two days Scharq would present San Cristo's elderly interim president with a ceremonial deed to a vast area of rainforest on Mount Azcalatl. The gift would double the size of San Cristo's major national park and advance The Mobys Foundation's global mission to protect the environment. For public relations purposes, the papers would be signed right after the grand opening of Mobys' first store in Ciudad San Cristo. The transfer would, of course, depend on certain concessions by Quijano's government in deference to Mobys as the largest landowner in San Cristo and master of a labyrinth of holding companies and dummy corporations the Quijano government could never hope to navigate. Wells' support would provide an ace up Scharq's well-tailored sleeve.

No one, after all, had more right to special consideration than Whitman Scharq. He had pioneered the espresso craze from a closet-size storefront in San Francisco's Financial District. Now, as his ad folks put it, Mobys' "If we're not there there's no there there" panache represented a key lifestyle choice for coffee lovers in ninety-nine countries. On October 31, San Cristo would take its honored place as nation number one hundred. True, the new store represented only a drop in the pot. Mobys' operations, even after a modest restructuring, included 15,000 owned or licensed stores, kiosks and in-home dispensaries. If Scharq was proud of anything, it was soccer moms, stay-home dads and stuck-in-the-job-search unemployed of all demographics hustling a little extra cash by selling coffee out of their garages and living rooms.

Even more true-blue American, Mobys was an equal-opportunity opportunist. His people were brainstorming *Yo Mobys!* and *¡Mobys Aquí!* handcarts for the nation's ghettos and barrios—a bootstrap operation designed to reduce poverty while keeping America's underclass awake and alert. Meanwhile, the company licensed an ever-expanding line of products bearing the Mobys logo—jewelry, school supplies, underwear, children's toys, auto accessories and religious items for mega-church gift shops.

María's cell phone rang. She glanced at Scharq then drifted towards the kitchen that opened onto the deck.

Scharq smiled in the subtle, unforced way in which couples communicate private feelings. The expression came naturally. He and María attended the same Catholic grade school as well as Lowell, San Francisco's select public high school. After going their separate ways, they reconnected years later at the expense of Scharq's second wife and María's sole husband.

After the affair ended by mutual consent, María accepted a position at Mobys, troubleshooting throughout Central and South America. He had her to thank for helping the company exploit interests in land, processing and exporting to maintain an ample supply of coffee beans at below-market prices.

María returned, whispered into Scharq's ear then held up a small tray with four glasses. "Bourbon, Congressman?"

"Hell, yeah! Fuel for body and soul."

Scharq raised his glass. "Well put, Gusher. Your comment about fuel. Because that's the business I want to talk to you about."

Wells took a long, welcome sip. "So just what's on y'all's mind, Whit?" He chuckled, although his eyes—had they not been hidden by dark lenses—would have revealed little sense of mirth. "Y'all gonna take over San Cristo with your private army and make coffee into one of those crazy new biofuels?"

Scharq nodded.

Wells stared.

"Seriously, Gusher," said Scharq, "you hit the nail right on the head. Or if you like, the ball square on the sweet spot." He turned to Khan. "I.A., you tell Congressman Wells. It's your baby."

Khan sucked in a deep breath to counter the sudden touch of nausea occasionally brought on by his daily heart medication. It was only fitting that Whitman defer to him, a man who had earned a doctorate at Oxford and instructed fellow military officers at the National University of Sciences and Technology in Rawalpindi—a scientist honored extensively for his work on biological weapons before being forced to flee by a misunderstanding arising from his relationship with the wife of a senior officer. "Congressman, I am about to reveal how research at the Mobys Foundation will soon change the course of history."

Wells transferred his stare to Khan. "The course of history?"

Khan stroked the dyed-black military mustache that betokened his exceptional virility. "I can tell you, sir, that a new discovery is about to lead to a dramatic reduction of global warming by orders of magnitude. Orders of magnitude, sir!"

"Bottom line," Scharq cut in, "I.A. is brewing up the *ultimate* biofuel."

Wells brought his right hand up to his hip like a gunfighter preparing to draw then hitched his pants up. "Whit, just what the fuck is this Paki talkin' about?"

Khan clenched his jaw.

Scharq patted Khan on the cheek. "What I.A. is talking about, Gusher, is caffuel."

"Caffuel?"

"A derivative of coffee blended with gasoline," María answered. "Major Khan assures us that caffuel will deliver incredible fuel efficiency."

"Beyond incredible, sir!" Khan interjected. "Caffuel will provide your average internal-combustion vehicle with well more than one hundred miles to the gallon in no more than a year. Two years perhaps. However, one hundred-fifty miles per gallon would not understate caffuel's short-term potential."

Wells leaned forward like a pine about to be upended by a Blue Norther. "And long term?"

"In five years," said Khan, "and certainly no more than ten, one must anticipate *two* hundred-fifty miles per gallon! And why not *three*-fifty, sir?"

Wells' jaw slackened. His mouth agape, he seemed to struggle for air. Then he straightened, clapped Scharq on the back and burst out laughing. "Goddam sumbitch, Whitman. You had me. You really *had* me."

Scharq emitted an even bigger laugh not unlike a burst from a .50-caliber machine gun. "There are so many nuts out there, right Gusher?"

"Well, California's the land of fruits and nuts, so y'all ought to know." He raised his glass. "Damn if I didn't almost spill this. I love oil as you know, but you can't drink it."

"Amen to that!" Scharq responded. "But Gusher, let's be serious about alternate forms of energy. Take electric cars. I love the concept. *Love* it. But I have to ask, where will we get enough lithium for those batteries? Bolivia mines half of it, and how reliable do you think any lefty government's going to be? And what about charging stations and battery swaps? How soon do you think we'll see a network of those that Americans can count on? All this talk about moving away from gasoline . . . that's all it's been is talk. But America . . . the planet for God's sake . . . needs something better *now*."

The creases running from Wells' nostrils down to the corners of his mouth deepened like cracks in a drought-stricken prairie. "So y'all are telling me that with caffuel, Americans'll keep drivin' but with a whole lot less gasoline in the tank. And then not fillin' up much, either." His chest puffed out like that of a Texas Longhorn getting ready to gore a rodeo clown too many steps from his protective barrel. "Over my dead body. The oil bidness is as American as pecan pie."

"On the other hand, Mr. Congressman," María interjected, "oil is killing the environment while caffuel is incredibly green."

"In all humility," Khan interjected, "caffuel will reduce CO2 emissions by up to eighty-eight-point-six percent while emitting water vapor scented with the faintest aroma of freshly roasted coffee."

"You'll choose a flavor at the pump," added Scharq.

Wells' face turned almost as white as the sheet his grandfather in the East Texas Piney Woods had worn as a member of the Klan. "Bullshit, you cocksuckin', motherfuckin' bastard-sumbitch," he gushed, revealing the origins of his nickname. "And I don't give a rat's ass if there's a woman present. Notice I said woman and not lady." He prodded Scharq's chest with a long finger. "Every *real* American knows, it's oil or nothin'!"

María pressed a slender thumb on Wells' wrist.

The congressman winced. His hand dropped to his side.

Scharq smiled broadly, baring perfect white teeth. "Get over it, Gusher. Do you know just how much the high price of gasoline sucks out of Americans' purchasing power?"

Wells snorted like a Brahma bull in heat. "Fuck the American people! I represent the Great State of Texas!"

"Gusher, look at the big picture," Scharq prodded. "With you behind us, Mobys can broaden its position in San Cristo and then the rest of Latin America. And then the rest of the world. We'll own all the patents for caffuel and corner the market on beans. Which means America can finally tell the Arabs . . . and the Iranians, too . . . not to mention the Chinese . . . to go take a flying leap."

Wells spat. "Let me tell you somethin'. If caffuel works like you say, y'all're gonna piss off a whole lot of important folks from Houston to Midland to out El Paso way. Friends of mine with deep pockets. Re-election comes up every two years, you know."

Scharq squeezed Wells' elbow. "Aren't *I* your friend? Don't six-figure gifts to a super-PAC show a friend's loyalty? Devotion even? Besides, it's not like I'm asking Congress for legislation to give Mobys a billion dollars a year in tax credits and cash payments . . . two's more realistic though three's not out of the question . . . for *not* developing caffuel just to help keep oil prices up and your other friends happy."

"And just who the fuck do y'all think you are?" sputtered Wells. "Jesse James?"

"Gusher, you know me. And I know *you* the way others don't."

Unseen, Wells' eyes narrowed.

"Hypothetically," said Scharq, "that billion or three per annum . . . That's chump change compared to the tax breaks your oil pals are getting. Not to mention what corn growers used to get at the public teat. Still do, I suspect, because nobody knows how all that legislation really works. And don't even talk to me about AIG and all those banks Washington bailed out . . . including other friends of yours . . . after the subprime mortgage mess. A grateful America's going to owe a big debt of thanks to Mobys for developing caffuel, and you can share in the glory. As a champion of caffuel, you'll be . . . well, almost as big a hero as Major Khan here."

Khan beamed. He'd expended substantial energy in the effort to propel caffuel from abstract theory to potential reality with copious documentation to support his work should Washington or the media raise questions. Granted, more extensive testing of caffuel remained. He'd also have to deflect the usual professional backbiting. Scientists were as political as anyone else. But one principle he stood by. No one had the right to impede scientific progress. That included him, as well. If during the course of his work he had uncovered numerous questionable expenditures on the part of Mobys Foundation relating to caffuel development, deference to the greater good mandated his silence. His upcoming four-week working vacation in San Cristo would enable the caffuel project to move forward. If it also distanced him from a certain Quran-obsessed husband furious with the sexual attraction I.A. Khan held for more than a few of the Bay Area's lovely but bored Pakistani housewives, so much the better.

Wells searched for another drink. "Y'all got balls, Whit. But y'all better listen up. Don't fuck with the oil bidness. Do that, and y'all're getting' in way over y'all's head. Just like messin' around in a country like San Cristo where a man's word ain't worth a pile of cow shit, and they all hate America no matter how much we do for 'em."

Scharq looked at María. "Oh, I think we've got a pretty good take on what's happening down there, Gusher. And that includes a lack of gratitude for American guidance. For example, María informed me when she brought out our drinks that one of President Quijano's . . . and America's . . . most vocal critics arrived in the United States yesterday. While we sit down to dinner, he intends to sell his message of hatred for America right across the Bay."

Wells' face reddened to a near match with the bridge beyond his shoulder. "Who?" he exploded. "And how the hell do *you* know?"

"We have our sources," said María.

"I'm gonna have to lay some whup-ass on my staff," said Wells. "They're supposed to know shit like this." He held his hands out, palms opened and facing each other, as if he were about to squeeze someone's neck. "Call that limo guy of yours and tell him to come back. I got half a mind to go over there and kill the greasy sumbitch."

Scharq pointed towards the house. "Let's go inside for dinner, Gusher." He led him inside. "Anyway, we both know there's a free-speech clause in the Constitution. Even for foreigners. But if it'll make you feel any better, I could have María dump the guy's body in the Bay before we start dessert."

"¡Trabajo del Diablo!" Jesús Garcia-Vega muttered as the black Escalade ascended higher into the Berkeley hills.

"¿Pardón, jefe?" asked Carlos, his trusted bodyguard, lifting an earpiece from his black iPod. From his shotgun seat up front, Carlos kept his one sighted eye—his left—on the road ahead. Over the years, he had demonstrated unshakable loyalty to his *jefe*. He would lay down his life for his *jefe*. All he asked was his weekly paycheck

with an appropriate annual raise and an appreciative bonus at Christmas. A man with a family had responsibilities.

"Work of the Devil!" Garcia-Vega spat out in English as he observed the palatial homes lining the leafy street transformed to spun gold by the early-autumn California sunset. He endured visits to such degenerate places only to serve the people. These ostentatious homes belonged to blue-eyed white people who underpaid dark-eyed brown people to maintain them. In this way, America and San Cristo were no different. The wealthy, addicted to relentless over-consumption, deserved the disdain of those who understood the progressive, humane principles of Marx and Lenin, venerated the steel-willed efforts of Stalin and Mao, and sought to duplicate—and, God willing, surpass—the heroic stands of Fidel, Ché and Chávez.

"Right on!" agreed Lenny Birnbaum, the comrade who drove them and had arranged the evening's fundraiser. A retired professor of anthropology at Berkeley, Birnbaum now lived off his generous pension with health benefits but nonetheless selflessly considered himself to be nothing more than a "working stiff."

Readjusting the earpiece to his iPod, Carlos glanced at the Escalade's navigation screen. "Just ahead, *jefe*."

The Escalade slowed. Mercedes, BMWs and Lexus SUVs lined the narrow, winding street along with a small fleet of Priuses, more modest Toyotas and Hondas. Garcia-Vega's two good eyes studied a vintage Vanagon displaying not one but two REAGAN SUCKS stickers among dozens, creating a comprehensive overview of late twentieth-century, liberal-American political expression. All was in order. The contributors had arrived, hungry for wine and cheese, beer and pupusas, and sage words sticking it to the man.

The Escalade halted at a massive wrought-iron gate flanked by high, cream-colored walls embedded with glass shards. Lower walls, thought Garcia-Vega, would have formed a sufficient barrier to indigenous Cristanos who maintained a stature, as well as a culture, closer to the earth. The architect, however, designed these to withstand taller, more rapacious men of European blood. Just inside the walls and soaring above them stood a second barrier of bamboo the green of unripe bananas. Above the bamboo towered oak trees dappled in light and shadow. Birds chirped from their branches. The wooded setting reminded Garcia-Vega of his boyhood home, except that his entire village could have found shelter in the house to which he'd been invited.

The gate swung open. The Escalade pulled forward into a cobblestone courtyard.

Carlos leaped from the vehicle even before it stopped, peered around to bring everything within his monocular view and opened Garcia-Vega's door.

Birnbaum exited on the other side.

Garcia-Vega approached the house's arched, custom-carved wooden front door.

Birnbaum dropped his arm around Garcia-Vega's shoulder. "Like I said, the living and dining rooms can hold close to a hundred people. We can squeeze in a few dozen more on the deck."

Garcia-Vega frowned. The owners' wealth disturbed him. But then, they were major contributors—capitalists with sufficient social conscience to undermine capitalism. They fully supported his efforts to make San Cristo the world's prime example of what humanity could achieve when all people were equal in every way. Years earlier, his passion for justice had compelled Garcia-Vega to found the *Asociación Nacional de Tierras Indígenas*—the National Association of Indigenous Lands. Over time, ANTI's contributors enabled him to leave his frustrating post as San Cristo's minister of housing for more important work on the people's behalf.

The door opened, revealing a woman almost a head taller than Garcia-Vega. Short, white hair and turquoise eyelids set off her pronounced cheekbones and wrinkle-free skin. Dressed in a flowing shift woven from Senegalese cotton, silver bracelets on both wrists, she artfully concealed the passing of her sixtieth birthday several years earlier. The woman embraced Birnbaum then turned to Garcia-Vega and pressed her yoga-toned body against his.

"*Mucho gusto,*" he whispered, fearing that he might stutter.

"Shall I call you *jefe?* Or would comrade be right?"

"Whatever you wish, *señorita.*"

"*Señora*, thank you. Bettina Owens. Formerly Starbird. In another life."

"Then please, Jesús. Simply Jesús."

She studied his eyes. "It's been *señora* for thirty-eight years now—not that Harvey and I really believe in such bourgeois ideas as marriage. And I must extend my regrets that Harvey is away on business. All week."

Garcia-Vega followed his hostess into the entry. Its gleaming hardwood floor set off a rug of deep, rich reds woven by women in a remote Afghan village grateful for their two modest daily meals. On the wall to his right hung a large mirror framed in Philippine mahogany carved to resemble tree branches and finished with quasi-gold highlights.

He peered at his reflection. How fortunate, he thought, to have both eyes. His faithful Carlos—practically a brother since childhood—had lost his right eye when a group of boys attacked them with rocks and sticks. The bigger, burly Carlos fended off the attackers with his fists and accepted his wound without complaint. Of course, Carlos' injured eye might have been saved had adequate medical assistance been available. Health care remained a dream in villages as remote as theirs.

The loss of an eye, however, had not freed Carlos from then-compulsory military service alongside Garcia-Vega. But this proved fortunate. A more enthusiastic and far better soldier, Carlos acquired many useful skills, later put to use in the employ of one of the government's security agencies before joining the cause of the people. Garcia-Vega, better suited as a clerk in their undermanned infantry company, attempted to organize a soldiers' union and spent eight months in a military prison for his efforts.

Satisfied, Garcia-Vega shifted the examination of his appearance to the army-replica jacket he wore every day in homage to Fidel and Chávez. Each year, a tailor in Miami made him half-a-dozen such jackets along with matching trousers. Shirts he could always buy off the rack. The uniforms represented a sound investment given how critical his appearance was to the movement.

With a final glance in the mirror, Garcia-Vega studied his hair. His stylist clipped it weekly to keep it short and suggest the image of a ferocious warrior for justice and dignity—ideals to which he had consecrated himself to the point at which he foreswore any long-term relationship with a woman. A night? A week? *Sín duda.* An affair of two or three months? Perhaps. But no longer. Jesús Garcia-Vega belonged to the people.

Of even greater importance, the cut avoided the embarrassment of his hair's naturally medium-brown, slightly wavy character. He would otherwise require unending coloring and straightening to reinforce the image of his mostly indigenous heritage. His hair, hazel eyes disguised by contact lenses and skin too pale by at least one shade—if not two, he worried—continually threatened to reveal the bloodlines of the European seducer who abandoned his mother's mother after viciously contaminating the family's gene pool. No matter how often he spoke of the poverty of his rural childhood, of arduous days picking coffee berries and long nights resisting hunger as he studied the few worn textbooks available to him, his body threatened to betray him.

Birnbaum nudged Garcia-Vega into the kitchen.

Garcia-Vega inspected the European oak cabinets with hand-brushed glaze and crystal knobs, the island with a sink and gray-green, polished-concrete top, and the gleaming copper range hood. All suggested a recent remodel.

"Great crowd," said Birnbaum, several grapes and a lump of Brie swelling his cheeks. "And our biggest donors are here."

"So we are, as they say, good to go?"

"Just about. Let me get some more wine, then I'll introduce you."

Birnbaum's remarks had been prepared for him. He would relate the degrading working conditions that killed Garcia-Vega's father when their guest of honor was still a child. He would detail the appalling health conditions in the rainforest, the lack of educational opportunities, the patronizing missionaries who sent Garcia-Vega to their high school to destroy his cultural integrity, the army debacle—every detail that could elicit top dollar.

Naturally, Garcia-Vega took great pains that his speeches appear, as the American idiom went, off the cuff. He had labored long and hard with two university graduates in literature and the director of a small, politically active theater company in the capital to create several modular components for his speeches. These he combined in various ways depending on the occasion.

Birnbaum caressed a glass of Napa Valley chardonnay. "Okay then. Let's liberate some ill-gotten capitalist cash." He went into the living room.

Humming softly to prepare his voice, Garcia-Vega examined the twin Sub-Zero refrigerator/freezers on the wall opposite. They looked as if they could hold an entire steer. He could not help but wonder how much this kitchen cost with its two pizza ovens, custom ceramic backsplash tiles glazed with children's and grandchildren's names, full-height wine cabinet and flat-screen television framed into the wall. And might that be an all-natural Marmoleum floor on which he stood? How many children could he educate over the next year with the money Betty or Birdie . . . no it was Bettina . . . had spent on this kitchen? How did she feel waking up each morning and coming into such a kitchen for breakfast? How did it feel not to have a care in the world? How would *he* feel if such a kitchen were *his*?

Energized by the cause, Garcia-Vega entered the living room. Snippets of conversation about tennis clubs, brokers and au pairs assaulted his ears.

Birnbaum stretched his arms upward towards the huge wooden beams supporting the cathedral ceiling. "*Camaradas.*"

The room fell silent.

Garcia-Vega feigned attention while Birnbaum detailed his post-military scholarship to Texas A&M and "what a fascist environment that had to be for a man like our special guest." He spoke of Garcia-Vega's law studies at the University of San Cristo, his years as a community organizer followed by a seat in the national assembly, his elevation to minister of housing with opponents seeking to thwart him at every turn and his humble resolve to dedicate the rest of his life to the role of tireless revolutionary and willing martyr.

Waiting for Birnbaum to conclude, Garcia-Vega raised his shoulders almost to his ears then released them. The flight from San Cristo the day before and from Miami to San Francisco hours earlier had taken their toll in spite of his seat in business class—first class would have been unconscionably decadent. Nonetheless, his enthusiasm remained undaunted. He had news. Important news.

Shout-filled applause greeted him.

Garcia-Vega clasped his hands over his head, lowered them and brought his left index finger to his lips.

The commotion subsided.

Energized, Garcia-Vega began. This would not be one of Fidel's daylong speeches or a marathon typical of Hugo Chávez. One could not do that in Berkeley for an audience of Americans attuned to sound bites. Nor was it necessary. He might offer them a quote from Teo Ballvé on Chavez's socialism for the twenty-first century or something from Eduardo Galleano's *The Open Veins of Latin America,* but these bourgeois academics and their camp followers had not come for that. They wanted to hear about real life as it was lived in the mud and muck of the *bosque*. As one who had endured such poverty forced upon him by the powerful—as the only man who could unite the native peoples of San Cristo with their brothers and sisters throughout Latin America—he would forego an intellectual approach and speak with all the passion and conviction only long and arduous rehearsals could achieve.

He told them how the *indígenas* from whom he sprang continued to be victimized by their European colonizers—now their political rulers who only pretended to be their countrymen. He informed them of the natural dignity—indeed superiority—of native peoples whose close and respectful relationship to the earth—nature gave them their gods, after all—represented humanity's last hope for survival in this age of global warming. He decried the reactionary adherence to capitalism that led the United States—their own country—to oppress liberation movements in San Cristo and throughout Latin

America. And he praised his hosts for their offering of particularly delicious food and wine in such a beautiful setting.

"Victory to the people!" he concluded.

Cries of "bravo" and "right on" ascended above hearty applause.

Again, Garcia-Vega touched a finger to his lips.

Again the crowd stilled.

"*Camaradas*, there is more. The seeds of revolution have been planted in the parched soil of a nation thirsting for justice. I submit to you in all humility that only one man can bring peace to our suffering fatherland. Upon my return, I will immediately announce my candidacy for the presidency of the Republic of San Cristo. I pledge to you, the Quijano government *will* fall."

PLANTANDO

| Planting |

3 | TRES | 3

BOBBY WALKED WESTWARD on Avenida Plaza Azcalatl towards his appointment with Juan Suelo, deputy commander of the *Seguridad Nacional.* Several blocks ahead, the tree-lined Avenida formed the northern border of Plaza Azcalatl, the hub of Ciudad San Cristo, across from which workers rushed to complete a four-story building housing the country's initial Mobys store. He'd visited the site in the morning at María Skoronsky's suggestion and again that afternoon to monitor the security arrangements he'd coordinated with Juan.

Late-afternoon traffic crawled along the Avenida in both directions. Here and there a showroom-new SUV darted among grime-spattered delivery trucks, vintage Chevy Impala taxis and snaking lines of buses belching exhaust fumes into the soft, damp early evening air. Horns bleated like lost sheep. Radios and CD players, in a fit of mass nostalgia, blared out *"La sirenita,"* one of the Mexican rocker Rigo Tovar's golden hits.

On guard for pickpockets with little regard for the clusters of police and *Seguridad* personnel at every corner, Bobby tried to keep pace with the mass of *capitalistas,* as residents of the city called themselves. They performed a series of massive yet intricate line dances, which took them in competing directions while enabling them to keep in step with the complex, erratic rhythm of the city. The going was anything but easy. Bobby's knee still troubled him following his unanticipated and fateful excursion into the chilly highlands the previous day ending with a chopper ride back to General Gomez' base and a late-night drive to the capital.

From time to time Bobby glanced at the shops and cafés, whose modest prosperity suffered the occasional betrayal of a ripped awning or a cracked window. He had left the city's wealthy boutiques and restaurants behind after crossing Avenida Londres, where Mobys put him up in the Hotel Azcalatl Grande, the capital's sole five-star hotel. María Skavronsky had just checked in along with Major Khan, who wished to learn more about Bobby's time in Pakistan. Whitman Scharq would occupy the penthouse for the next four weeks, although he would be in and out of the country. The Azcalatl Grande would have been way out of Bobby's price range if he'd been traveling on his own dime, and he found it a bit pretentious, but he wasn't about to complain. His room was large, the bar downstairs stocked Pikesville Supreme, and the health club offered free weights, which he preferred to machines.

At the end of the block, Bobby reached the northeast corner of the rectangular plaza, centered in a grid that replaced the haphazard layout of the original colonial town following the last of several revolutions in the mid-eighteen hundreds. There, the capital's largest thoroughfare, Bulevar Azcalatl, ran south from the Presidential Palace to the plaza and dead-ended. On the plaza's south side, Bulevar 8 de Abril continued down to the National Assembly building, a classical structure with imposing columns. The broad boulevards and expansive plaza left the Presidential Palace and the National Assembly to face each other or, in terms of Cristano politics, face each other down.

The areas north and east of the central city—above and right as the locals called it—hosted upscale and middle-class condos, shops, restaurants and clubs. The elite often shopped and played there, but most lived in gated communities in the northern suburbs. Two blocks north of the plaza, the steel-and-concrete American embassy stood a short distance to the right of the Presidential Palace. Below and to the left—or south and west of Plaza Azcalatl—a jumble of apartments, shops and restaurants ran from humble to downtrodden. The National Cathedral fronted the plaza's left side.

Bobby stopped at the corner of Avenida Colón to glance down the street at the new Mobys building. He'd arranged with Suelo to have at least one *Seguridad* agent posted on site around the clock and for police patrols to constantly pass by to help prevent the frequent protests from getting out of hand. They would also report lapses by the private security guards hired by the construction company. More often than not, "third world" and "first-class security" proved to be mutually exclusive terms.

Ready to move on, Bobby crossed the street among a swarm of Cristanos evidencing as much use for traffic lights as snowshoes. Reaching the sidewalk, he looked up. Strings of red, green and blue lights crisscrossed the huge plaza, the crowning work of a nineteenth-century German-Mexican landscape architect, who soon after became insolvent, robbed the city's largest bank at gunpoint and bribed his way to Cuba. He died of syphilis in a Havana brothel twenty years later.

Beneath the lights, men and women strolled on cobbles glistening from the late-afternoon rainfall. All paths converged on the fountain of *las tres señoritas.* Legend had it that a thousand years earlier—or more, or less—invading Mayans—or Pipils, or Lencas—ravished and slew—or slew then ravished—three indigenous virgins of exceptional beauty and saintly character. The *señoritas'* blood flowed freely into the baked earth of what was then a small village. In response, a broad-winged azcalatl descended from the heavens to weep over the site. The invaders hurled stones. Fire from the azcalatl's beak melted the projectiles. Then the azcalatl assumed the shape of a giant phallus. Its tears fell like seed, raining down upon the blood of the martyrs. The entire area of what was now the plaza burst forth with springs of fresh water, rose bushes and banana trees.

Some versions of the legend mentioned coffee trees, although everyone knew that the European elite had introduced coffee in the late eighteen hundreds, long after the Mayans had been removed from history—or the ancient Pipils, or Lencas had lost power. Of course, even if that part of the legend was apocryphal, no one could deny the importance that coffee played in the Cristano economy. It *was* the Cristano economy.

Bobby skirted a large puddle shimmering with reflected light and approached the fountain. Around its stonework edge, young women sat on plastic ponchos, shopping bags or folded newspapers.

Their shoulders covered with shawls or sweaters, they watched demurely as preening young men circled in twos and threes.

Stopping, Bobby flexed his right knee then reached into his pocket for his cell phone. He'd have just enough time to try to reach Bobby, Jr. again, although he'd left a voicemail just before leaving the hotel. While not a man to embrace guilt, Bobby had not only grown lonelier over the years but also remorseful. After the divorce from Sandi—who claimed he preferred life in the field to home, and not without cause—he saw little of his son and received only an occasional Christmas photo. Admittedly, he hadn't put much effort into keeping in touch. For that matter, he'd long lost track of his second wife, LeeAnne, who lodged the same protest by hitting the road with a guitar playing insurance salesman seeking fame in Nashville. All he knew now was that Bobby, Jr. had graduated from North Carolina State, married his college sweetheart—whose name slipped Bobby's mind—and moved clear across the country to California. Also that he would become a grandfather sometime in the winter.

He had, he considered, a great deal to atone for. And if not today, when?

Deciding against leaving another voicemail so soon after the last, Bobby headed to the plaza's below-left corner where a ceiba tree stretched itself nearly one hundred feet aloft into the hovering darkness. Birds filled its huge, umbrella-like canopy, chirping a welcoming chorus to the approaching night.

Bobby paused. The ceiba, like the fountain, was the stuff of legend. When San Cristo achieved independence from Spain, the government of the new republic attempted to remove the fountain of *las tres señoritas*. Their Christian duty demanded that they obliterate any trace of the godless culture of the indigenous people who tilled their fields and cleaned their houses. Both *indígenas* and *mestizos* rose against them. A truce protected the fountain in perpetuity. But the lords of independent San Cristo insisted on their own monument. They planted the ceiba tree, whose canopy would symbolize the protective, fatherly rule of the oligarchy blessed by God and Holy Mother Church.

Bobby crossed the intersection and entered a café catty-corner from the plaza. Inside, perhaps two-dozen legislative assistants and female clerks were getting an early start on the evening.

He chose a table near the large windows offering a view of the National Cathedral. Its southern wall displayed gargoyles that might have graced the façade of Notre Dame. The ceiba stood in plain sight.

A heavyset waiter with a 1940s-style pencil mustache approached.

"*¿Tiene usted* Pikesville rye?" Bobby asked.

The waiter shrugged. "*No, señor. Lo siento.*"

Bobby smiled. "*Cerveza Azcalatl, por favor.*" Beer would do fine. He was in someone else's country and not about to embarrass his hosts. If he'd learned anything in thirty years of serving the USofA in some of the most remote locations on God's good, green and not-so-green earth, he'd learned that.

Darkness quickly enveloped the city. The lights strung across the plaza suggested necklaces of glowing, multi-colored beads. Moonlight peered through the clouds. American rock music on the café's sound system caught Bobby's attention. He couldn't place the song. His musical tastes ran in other directions. A two-year tour in the military attaché's office in Moscow had introduced him to classic Russian composers like Mikhail Glinka and Alexander Kopylov along with Borodin, Mussorgsky and, even if it suggested a cliché, Tchaikovsky. For that matter, he'd also accumulated an eclectic selection of Middle Eastern music from Oum Kalthoum to more modern Lebanese singers like Najwa Karam and Maya Nasri. You could take the boy out of McKeesport, Pennsylvania, and he just might find it impossible to go back.

"Bobby! Bobby!" a voice called. "*¿Qué tal?*"

Startled, Bobby jerked his head up. Then he stood, bent down and spread out his arms to share an *abrazo* with Juan Suelo, a former Cristano army officer of great promise he'd helped train at the School of the Americas years earlier. "Juan, you could have slit my throat, and I wouldn't have seen it coming!"

Suelo reached up and patted Bobby solidly on the back. His thick hands produced sounds like thunderclaps. He grunted.

"What's the matter?" asked Bobby.

"Just my back. It goes in and out lately." He motioned Bobby to sit. "Long time no see, huh?"

"You're looking good, Juan. *Doing* good, too."

"Maybe you better call me 'sir.' I outrank you now."

Bobby saluted.

"I owe you, *amigo*. Drinks and dinner, they're on me."

Bobby held up both hands to protest any thought Suelo had of debt. He was proud that Suelo, honest, skilled and educated—the USofA had paid for his bachelor's in European history and a master's in management—had climbed to the rank of full colonel. That promotion represented no small feat for a short, squat *indígena* nicknamed *el buldog* in an officer corps dominated by European blood. Now, as deputy commander of the new *Seguridad Nacional*, Suelo was in the middle of reorganizing half-a-dozen inept military and civilian security agencies into one. Success could earn him a star. Then again, it would be easier for Suelo to change the security apparatus than his skin.

The waiter placed a bottle of *Cerveza Azcalatl*, a glass and American-style tortilla chips on the table. He turned to Suelo.

Suelo, dressed in civilian clothes, pointed to Bobby's beer. "No glass."

The waiter spun on his heels and hurried to the bar.

Bobby pushed the glass to the middle of the table. Drinking from the bottle would do fine.

"We'll start catching up here," said Suelo. "Then we'll head to dinner. You hungry?"

"Does San Cristo grow coffee?" Bobby'd downed two slices of toast with coffee that morning but skipped lunch. The missed meal hadn't been an oversight. Today was Yom Kippur, the Day of Atonement, when Jews traditionally fasted. The fast began the night before at sundown when the patrol he'd accompanied had been unexpectedly attacked. He felt himself a fool for accepting General Gomez' assurance that despite concerns in the capital, the bank robbery in Maquepaque had been a criminal one-off, that no would-be revolutionary would dare raise his head so close to San Cristo's largest army base. But after the chopper flight back to Ciudad San Cristo, he had to get something on his stomach. Besides, he'd developed his own Yom Kippur ritual over the last few years by foregoing one meal, usually lunch. In this way he acknowledged the Jewish world his parents had abandoned after surviving the Holocaust—a willful erasure of history that left Bobby unaware of his heritage until his father revealed their secret on his deathbed. Maybe some year he'd pass on two meals then all three. For now, reading Jewish history and the Old Testament—no, he really should be calling it the Hebrew Bible—was the best he could do. And then there was the matter of atonement. Perhaps missing lunch might help him make amends in some small way for deserting Bobby, Jr. And now he add to that the attack on the patrol, which he felt strongly could have been averted if only he'd taken a more active role before they were fired on—although doing so was strictly forbidden by his contract. He served as a consultant to Mobys and nothing more.

"So look," said Suelo. "There's a little French place a block left of the bus station. You wouldn't expect it in this part of town, but it's good. Real good. Anyway, Carolina's fine, the kids are great, and I'll fill you in on the Pope's visit when we eat."

The waiter returned and gently placed Suelo's beer on the table.

As if manipulated by a skilled illusionist, the bottle began to rattle on the polished wood. A low rumbling filled the café. Glasses and dishes clattered on the tables. Bottles clinked behind the bar. Then everything stilled.

"*Terremoto*," said Suelo.

Bobby glanced around. No one in the bar seemed particularly disturbed. Cristanos were more than familiar with earthquakes, and this temblor had been minor.

Suelo lifted his bottle "*¡Salud!*"

"*¡Salud!*" Bobby toasted in return.

"*¡Salud* and what the fuck!" bellowed a third voice. A big man, not as tall as Bobby but even more heavily muscled, approached the table. His cropped red hair was shaved at the sides. His neck was linebacker-thick and encircled by a gold chain from which dangled a small, white ivory skull. He extended his hand. "Bobby fuckin' Gatling! How's the knee?"

Bobby accepted the hand, anticipating the grip that attempted to dominate his while concealing his annoyance. The crushing grip was high-school stuff. More important, someone again had approached him without his noticing. And the reference to his knee after all these years flat out pissed him off. He'd taken a round fired into the sky during a Kurdish celebration in northern Iraq. No purple heart for that. But he'd lived to tell the story. The Peshmerga colonel who'd accompanied him and stood at his side as they both took a pee break had taken a round in the head. But the knee only served as an excuse for the derision expressed by some of his peers, who resented his continuing questioning of the violence produced by American strategy in the Middle East and elsewhere. Combat zones and promotions generally went hand in hand.

The red-haired man sat. "So, Bobby, buy me a beer or what?"

Bobby glanced at the ivory skull. "Kill anyone interesting lately, Lewis?" He caught Suelo's eye and looked back to the red-haired man. "Lewis Kennan, this is Juan Suelo."

"Heard a lot about you, Colonel," Kennan offered.

"Juan, Lewis Kennan. Used to be Major Kennan, U.S. Army and a proud member of Delta Force before Crimmins-Idyll recruited him.

Kennan extended his hand and smiled. "If Bobby revealed anything more, I'd have to kill him. And you."

Suelo accepted a grip intended to send a message and returned a message of his own. "I'm sorry we didn't meet when you first arrived, Major. I hope you're enjoying Lake Azcalatl."

"*¡Cerveza!*" Kennan roared at a waiter three tables away. He turned back to Suelo. "Not here to vacation. Figure you know that. Spending most of my time out in the boonies. Chasing bank robbers.

And revolutionaries. Same people probably. No hard feelings, us being outside your chain of command?"

Suelo betrayed no response. He had no choice but to acknowledge that the embryonic *Seguridad Nacional* wasn't yet ready for prime time. Kennan's force of American contractors, complete with helicopters, had arrived a month earlier to secure the area adjacent to Azcalatl National Park. The region was within General Gomez' command, and although Gomez had plenty of men, he'd earned his post through political connections and never demonstrated anything near the level of leadership required to deal with more than the most amateurish of criminal acts. President Quijano's signing the order bypassing the Cristano Army, the police and *Seguridad* hinted that a challenge of some magnitude might be brewing in the highlands. However, one had to be careful about describing the situation. The president's office had strictly forbidden the use of the word "revolution."

The waiter with the pencil mustache now turned down to reveal a frown of displeasure appeared with Kennan's beer. The bottle hit the table with a sound resembling a shot from a small handgun.

Kennan's cheeks flushed.

Suelo stared at Kennan's ivory skull.

Kennan shrugged and held the skull away from his chest. The black shirt he wore loose over his slacks to conceal a Mark 23 pistol set the trinket off as if it rested in a jewelry display case. "Found it with a body in Central Africa. Can't tell you where."

"Africa?" Bobby asked. "Was that *before* or *after* the company pulled you out of Iraq?"

"Not sure that deserves an answer coming from the guy who held his dick while Moq'tar slipped away from America. Talk about a changing Middle East! I hear you were out of work until Allen Crimmins set you up with Mobys for the month. But I guess being a hands-off consultant beats looking for sea shells at the beach."

"So, Major Kennan," Suelo interjected, "it appears *you* know where to go for souvenirs."

Kennan clenched his jaw then winked. "One of our guys back in Alexandria . . . the home office . . . offered me twenty-five hundred bucks for this skull. Twenty-five hundred! Not even a week's pay. Make me an offer I can't refuse or get the fuck out of my way."

Bobby shook his head. "I don't know, Lewis. It's all profit, figuring you only paid for the chain. Maybe."

Kennan grinned. "Package deal. Skull came on the chain." He drained his beer. "What the fuck was I supposed to do? Post a found notice on Craig's List? Sell it on EBay? Send the proceeds to the guy's tribe? Never even found his fucking head. Not that we looked." The grin morphed into a grimace. "Fuck all this bleeding-heart shit, Bobby. And fuck all these so-called innocent native people who don't know anything but how to be victims."

Suelo squeezed his bottle. The skin across his knuckles grew taut.

Bobby reached under the table and touched Suelo's knee.

"My apologies," said Kennan. "Seems like the natives in San Cristo also know how to rob banks and massacre working people. Not to mention the local troops."

Suelo gripped the edge of the table. "We have troublemakers. Radical politicians and others who romanticize terrorist groups like the Zapatistas, FARC and Sendero Luminoso. We can deal with them."

Kennan slammed his fists on the table. "Let me show you a trick."

Suelo's eyes widened with confusion.

Kennan laughed. "Got your attention, didn't I?"

"Give us a break, Lewis," said Bobby.

"One trick. Just one," said Kennan. He withdrew a deck of playing cards from his shirt pocket.

Suelo scratched his head. "You learn this with Delta Force?"

Kennan smiled. "Got a magic set for my tenth birthday. Every kid wants to be a magician. Control other people. Never lost my fascination. Earned good money during college performing at parties and meetings. Still show my stuff when I'm home."

Bobby raised his right index finger. "Just one."

Kennan shuffled the deck, expanded it and held it out to Suelo. "As we say, pick a card, any card."

Suelo fingered a card.

"No. Take it out of the deck. Look at it. Show it to Bobby. Just don't let *me* see it."

Suelo removed the card.

"Alright. Put it back in the deck. Anywhere."

Suelo followed Kennan's instructions.

Kennan held the deck in both hands and squared it. Then he riffled it with his thumb. Finally, he placed it face down on the table.

"You gonna find my card, is that it?" Suelo asked.

"Houston, we have a problem."

"Problem?" Suelo asked.

"Your card. It's missing."

"Missing?"

"Not in the deck. Vanished."

"No way," Suelo retorted. "I put it back in the deck. You saw. Bobby saw."

"Twenty bucks says it's gone."

"Be careful, Juan," Bobby advised. "And don't play poker with this guy, either."

Kennan waved his hand. "Give me a break. Do I look like the kind of guy who takes money from friends?" He held the deck out. "But your card's still missing, Suelo. Check it out."

Suelo turned the deck over and spread the cards face up across the table. "*¡Cabrón!*" Damn! "It's not there."

"Sure you're looking in the right place?" Kennan asked. He reached his right hand towards Suelo.

As if a theater had been rigged with special effects to reinforce the trick's big finish, one of the café's windows shattered. Outside in the plaza, the near-severed canopy of the ceiba tree hung at a right angle from its trunk then toppled.

The three men rose to their feet.

"*¿Terremoto?*" asked Suelo.

"You wish," Bobby answered. "Bomb!"

4 | CUATRO | 4

BOBBY HUSTLED WHITMAN SCHARQ and Alonso Quijano away from the rotor blades whirring atop the helicopter. Rented by Mobys, it promised far more reliability than President Quijano's Vietnam-era Huey, which the American Ambassador continually promised to replace. Around them, a company of Cristano soldiers—barely at half strength but according to General Gomez, fully enthusiastic—secured the landing zone in an isolated clearing on the northern slope of Mount Azcalatl unobservable from the lake and nearby towns. A Super Cobra gunship owned by Crimmins-Idyll hovered overhead along with a UH-60 Black Hawk ready to set down Lewis Kennan and a squad of play-for-pay commandos should a challenging situation arise.

They crossed the LZ with Scharq pulling the stumbling Quijano along like a skittish dog resisting the leash. Colonel Gatling's security preparations were all well and good, Scharq acknowledged, but he had work to do and little time. Two-bit revolutionaries could never intimidate the self-made billionaire who faced down Wall Street bankers, London commodities traders and Eurotrash bureaucrats the way ordinary men ordered parking valets to bring around their cars.

President Quijano struggled to keep pace with his host. The situation left him uneasy, given that the American had virtually rendered him a guest in his own country. María danced forward just behind the president. Khan, slowly falling back, completed the party at a more deliberate and dignified cadence.

Scharq, Bobby at his shoulder, stopped at the edge of the jungle.

Quijano, breathless and just short of gasping, dabbed his forehead with a white handkerchief.

Bobby watched María approach. He'd never worked for a woman before, although he'd had an offer of sorts from the Sultana of Moq'tar. But he had no intention of screwing up what he'd been told would be a low-key, four-week consulting job—almost a paid vacation—to get him back into the swing of things. In San Café only four days, he'd already come under hostile fire and witnessed the bombing of a public square. Today might be calmer, but he certainly wasn't about to let María Skoronsky distract him. He bit his lip. The fact that he was even thinking about that demonstrated that ignoring María, whom he hadn't met until the other day, might put up a tougher challenge than he anticipated.

"There's a whole lot of trees out here, isn't there, Mr. President?" said Scharq.

Quijano glanced down at his mud-splattered shoes. "I must thank you again, *Señor* Scharq, for all this land the Mobys Foundation has donated to Azcalatl National Park."

"*Will* donate, Mr. President. After we sign the agreement."

"Always the legal documents, yes. I understand. But then this land will be protected forever."

Scharq noted the mud covering his own Italian slip-ons. He could give them to the concierge to clean and shine, but shoes like these . . . He'd have María donate them to a homeless shelter. Have his people send out a press release, too. He could have another pair flown down from San Francisco. Two pairs. "Land like this," he said. "No one should screw with nature."

Quijano tucked his handkerchief into his jacket pocket.

"The thing is," said Scharq, "there's a *lot* of land up here." He shivered in spite of his fleece-lined jacket. "And let's be honest. Environment or no, some of it's just going to waste."

Quijano clasped his hands together. "To waste?"

María patted Quijano's arm. "Mr. President, no one's suggesting that anyone build a town up here or develop an office park. It's kind of a long way from anywhere."

"I do not understand, *Señora*."

Scharq turned to Bobby, whose eyes remained in constant motion. "Colonel, did you bring any bug spray?"

"Sorry, sir," Bobby replied.

"The trees, the birds, the butterflies," Scharq continued, "and whatever else grows or creeps or flies in a beautiful place like this . . ." He swatted at an unseen creature buzzing in front of his face. "The Mobys Foundation is here to protect them. Goes without saying. But don't forget about *people*."

A V-shaped wrinkle emerged between Quijano's eyebrows. "People?"

"Nature, people . . . one big happy family."

"I am confused, *Señor* Scharq."

"You're a poet, Mr. President. I hate to say that I haven't read anything you've written, but I will. God's honest truth. But I'm a businessman. Put it this way. A tree's a tree, right?"

Quijano made no reply.

"So what does it matter what kind of trees grow up here? If our agreement lets us plant a few acres or hectares or whatever of coffee trees on land *we* donated, all as part of a little research effort, okay. God's still in his heaven and all's right with the world."

"Plant, *Señor* Scharq? In a national park?"

"A simple lease-back deal, Mr. President, with a few tax breaks thrown in. It's done all the time. And don't concern yourself with pushback from the crazies who claim people are the problem, not the solution. We're visionaries, you and me." Scharq gripped Quijano's shoulders and spun with him in a circle like paired figure skaters testing the ice in an arena. "And while we're at it, we'll put in a road, power lines, all that stuff. They'll all lead right up here to our . . ." He paused.

María reached out and gently patted Quijano's hand. "Mr. President, you understand that what you are about to here is privileged information." She stepped closer. "*Naturalmente*," she whispered formally, "*si diga algo a alguién, tenemos que matarse.*"

Quijano's face took on a pall of rain-cloud gray.

Bobby, whose Spanish was more than serviceable, glanced at María.

Scharq, who knew little more Spanish than *tequila por favor*, grinned. Quijano's reaction confirmed that he'd received the message. If the president told anyone, they would have to kill him.

"So in a nutshell," Scharq concluded after delivering a sketchy briefing augmented by Khan as the respected man of science among them, "we'll produce small quantities of caffuel and run test engines up here. And of course, we'll increase our coffee growing capacity all over the country. A win-win situation, right?"

Quijano pursed then released his lips. "But if more land is cultivated for coffee in San Cristo, *Señor* Scharq, will not less land be used for growing food?"

Scharq patted his chest. "You've got a good heart, Mr. President. But as someone said, 'Let them eat cake.'"

"Marie Antoinette," Khan offered.

Scharq smiled. "And who doesn't like cake?" He flicked a small silvery-green bug off Quijano's shoulder. "Oh, and more good news." He winked at María. "Guess who's cutting the ribbon at the grand opening of our Mobys store?"

Quijano stared blankly ahead.

"The Pope! Since the Vatican added San Cristo to the Holy Father's Latin American tour, we've been in touch. He loves our double-heavy-foam-light-sprinkle-of-cinnamon-dab-of-whipped-cream latte."

"But why . . ." Quijano sputtered. "Why have I not been informed?"

"Everything in due time," said María like the mother she was comforting a bewildered child.

Quijano shook his head. "Caffuel . . . and now your business with the Holy father. *Señor* Scharq, your gift of land is most generous, but I should require some time . . ."

Scharq cut him off. "Mr. President, I'm disappointed. Considering all we're doing for you, I'd hoped you'd share our enthusiasm."

Khan raised his right palm. "Not to fear, Mr. President. The new research facility will be kept out of the public eye. One wishes, sir, to avoid scrutiny when one's research is as sensitive as that for caffuel."

"And when," Quijano asked, "do you propose to begin construction?"

Scharq threw his arm around Quijano. "Well, Mr. President, that depends on you. And I think you'll pull your weight, if you know what I mean. In fact, I'm sure."

"And why, *Señor* Scharq, will I do that?"

"A simple axiom of business, Mr. President. One hand washes the other. By which I mean I've had several conversations with important people in the capital. We agree that *you,* a man who understands business yet remains a friend of the little people, are our man in April's presidential election."

What was not to like about a freely elected President Alonso Quijano? The army had staged its bi-annual coup the previous spring. Under pressure from Washington and following quiet discussions with Scharq, the general staff approached the nation's acclaimed professor of literature and beloved poet laureate whose epic fantasy, *"Todo y nada"*—"All and Nothing"—charmed generations of children with tales of the magical azcalatl bird that took the physical form of anyone's fantasy. The nation would hold an election for interim president before the next regularly scheduled election. Quijano would run. Quijano would win. Quijano would be hailed as a representative of enlightened moderation in a region in which the forces of right and left had so long struggled. And so it had happened.

Quijano bent his head. "With your help and God's . . ."

"In that order," Scharq cut in. "I mean, God helps those who help themselves, right? And it's no secret that radical elements in San Cristo oppose Mobys' establishing our retail presence here. Hell, they hate anybody with a little capitalist spirit who wants to make a buck."

Khan stepped forward. "Mr. President, I have staked my career on making Whitman Scharq the father of a radically new supply of energy. Rest assured, sir, the entire world will reap its benefits and sing his praises as the savior of our planet."

A small insect fluttered by.

Scharq clapped his palms then wiped them off. "Let's go back to the capital."

Garcia-Vega studied the television's close-up of the goalkeeper with blonde, shoulder-length hair. The keeper rocked from side to side, delaying his commitment until the shooter ran forward and attempted the penalty kick.

The referee blew his whistle.

The shooter approached the ball.

"*¡A la izquierda!*" urged Garcia-Vega. To the left!

Fool that he was, the goalkeeper flung his body to the right. The ball rocketed in the opposite direction past the helpless keeper's feet and into the net.

"*¡Comemierda!*" Garcia-Vega let loose. Shithead! He looked around the conference room for Carlos' approval only to realize that Carlos had not yet returned to ANTI's dark, cramped offices.

Garcia-Vega calmed himself. A league match between two German teams meant nothing as regarded his personal loyalties. He watched *futból* solely for the sake of the sport, the gripping poetry of two sides working patiently for the slightest advantage that might lead to a goal. *Futból* infused his blood. Although an undersized, scrawny child, he'd played *futból* fiercely, always with Carlos on his side to punish any opponent who returned one of his elbows to the head or kicks to the shins.

Now he had another reason to watch *fútbol*—a fifty-inch plasma television, which added a whole new dimension to the game. He'd had the TV installed in ANTI's conference room after returning from California. And why not? He'd raised more money than anyone could have expected. Surely, a man who dedicated every moment of his life to the people and risked all was entitled to a little relaxation.

Garcia-Vega crossed the room and opened the small refrigerator purchased from a Wal-Mart super bodega—on sale, of course—to accommodate the staff while workmen slowly installed ANTI's new kitchen. He withdrew a Sierra Nevada Pale Ale, ambled back to his seat and, as he had done half-a-dozen times earlier, studied the front page of *La Patria*. The capital's elite-dominated daily newspaper continued to torment him.

The offensive headline and accompanying photo, which suggested that he'd gained a little weight, held over him an almost-hypnotic power. As president, his first official act would be to shut down *La Patria* and show San Cristo's media whores that they could no longer spew one lie after another to advance the cause of the rich. Cristanos who valued the truth found it only in *Dar Voces*, the newspaper ANTI published every Friday.

Although Garcia-Vega now knew the story practically word for word, he slammed his hand down on the table. His palm stung. So be it. Pain had never interrupted Jesús Garcia-Vega's unending quest for justice. Nor had lies. *La Patria* had the nerve to belittle his presidential candidacy and deprecate his record as minister of housing. And who was this emblem of corruption to raise old accusations regarding government-paid trips to Havana, Caracas and La Paz, as well as to Buenos Aires during a major *fútbol* event? Bullshit! Not one hotel room, not one meal in a restaurant worthy of the name, not one seat in a stadium served any other purpose than to advance the cause of the people. The people always came first. Why else had he paid for that lovely young blonde companion in Lima out of his own pocket?

Garcia-Vega took a deep breath and held it to center himself. The media's time would come. After his victory in April, ANTI would publish *Dar Voces* daily. It would become the capital's official newspaper, giving every Cristano access to the truth, as he and ANTI knew it to be. In spite of the Internet, which his government would carefully scrutinize—the Chinese did so, although they had betrayed socialism—*Dar Voces* would gain major advertising revenues to support the foundation and the party it spawned. Advertising, however, was secondary. Such financial concerns represented the old politics of the elite. Truth had no price.

Garcia-Vega stood, left the conference room and walked several paces down the hall to the kitchen area. The contractors had stripped its walls down to the studs, pulled up the old flooring and removed the ceiling. But demolishing something old always proved easier than building something new. The contractor had called that morning to explain that his crew could not come in. A project in the upper suburbs required them. The idea of wealthy Cristanos living in the hills—traditionally the home of the poor—disgusted him. These people sought to ape their American counterparts in Berkeley and other cities at every turn. But at least, the crew would return tomorrow. Or the next day. Garcia-Vega asked if the other client could wait, implored and finally cursed. But what he could he do? Working men—even contractors—served many masters.

Still, just looking at the new PVC pipes and color-coded wiring in the bare but larger room—they had knocked out a wall and eliminated a small office—heartened him. ANTI's leaders and workers had to eat as did all other human beings. With the kitchen completed—and the contractor had better take this job seriously if he wished to stay in business after the election—Garcia-Vega would again prepare meals for the staff, but now with an even greater flourish. He had established an enviable reputation for his creative ways with simple Italian and French peasant dishes—pan-seared gnocchi, pasta fagioli, ratatouille and cassoulet. Moreover, the new kitchen would boast an electric grill for steaks. Man did not live by pasta and vegetables alone.

Down the hall, the entry door opened and slammed shut. Carlos' familiar footsteps echoed off the newly tiled floor as he plodded to the conference room. Without a kitchen, the staff had no choice but to patronize nearby *pupuserías* or *bodegas*, or return home for lunch and a nap—a practice Garcia-Vega frowned upon as an unproductive relic of Spanish colonialism. Today, however, he had ordered an extended lunch hour. He had important business to conduct—business demanding absolute privacy.

"Way to tackle!" Carlos cheered in the conference room.

Garcia-Vega sipped from his Nevada Pale Ale and went to join him.

Carlos pointed to the plastic bags on the table. "Smells good, huh, *jefe*?" He glanced up at Garcia-Vega. "Is that my beer?"

"Sorry, I just got one for myself. I was thinking."

Carlos fiddled with the volume control on his iPod so he could listen to his music and the *jefe* both.

"So?" asked Garcia-Vega. "Go get one."

Carlos grinned. "You don't have to tell me twice, *jefe*. It may be *Yanqui* beer, but it's good, no?"

Garcia-Vega mimed writing with a pencil.

Carlos reached into his pocket, fished out a crumpled paper receipt and dropped it on the table.

Garcia-Vega flattened the receipt and tucked it in his shirt pocket.

Carlos went to the fridge. "Those Germans play tough defense, huh? My Miguelito, he is going to play in Europe some day. All three boys, they will play in Europe and pay for their sisters' weddings. A family is expensive, *jefe*. It is never easy for the working man, no?"

Garcia-Vega sat and pushed the front page of *La Patria* across the conference table.

Carlos unscrewed the cap on his bottle, sat and stared at the plastic bags.

Garcia-Vega wondered if his friend, like Pavlov's dog, would begin to salivate as soon as he heard the bag's contents being removed. His own appetite aroused, he withdrew three steak sandwiches and three portions of pommes-frites along with packets of mayonnaise. The French restaurant down the block always pleased him and offered, in his knowledgeable opinion, a better wine list than even the restaurant at the Hotel Azcalatl Grande.

Carlos waved a beer. "You know, *jefe* . . . sometimes life is pretty good."

Garcia-Vega unwrapped his sandwich, careful to avoid dirtying his hands.

Carlos stuffed three pommes-frites in his mouth.

Garcia-Vega bit into his sandwich and chewed slowly. What could be more important to a man than good food? Good pussy, yes. But you could live without women if you absolutely had to. He took a single pommes-frite, dabbed it in mayonnaise, held it aloft and savored it before sliding it between his teeth.

Carlos nodded at the newspaper. "That article in *La Patria* . . . I read it."

"Those fascists will do anything to stop us. And the elite who support them, they have money we cannot even dream of getting our hands on no matter how many banks the people rob."

Carlos bit into his sandwich. He chewed with gusto.

Garcia-Vega lifted his right hand to his ear to remind Carlos that he could not possibly hear every word his *jefe* offered with music continually playing on that damn iPod. He had half a mind to make Carlos leave it at home but dismissed the thought. He knew Carlos would do as he was told, but he valued Carlos' friendship and loyalty far too much to disappoint him.

"Don't worry, *jefe,* I hear you," Carlos acknowledged. He licked his lips. "Quijano, that scrawny puppet who understands only children, has a very unfair advantage. But you will think of something, no?"

Garcia-Vega looked at his sandwich. "Quijano has money and momentum. But it is very early. Not everyone is thinking about the election yet. This is not the United States, you know."

"True, *jefe*. But with the Pope coming, people are saying good things about Quijano. And they will see his picture with the Pope all through the campaign."

"Cristanos and their childish faith! But even in the Church, we have our supporters."

Indeed, Archbishop Dantón, the highest-ranking member of San Cristo's Roman clergy had long supported ANTI in defiance of the Vatican, which had many interests to consider. Dantón also had accepted his fate. His clashes with his superiors had cost him any hope of attaining the red hat of a cardinal.

Carlos tilted his head back, finished his beer and rose. He held the empty bottle towards Garcia-Vega. "Another, *jefe*?"

Garcia-Vega motioned Carlos to sit. "You said I would think of something."

"Yes, *jefe*. You always do."

"I *have* been thinking."

Carlos' face reflected a look of reassurance, which quickly changed to uncertainty as he stared at the third, still-unwrapped sandwich and sack of pommes-frites.

The doorbell rang.

"Who could that be?" Carlos asked.

Garcia-Vega stood. "Archbishop Dantón. That sandwich and pommes-frites you have been eyeing, they are for him."

Carlos shrugged.

"Leave the beer for now. The archbishop wants to discuss a favor we can do for him."

"Sure, *jefe*. Whatever it is, I know we can help him out."

"And stop playing with that damn iPod. This matter . . . We do not have a lot of time. I need you to hear every word." Garcia-Vega held out his index finger as if he were warning a teenager about to run a complex errand. "And remember like it was recorded in your head."

Bobby pushed his desk chair back and raised his glass. A nightcap—this was his third, but he had no plans to leave his hotel room—was just the thing. He let the rye trickle slowly over his tongue then reached for Suelo's report on security for the Pope's visit, still three and-a-half weeks off. He'd already read twice, but María Skavronsky was concerned. The government was nervous. And the Vatican seemed more than a bit skittish given the bombing in the plaza the other night.

There also was the matter of a Vatican emissary flying in the next day, although he was a bishop no one had heard of and unlikely to be on anyone's hit list. As a precaution, neither the government nor the Vatican announced the visit and agreed to allow private arrangements for bringing the bishop downtown. The focus remained on P-Day, October 30, the day of the Pope's arrival and one day before Mobys' grand opening. Suelo was on it. Bobby, in consultation with María, would advise when asked.

Bobby stared into the remains of the whiskey like a magus consulting an oracle. California was what—two hours earlier? No, one. San Cristo, like the rest of Central America and every other country close to the equator, remained on Standard time. That made it a little after eleven where Bobby, Jr. lived. He could call. *Should* call. He finished the rye then reexamined the matter. Given that his daughter-in-law—now he remembered her name, Kimberly—was pregnant, they probably went to bed early. Why make a difficult situation worse? He glanced at his laptop. He'd email.

He placed the empty glass down, began to type and stopped. Maybe he should have insisted to María Skavronsky that *he* go to the airport tomorrow to meet the papal emissary. If San Cristo was in the midst of a budding revolution—although no one was certain that was the case—even the most routine matters could get complicated. And complications represented danger.

5 | CINCO | 5

BISHOP THOMAS GROELSCH NUDGED HIS GLASSES back up the length of his prominent, bony nose and peered out the window to follow the jetliner's initial approach into San Cristo International Airport. The plane flew nearly due south with Mount Azcalatl, the shimmering blue lake concealed behind it, on the western horizon.

Father Giovanni Sabella, the young priest next to him and the bishop's aide for the past several months, put down the Harry Potter book he was reading and craned forward to share some of the view partially shrouded in cloud and mist. "It's so beautiful, Bishop. Everything is so green."

Bishop Groelsch nodded.

"I've never seen green so intense, even in Italy," Father Giovanni continued. "The physical world can be so . . ."

Bishop Groelsch patted Giovanni on the knee and continued his gaze out the window. There was no lack of greenery in the forests of his native Germany, but young Giovanni was correct. This particular green seemed a color only an artist might have mixed. Or God. God certainly. The Supreme Artist. Of course, Bishop Groelsch didn't know all that much about painting. His career as a Vatican functionary—one of modest achievement in all humility—had kept him thoroughly occupied. He had, however, visited many of Europe's important museums over the years and never tired of the devotional art that placed the Lord Jesus Christ at the apex of Western culture. Of God's handiwork he was certain. In the beginning, God created the heavens and the earth. What more did any man need to know?

Giovanni, his face radiating an intense wonder, turned to the purple-haired woman across the aisle to his left—their companion on the flight with whom they would spend a few moments in the capital. She appeared to be in her forties like his mother in Perugia, although her thin, drawn face suggested someone whom life had not always treated kindly. He knew her from the television, of course, and understood that her life in no way resembled that of his mother. Nor did her appearance. Her blue eyes in particular revealed a beauty not eroded but burnished by a life of passion, commitment and—living.

Giovanni hated to interrupt her while she concentrated on the purple wool with which she knitted a sweater or scarf—perhaps it was meant to be a cap—to match her hair. But with the plane descending, the view out either side was too breathtaking to miss. He thanked Christ for this moment, never before having traveled out of Italy, then asked, "Signorina Rozen, have you seen . . ."

"I've seen it all, sonny."

"I have never . . ."

"I *have*."

Indeed, Adella Rozen had shared joints with narco-revolutionaries in Colombia, taken tea with Pashtun warlords in Pakistan's Northwest Frontier, gotten drunk with rebel leaders in Congo after Angolan troops intervened and trekked the jungles of Mindanao with Moro separatists. Her experiences were legend, earning her not only an international following but also the respect and envy of fellow journalists.

"It's just that from here," Giovanni declared, his voice suggesting a childlike joy, "everything reveals itself to be the loving work of Our Lord." He gazed down at the small gold ring on his right hand—a gift from his parents. An engraved cross expressed his commitment to Christ. "You must be thrilled to be here."

"Very inspirational," said Adella, not wishing to offend, although offense more often than not served as her stock in trade. She raised a pair of knitting needles. How, she wondered, could she not tell truth to power, even in the form of a young priest who had no affect on the world at all? "You already know that my network is forcing me to gather background on the Pope's visit to an insignificant country." She rolled her eyes. "Such an inconsequential assignment I take as a grievous violation of my professional standing and a personal affront. And when I want to hear a travelogue, I will request one." She resumed her stitches. "God, I need a cigarette."

Father Giovanni, his cheeks as purple as Adella's hair and wool, turned away to peer through the window that continued to hold Bishop Groelsch's attention. What sin of commission or omission tarnished their souls that the Vatican press office consented to have *this* woman accompany them?

Giovanni's discomfort was not unnatural. That Adella Rozen was an alcoholic and a drug addict was public knowledge—and for good reason. She infused her work with a steady stream of public confessions regarding her failings—liquor, cocaine and also men, particularly other women's husbands. Just as sinful, the media conglomerate that employed her to cover edgy issues for its television network and chain of newspapers encouraged her to promote the spectacle of each and every one of her latest recoveries.

Adella freely acknowledged that she had critics. What truth they uttered she dismissed as water under the Ponte Rotto. You lived your life, and you accepted the fallout. It was no accident that the person she held in highest esteem was Edith Piaf. But the lies—the vicious lies she could not abide.

The worst lie was that she was a Jew. This lie particularly galled her because her detractors sought to define her as the Nazis had defined Jews—through genetics. Admittedly, her great-grandparents, Shlomo and Malkeh Rozen, were Jews who fled Tsarist Russia only steps ahead of the secret police. Atheists and socialists, they found their way to Rome where Shlomo spent days buying and selling second-hand luggage and evenings attending socialist lectures with Malkeh, before she bore children. Adella's grandfather, Shlomo and Malkeh's son, Giuseppe, named after the great Garibaldi rather than the biblical Joseph, trumped his parents by marrying a nonreligious Catholic. Shlomo and Malkeh neither cursed nor mourned but celebrated universal brotherhood—and sisterhood. Adella's father, Antonio, was not recognized as a Jew by Jewish law, since his mother was not Jewish—a matter to which Antonio gave not a single thought. The Nazis gave it great thought. During the War, nuns in the countryside hid Antonio from the German occupiers. Giuseppe ascended to the heavens at Auschwitz.

Father Giovanni stared into the back of the seat in front of him. To his amazement and regret, Signorina Rozen had made no mention of the healing power of the Lord Jesus Christ. He would pray for her. Whether the God of love and mercy would answer his prayers, he could not say. Adella Rozen might have strayed too far off the path for the Shepherd to reunite her with the flock, and if she did not make confession . . . Although he suffered endless guilt regarding his less-than-perfect faith in the power of love, he would ask God for the strength to endure her presence on the rest of a journey that marked the highlight of his young life—other than once having been allowed in the presence of the Holy Father. And earlier, as a small boy, glimpsing on more than one occasion the naked thighs of an older cousin in a short skirt as she climbed the stairs ahead of him to her family's apartment.

Bishop Groelsch turned to the young priest. "Giovanni?"

Giovanni startled.

"You say Archbishop Dantón will meet us. Will there be . . ." He peered across Giovanni's pensive face to observe Adella, knitting furiously as though she were being paid by the piece. "Will we have to confront the media?"

"I don't believe so, Bishop."

Bishop Groelsch chuckled his assent. Senior advisors had already handled all the important details concerning the Holy Father's visit. Elevated to bishop only months earlier as a reward for years of performing mundane but essential tasks with resolution and humility, he would tidy up a few minor matters on what was, in reality, a pre-retirement jaunt. "Truly, Giovanni, an old priest and a young one would hardly draw much attention from anyone. Well, except from . . ." He looked again at Adella.

Father Giovanni shook his head. "Signorina Rozen won't really be reporting on *us*, Bishop."

Indeed, while Adella would cover the Pope's brief visit, her early arrival represented more than the opportunity to acquire background on San Cristo. Of course, the conglomerate's chairman considered that the papal visit would appeal to Europe's few remaining faithful—a shrunken demographic but still a component of the marketplace from which a profit could be wrung. But more important, sending Adella away from Rome and out of Europe raised the odds that her annual reentry into sobriety might evolve into a more permanent state. Of at least equal concern, the conglomerate's legal team would enjoy a greater opportunity to calm a delicate matter threatening to embarrass not one but two ministers within the Italian government and destroy years of goodwill the chairman had so carefully nurtured.

Anticipating Adella's expected lack of enthusiasm, the chairman had dangled a book offer, although her last two books had fallen well short of expectations. In San Cristo, Adella's penchant for leftist politics would prompt her to meet with Jesús Garcia-Vega, a minor character on the world stage but a symbol of continuing political ferment in Latin America. Follow-up jaunts to Havana, Caracas, Lima and La Paz might keep the fearless, trendsetting and newly clear-eyed media diva's passion focused sufficiently to produce an entertaining geopolitical work appealing both to intellectuals captivated by revolution and the public, whose appetite for titillation remained insatiate.

The plane began its final descent. Without warning, an air pocket caused it to drop. Cries of alarm sounded. Objects of various sizes and shapes rose towards the ceiling. Then, as if the captain had been playing a joke, the plane steadied and proceeded smoothly towards the runway.

"Someone give me a fucking cigarette!" Adella exclaimed.

Father Giovanni reached across the aisle and lightly touched Adella's shoulder. His fingers trembled as if he'd come in contact with a live electric cable. The sensation frightened him. He'd sinned continually over the past months by being unable to cast off thoughts forbidden to a man of the cloth. What, he wondered, would it be like to live like the sheep and not the shepherd? To work in a factory or shop or office? To play football on warm Sunday mornings instead of leading or attending Mass? To know a woman?

What would happen if he simply walked away from everything he knew into a world that both terrified and fascinated him?

Sadly, he could no more resist his impure thoughts than still the waves of the Adriatic or the Mediterranean. Naturally, each time the evil impulse seized his soul he dutifully confessed and eagerly accepted his penance. His commitment to Christ remained strong. His longings, his confessor instructed, served less to torment him than to strengthen his soul by testing his faith. But didn't husbands and fathers have faith?

With a practiced but worn charm, a flight attendant began the usual announcements to ready the passengers for landing.

"A car will pick us up?" Adella asked.

"Oh yes," Giovanni responded. "We will be at the hotel in no time."

Father Giovanni approached the curb outside the terminal with hesitant steps. Unsure of what he could expect in a small and perhaps dangerous Central American country, he tapped his side as if scratching an itch. Reassured that his passport remained secure in the slender pouch his mother had sewn for him to wear under his shirt—he'd stopped in the restroom after clearing customs to conceal it—he yielded his and Bishop Groelsch's suitcases to the one-eyed man who had greeted them bearing a card from Archbishop Dantón.

Carlos tucked his black iPod into his shirt pocket, opened the trunk of a blue 1995 Ford Taurus, shifted a shotgun and hoisted the bags into place.

Adella, a cigarette dangling from her lips, handed Carlos her small carry-on. No one packed more quickly and efficiently. She could, after all, expect to go anywhere in the world on a moment's notice. And her expense account would cover anything she forgot, needed or desired.

Carlos glanced at Adella's handbag.

Adella scowled.

Carlos slammed the trunk closed then stepped to the left-rear door, opened it for the bishop, who had drifted from the curb, and nudged him gently but firmly inside. Circling around the front of the Taurus, he motioned to Father Giovanni then entered the front, passenger-side seat.

Father Giovanni opened the right-rear door and stepped back to allow Adella to take the middle seat.

Adella scowled.

The young priest slid across the seat to take his place at his superior's right hand.

Adella followed. Settling in, she opened her window, tossed out the remains of her cigarette and lit another.

Bishop Groelsch leaned slightly forward as the driver pulled away behind a gray Honda Accord even older than the Taurus. Its trunk looked like someone had pounded it with a baseball bat. Half of the left taillight was missing, and the bumper jiggled as if it were about to fall off. "I am sorry, Carlos," Bishop Groelsch said in Spanish, "but does Archbishop Dantón really believe we might be in any danger?"

Adella turned towards Bishop Groelsch and exhaled.

The bishop and Father Giovanni each emitted a small, choking cough.

"Welcome to San Café," she said in Italian. "And that car, that Honda in front of us," she asked Carlos in flawless Spanish. "We are following it?"

Carlos turned to Bishop Groelsch. "They are with *us*. Off-duty *Seguridad* men making a little extra money. After the army, I served in one of the security agencies for several years. But the pay . . ."

"We know how that goes," Adella responded.

Carlos handed a photograph to Bishop Groelsch.

"Your family, Carlos?"

Carlos smiled.

"It looks like a very wonderful family. Three handsome sons."

"And four beautiful daughters," Carlos replied.

"Indeed. I trust that at least one will be a bride of Christ."

Carlos shrugged, took back the photo and tucked it behind his iPod.

Giovanni swiveled his head and looked past Adella. "Didn't we just pass the entrance to the highway?" he asked in serviceable Spanish.

"Traffic," Carlos answered.

The gray Honda pulled further ahead.

"The highway into the city is not like the . . . how you say in Italian . . . the *autostrade*," Carlos explained. "In this traffic, it will take an hour and a half to get downtown. Possibly two. But we can take Avenida San José. The other car will go ahead of us. What does the Bible say . . . a pillar of fire led the Israelites through the wilderness?"

Bishop Groelsch leaned back. "Very good, Carlos."

Carlos held up a small radio. "If the traffic is too heavy on San José, no problem. I know these streets. I live close by. With seven children, it is hard to find a decent house you can afford."

Open countryside quickly yielded to the poor, crowded neighborhoods of the city's down, or southern, flank. Small assembly plants and tin-roofed warehouses lined the avenue along with auto repair shops and junkyards showcasing stacks of rusted cars and decades-old kitchen appliances for which even the poor had no use. Gas stations, small grocery stores and pharmacies displayed windows masked by posters hawking Coke, Pepsi and lottery tickets. Burger and pizza joints competed with vendors selling pupusas, ice cream and sugary soft drinks from umbrella-topped carts. Three—and four-story walk-up apartment buildings in various shades of peeling pastels stood among rubble-filled lots.

Giovanni stared at dark-skinned men and women carrying plastic shopping bags, jugs of water and metal toolboxes. He noticed how they walked unhurriedly but deliberately since no sidewalks had been built this far from downtown. Others gathered patiently around telephone poles painted with red and white stripes identifying bus stops. At irregular intervals, narrow streets, some cobbled and some dirt, ran off at an assortment of angles past small houses. Their exteriors, Giovanni imagined, suggested that roofs would always leak, foundations crumble and walls provide no barrier to creatures seeking secure nests for their young.

The Taurus made modest progress—the Honda was now just out of sight—hopscotching from lane to lane in bold attempts to pass the endless flow of trucks, buses, autos and scooters also avoiding the highway. In turn, it slowed as others employed the same ultimately fruitless tactic. A succession of irregularly timed traffic lights added to the delay.

Carlos radioed the Honda. A moment later, the Taurus turned right at a small traffic circle.

"San José is no good," Carlos informed them. "We will go a little out of our way, but we will get downtown more quickly. Thirty minutes at the most. Or forty."

Bishop Groelsch stroked the beads of his rosary.

Giovanni peered intently out of Adella's window. His few travels within Italy had never revealed sights like this.

Adella pulled her knitting from the handbag between her feet. Ciudad San Cristo offered nothing she hadn't seen before only worse.

The Taurus turned left and bounced with jaw-rattling force over a street once fully cobbled and long neglected.

"Who lives here?" asked Giovanni. "In this neighborhood, I mean."

"*Indígenas*," Carlos answered. "Indians who come from the countryside to find work."

"Do they?"

"Some. Sometimes."

Several blocks ahead, the quality of the roadbed improved while the traffic worsened. The driver pressed down heavily on the brake pedal. The Taurus squealed to a halt.

"*¿Hay problema?*" Carlos asked.

The driver pointed ahead.

Traffic was stopped in both directions, blocked by a crowd gathered in the middle of the street.

Carlos got out of the Taurus and crouched at Adella's window. "Wait here. Everything is fine, I am sure." Straightening, he reached his hand under his shirt and walked forward.

Adella put down her knitting.

Bishop Groelsch squeezed his rosary beads.

"It happens all the time," the driver confided. "The Honda will wait for us. No need to worry."

Carlos returned, his gun tucked away. "A man in a white pickup truck and his wife. He has had a heart attack maybe. He is unconscious."

"We should see to him," said Groelsch.

"Someone is calling for an ambulance. And police, of course." He gazed ahead and behind. "This may take a few minutes."

Bishop Groelsch opened his door.

"It is better to stay in the car, Bishop," said Carlos. "Unless, as a religious duty . . ."

Bishop Groelsch got out and walked towards the crowd.

Carlos followed, trailed by Adella and Father Giovanni.

The knot of small, dark men, women and children parted amidst whispers of "*cura*." Priest.

Bishop Groelsch approached the driver's side of the pickup, made the sign of the cross on the unconscious man's forehead and looked across to the woman, her face frozen in fear. Returning his gaze to the man—his head lolling against the back of his seat, mouth open and eyes closed—the bishop opened the door. Whether the man was pale he could not tell, but his breathing sounded unnatural, surely a sign of a struggle with impending death. Taking the unconscious man's hand, he smiled at the woman and prepared himself to administer the Sacrament of the Sick.

"Bishop," Giovanni asked from behind his right shoulder, "may I . . ."

The metal-crunching sound of a collision cut him off. At the intersection behind them, two trucks stood, their grilles entangled like rams' horns.

Bishop Groelsch turned to Giovanni.

The young priest had taken only a step away when a small explosion from one of the trucks spewed a cloud of dark gray smoke into the air. It resembled a newly drilled oil well gushing crude.

Cries arose from the crowd. The men, women and children who had gathered around the pickup to observe or pray scattered. Those inside shops, cafés and homes ran out to see what had happened. Bodies collided like molecules in a heated solution.

In the distance, sirens wailed.

"You would think the world was ending," said Adella from behind Carlos, who tugged the resistant bishop away from the pickup. She shook her head. "I know what the end of the world looks like. It's not pretty. And this isn't it."

Bishop Groelsch protested. "Christ's work is here. Now."

Carlos led the bishop back towards the Taurus, pushing away those who blocked their path without regard to sex, age or infirmity.

Adella followed.

The Taurus' driver, his gun drawn, met them.

The sirens grew louder. Flashes of red and blue lights reflected off walls and windows as two police cars and an ambulance crept closer.

Just as quickly as the crowd had swelled, it evaporated.

A policeman began directing one lane of traffic at a time around the pickup and the ambulance.

Drivers up and down the street revved their engines adding to the dense, gray cloud of exhaust overhead.

Carlos guided Bishop Groelsch into the Taurus and closed the door behind him. "The Honda has another route for us. God willing, we will be downtown soon."

Adella stood by her door, revolved slowly in a determined journalistic pirouette then stared at Carlos. "So where is our young priest?"

6 | SEIS | 6

"TELL US AGAIN," BOBBY INSISTED. He stretched his right leg beneath the large gray metal table. "What happened when you went back to the car?"

Carlos looked past Bobby to Suelo, propped against a wall in response to the pain in his back. "Now *Yanquis* are asking questions? Why is this man even here?"

If Carlos appeared belligerent, Bobby felt awkward. This *was* Suelo's turf. The last thing he wanted was the student resenting the teacher. But the missing priest was tied to the Pope, the Pope was tied to Mobys, and Vatican security was expressing concern, which could untie the arrangements for the visit and the Pope's attendance at Mobys' grand opening. Bottom line as María Skavronsky had made clear was that anything that happened in San Cristo was Mobys' business, which made it Bobby's business. Moreover, he'd spent his share of time questioning enemy soldiers and jihadis, sheiks and tribal elders, farmers and grocery clerks, grandmothers and housewives. He knew what all interrogators knew—a story repeated often enough could reveal inconsistencies that compromised the bad guys.

"You have been very helpful, *Señor* Rivera," said Suelo. "But please, one more time."

Carlos took a deep breath then blew the air out of puffed cheeks as if he were playing a trumpet. "Archbishop Dantón requested through *Señor* Garcia-Vega that I go to the airport. You know that." He tapped his shirt pocket to be sure he still had his iPod. "Listen, how about something to eat? I am your guest not a prisoner."

"*Por favor*, just one more time," said Bobby then continued to scrutinize Carlos' face as he repeated what he had already told them half a dozen times. If a hole existed in his story, Bobby couldn't find it. Neither Suelo nor his interrogators indicated a different opinion.

Suelo stepped forward and placed his hand on Bobby's shoulder. "Anything else, *amigo*?"

Bobby shook his head.

"Go home to dinner," said Suelo to Carlos. "And don't worry. We'll find Father Giovanni."

Carlos stood and fished the earpieces of his iPod out of his pocket. "I hope you do. But I'll tell you this. If I *had* taken the priest, you would *never* find him."

Father Giovanni's attention focused on the sounds of an impromptu but unseen *fútbol* match that drifted through the closed window. Children's shouts and laughter rose above an airplane ascending overhead. They reminded Giovanni of his own childhood when he played with friends until darkness set impatient mothers to shouting their names. Those who dawdled encountered grim looks of displeasure, muttered threats and firm hands tugging painfully at ears or pinching the tender flesh of young arms. Of course, Giovanni rarely suffered such consequences. An eager altar boy who upheld the Fourth Commandment by honoring his parents—his father worked in the big chocolate factory, his mother in a bakery—he rarely failed to respond to his name and the filial duty demanded of him.

Now, experiencing a deep sense of solitude in the crowded city and sharply aware of the distance between him and everything he knew—home, family, country and even Holy Mother Church—Giovanni took comfort in the noisy street. In Genesis, God commanded Adam and Eve to be fertile and multiply. The street from which he remained hidden—the authorities doubtless were looking for him—teemed with life, young and old. He could hear, as well, the trucks and buses and automobiles that coursed through the neighborhood of workers, students, dreamers, and yes, lovers, like blood pumping through a body's veins.

Remarkably, he felt alive as never before, connected not to the next world of angels and heavenly choirs but to this one of flesh and blood. He gathered his thoughts. What new people would he encounter? Should he drink the water? What would happen to Harry Potter, since he'd tucked the book away in his carry-on bag the man Carlos had thrown into the trunk of the Ford Taurus? And like Harry, would he face dangers he could not imagine?

7 | SIETE | 7

"AND THE POPE WEARING A MOBYS APRON," declared Scharq. "You can't buy that kind of publicity. Only now . . ." He flung the morning's newspaper in disgust. It landed with a splat on the penthouse's dining room table. Thinking better of losing his composure in a moment of crisis, he closed his eyes and counted to seven.

María dug her small but powerful hands into his shoulders then stepped back. "It's not over, Whit. We can still pull this off."

Scharq stretched his arms overhead, lowered them slowly then gently set five crystal wine glasses on the polished-concrete counter separating the suite's gourmet kitchen from the expansive living/dining area with its 60-inch plasma flat-screen television. In all, the Hotel Azcalatl Grande's penthouse encompassed a virtual house perched atop the roof above the twelfth floor. Decks and patios—each landscaped with potted palms, rosebushes and raised flowerbeds—bounded three sides. Glass walls offered panoramic views of forested mountains that created a jagged horizon line resembling the fluctuation of Mobys share prices over the past months. Closer in, the penthouse looked west past its private pool and spa towards Plaza Azcalatl and the left side of the capital. Scanning clockwise, the view took in the Presidential Palace only blocks away to the northwest and the northern suburbs of the wealthy. To the east rose twin condominium towers dubbed by *capitalistas* "Manhood I" and "Manhood II." They abutted a neighborhood of modest homes and apartments leading to the green expanse of Parque Azcalatl. The penthouse's south wall offered only small windows at the roof line to let in light while shielding its occupants from various components of the building's heating, ventilation and air-conditioning system, as well as the city's sprawling slums.

"A little wine before we think about lunch?" Scharq called out.

"A most delightful idea," answered Khan. He was, after all, on holiday, if a working one.

Scharq extracted the cork from a 1990 Charmes Chambertin, Grand Cru. He maintained a fierce loyalty to California wines but never to the point of depriving himself. He poured a glass and handed it to Alonso Quijano. "Mr. President?"

Quijano hesitated. "Perhaps some other time, *señor*."

"It's happy hour," María warbled. "Somewhere." She rose on her toes as if on point then dropped slowly into a *demi plie*. The knee-length hem of her skirt—she rejected slacks for business occasions—revealed the muscular dancer's calves she maintained with vigorous workouts. Satisfied, she perched on the black-leather seat of a stool.

"Mr. President," said Scharq, "you wait for another time and before you know it, life's passed you by. What else do we have but time?" He placed the glass in Quijano's hand.

Quijano held it in front of his chest as if to calm his pounding heart.

"Colonel?" Scharq asked.

Bobby held up his right hand. "Not right now, sir. Thank you, sir."

Scharq shrugged. "Well, you *are* on duty. For that matter you're *always* on duty. Isn't that the way it works, María?"

María took third position, her feet pointed out, her right arm raised, her left extended. "Something like that, Whit."

Scharq poured glasses for Khan and María then set the bottle down. "Colonel, that newspaper on the table. If you don't mind."

Bobby handed the paper to Scharq.

Scharq turned to Quijano. "And which paper is this, Mr. President?"

"*La Patria, Señor* Scharq."

"*La Patria*. The *New York Times* of San Cristo." He held the paper up. "Read the headline to us."

"*¿Adónde?*"

"A headline consisting of exactly . . . count for yourself . . . one word. Which . . . and you tell me if I'm wrong, María . . . means 'where?' As in, where can he possibly be? In big, black letters maybe . . . what? Four inches high? Which is what . . . ten centimeters, Mr. President? And something else, I notice. The headline, although I'm no student of journalism, relates to the picture . . . the photo . . . of a young Italian priest named Giovanni something-or-other. And the newspaper reports that this priest has gone *missing*."

Quijano's eyes grew watery and unfocused. "*Señor* Scharq . . ."

Bobby recognized Quijano's response. He had seen the same deer-in-the-headlights helplessness in the eyes of presidents, prime ministers, kings, generals and sheiks who suddenly realized that ultimately they were not the masters of their domains. He turned to Scharq. "Colonel Suelo is working on this personally, sir."

"And?" asked María.

Bobby glanced at María. She clearly demonstrated the character of a woman not to be taken lightly. The trait left him somewhat uncomfortable yet very much intrigued. "And we know a few things."

Scharq poured a glass of Burgundy for himself with a deliberateness suggesting the venting of anger one drop at a time. "Which would be what, Colonel?"

"We've interviewed a man named Carlos . . ."

"Rivera," María cut in. "Jesús Garcia-Vega's right-hand man. I have a file on both of them from some time back."

All eyes fell on her.

María returned their collective gaze with a smile. Did they really think that a woman in her position would leave any bases uncovered?

"Might I see that file, Ms. Skavronsky?" Bobby asked.

María's eyes narrowed.

Scharq's mouth puckered. "This Garcia-Vega, he's a fucking communist from the old school."

"More of a populist," María advised.

"The worst kind," said Scharq.

Bobby waited to see if Scharq had anything else to say then continued. "We spoke separately with Garcia-Vega and Archbishop Dantón. Their statements check out."

"Those two guys in the front car," Scharq said. "What about *them*?"

"Clean so far," Bobby answered. "But this kind of work takes time."

Scharq threw his hands into the air. "Time! Everyone is so goddam patient. We've got a problem right here and now!"

"Whitman," Khan asked, "might it be possible to get the CIA involved?"

María's head snapped towards Khan like an opening switchblade.

Khan stared into his wine. "Not appropriate on second thought."

Scharq pointed at Bobby. "What I want to know, Colonel, is how do we get a kidnapped priest back? And soon!"

Bobby looked squarely at Scharq. "Sir, nothing confirms there's been a kidnapping. We have to think that way, but no one's claimed responsibility or demanded a ransom."

Scharq rolled his head back as if the answer to the mystery lie exposed in the midst of the blown-glass chandeliers hanging from the kitchen's ceiling of coffered teak. "What else could have happened? He slipped away to find his fortune in the jungle or see what sex is all about?"

"A priest is still a man," said María. "I can tell you stories."

"The thing is," said Bobby, "until we get something we can work with, we have to assume all the possibilities."

Khan raised his glass to his nose and spoke as if into a microphone. "Actually, Whitman may be on to something, Colonel. The missing priest is a young man, is he not?"

"Twenty-three. Bishop Groelsch wasn't sure, but Vatican security's been very helpful."

Khan lowered the glass and ran a fingertip along its rim. "I come from a nation . . . first-rate in many ways, sir . . . yet a nation in which so many young men have been sequestered from . . . from the pleasures of life. These young men, even when educated, often lack prospects. They cannot gain meaningful employment. Therefore they cannot marry, which is the only way they will come to know a woman. The only way, sir! As a result, they become repressed and often turn to religion for comfort. Yet they nevertheless remain . . . with all due respect to María as a member of the gentle sex . . . distant from the satisfactions men such as ourselves expect from life."

Scharq peered into the newsprint-blurred eyes of young Father Giovanni in a photo released by the Vatican. "In plain English, I.A., you're telling me you think this priest saw the chance to throw his collar away, get lost in an exotic foreign capital . . . exotic to him, at least . . . and get laid."

Khan raised his glass. "You inspired me, Whitman. I rest my case."

Bobby glanced at what was left of the wine and promised himself a shot of Pikesville at lunch. "Colonel Suelo has men all over the city. If the priest is here, we'll find him."

María's fingernails drummed a tango beat on the counter. "Any woman knows that any man will do anything . . . But let's not kid ourselves. The Vatican is upset. If Father Giovanni is just a horny kid, that's not going to matter unless this is all cleared up. And soon. Because photos of the Pope and President Quijano will make the election in April just a formality."

"Screw the election," said Scharq. "We can get a goat elected president if we want." He glanced at Quijano then looked down into his glass, empty except for a tiny residue that cast the appearance of blood. "It's all about the Holy Father enjoying a little indulgence at Mobys. Here. In San Cristo." He placed his glass on the counter. "At least it was a priest, not a bishop who . . . You hear something?"

A low rumble intruded into the penthouse as if many Marías drummed their expensively manicured fingertips to a common rhythm. The wine glasses accompanied them.

Just as quickly, everything fell silent.

"Earthquake," said María. "There was one the night of the bombing in the plaza."

Khan went to a window. "Nothing seems amiss."

Bobby wondered if someone or something was sending a message—a coded message for which they lacked the key.

María interrupted his thoughts to deliver a message loud and clear, her brown eyes boring into him in ways he found both unsettling and inviting. "Colonel Gatling, it's time you got back with Colonel Suelo and found out what the hell is going on here. Because one way or the other, Mobys' interests *will* be protected."

Bobby found himself assuming a position of attention. Whitman Scharq and María Skavronsky were, after all, his superiors for the next weeks—the people who paid the freight. Whether Father Giovanni had run away or been kidnapped, he didn't know. What he *did* know was that the first forty-eight hours were the most critical—and twenty-four of them were gone.

Garcia-Vega, Carlos by his side, walked slowly while Bishop Groelsch, several dozen priests, including the Bishop of Maquepaque, assorted deacons and the choir followed Archbishop Dantón onto the marble portico in front of the National Cathedral. Dantón had just offered a special late-morning Mass for Father Giovanni. His golden tongue shone no more brightly than when he declared that the Blessed Virgin had sent San Cristo a message during the Lord's Prayer as he uttered the words "Deliver us from evil" by gently shaking the cathedral as a mother wakes her sleeping child.

Garcia-Vega cocked an ear. The murmur of the crowd grew louder and more expectant as Dantón descended the steps with the majestic deliberateness of his office. He saw Dantón pause to look towards the sheared-off top of the ceiba tree in the plaza then quickly shift his gaze to the television cameras. A nod acknowledged the reporters from the broadcast media as well as those from the newspapers clutching their digital cameras, microphones and recorders. A second nod recognized the large crowd overflowing from the sidewalk into Avenida Catedral and Plaza Azcalatl beyond.

"This crowd, it's big, *jefe*," whispered Carlos.

"He likes a big crowed," Garcia-Vega returned. "These men of God . . . what can I say?"

Garcia-Vega had little use for religion beyond political convenience. After taking first communion under maternal duress, he had rejected any further pretense of faith. He counted Dantón as an ally but disdained the Church. The Vatican had never communicated more than a mild discomfort with the rule of San Cristo's elite and refused to support ANTI. Such hypocrisy! How could the Church plead the cause of San Cristo's downtrodden while resisting any effort to empower them? The Pope's advisors feared confronting the elite, which included the Church's main financial benefactors—men who would protect their interests at any cost. Garcia-Vega equally had no use for San Cristo's growing evangelical movement, which offered sinners mired in poverty faith in a Christ of the free market. Wealth in this life, they preached, would secure your soul in the next. What kind of religion was that?

Dantón approached a microphone clipped to a stand. A yellow extension cord snaked back into the cathedral.

A worker with an expression of utter boredom flipped a switch and blew into the microphone. A scratchy whoo-whoo-whoo exploded from large speakers on either side of the steps. The worker withdrew.

"Now," said Garcia-Vega.

Carlos pushed forward, elbowing aside the clerical sycophants who blocked their path, until they wedged themselves between Bishop Groelsch and Dantón. Standing with chin up and chest out, Garcia-Vega tapped Dantón's left shoulder and pulled him away from the microphone. "*Momentito*," Garcia-Vega whispered. He turned to Carlos, pulled an earpiece away from his head and instructed, "Go down to the TV cameras and make sure I am in the picture."

Carlos trotted down the remaining steps and paused. The purple-haired Italian journalist was pushing several media representatives aside. He continued on and positioned himself behind a cameraman from TeleCristo, the nation's largest television network. Satisfied, he held up his right thumb.

Garcia-Vega tugged at the cuff of Dantón's sleeve then gestured towards the mic. "*Por favor*."

The Archbishop covered his mouth, cleared his throat and lowered his hand. "Friends, countryman, children of Christ. On behalf of Holy Mother Church, I wish now to pray publicly for what I have beseeched our Savior during the Mass we have just concluded. May the Father, the Son and the Holy Ghost take in their keeping our brother, Giovanni Sabella. May he be . . . may he return to us this very day. Our brother, Giovanni, is a simple man like all of us who toil each day for our daily bread. May He who died on the cross to assure us new life protect this humble man and all the humble men of San Cristo . . . the native peoples denied their right to determine their own future . . . all men, and yes, women, crushed by oppressive capitalism and the injustices it perpetrates."

Garcia-Vega glanced down furtively at the creases in his trousers compromised by the public kneeling just forced upon him. Calling upon his iron will, he raised his eyes and kept his gaze fixed on Dantón. Better not to attract undue attention—at least, until the appropriate time.

"Even now," Dantón continued, "capitalism tightens its merciless grip on the people. Mobys, the very symbol of American corporate greed, will open its first store in our beloved city facing this same plaza. And more will follow you may be sure." He lifted his face towards the heavens then lowered it. "They will sell coffee that the workers on the *fincas* and in the processing plants cannot themselves afford."

An animated cheer rose from the small knot of ANTI supporters directly behind the media.

Carlos rejoined Garcia-Vega.

Garcia-Vega covered his mouth. "Put that iPod away. It looks unprofessional on television."

Carlos removed his earpieces.

Garcia-Vega took his measure of the crowd. Earlier, Cristanos concerned for the missing priest had filled the cathedral. Several thousand had waited in the plaza. Now, they responded enthusiastically to the Archbishop, who displayed both the eloquence that sparked his ascension through the clerical ranks and the political obstinacy that denied him the red hat. Both men understood that Cristanos were a proud people. A passionate people. A people longing for the justice to which Jesús Garcia-Vega eventually would lead them. He saw how Dantón held them close as the Virgin held the baby Jesús to her breast—assuming that the Holy Mother would do such a thing.

"I say to Mobys," Dantón declared, his voice more intense, "*Yanqui*, go home or we will *send* you home."

Although dark clouds presaged the usual afternoon rainfall, the day remained bright and shining within Garcia-Vega's heart. Dantón, he knew, would make it clear that duty and humanity compelled the people of San Cristo to rise up, demand their rights and take them—and do so, as Malcolm X had enlightened America's blacks, by any means necessary.

Garcia-Vega studied the ANTI workers and supporters immediately behind the media where their roars of approval would be picked up by the television and radio microphones. These were San Cristo's true patriots and sons of God—if there was a God. Their numbers would grow rapidly. This Garcia-Vega accepted as an article of faith. He took added satisfaction in the media leaning forward like dogs waiting for food to be placed in their bowls, not simply focused on Dantón's words but also mesmerized by them.

Then Garcia-Vega startled. What was that? A woman with purple hair and a cigarette dangling from purple, almost pouting, lips? Yes. Yes, indeed. And a very attractive woman.

"I say to anyone who may have taken our dear, innocent brother Giovanni from us," Dantón continued, "if you have done this to threaten us, to thwart us, to deny our right to protest against poverty and degradation and the worship of the dollar and the euro and the renminbi and the yen . . . return this innocent and selfless soul to us. And I say to you, as well, that I pray for you. In spite of what you have done, I pray for your souls." Dantón made the sign of the cross. The crowd followed suit. "In the name of the Father and the Son and the Holy Spirit, amen."

Garcia-Vega directed his attention to the journalist with the purple hair, who removed her cigarette and flicked it—heedless of the reporter whose midsection it bounced off—to the sidewalk.

His remarks completed, Dantón stepped back.

The same worker, his face as expressionless as if he had just wakened from a nap, ambled past the Archbishop and turned off the microphone.

The media charged up the steps. It seemed to Garcia-Vega that they thrust their cameras, microphones and recorders forward like the swords and knives of marauding Mayans, Pipils or Lencas—or more appropriate to the occasion, the arquebuses and muskets of the gold-seeking *conquistadores*.

He placed his hand on Dantón's shoulder and leaned in. "Beautifully spoken, Archbishop. I hope now that the Vatican understands the depth of our resolve." His right hand gripped Dantón's left wrist to maintain his position in the crush around them.

And then something drew his eye. Wasn't that the famous Italian journalist with the purple hair approaching, her lips fondling yet another cigarette, her eyes locked on his as if she were a heat-seeking missile? Yes, and she was coming towards him. And in doing so, she laid her soul naked before him. Clearly, she sought to get close to him, to ferret out the plans, dreams and secrets in his head. Jesús Garcia-Vega knew a thing or two about journalists and how they would do anything to get close to the men who moved the world. This particular woman was no different. He smiled. The possibilities intrigued him.

"You truly believe that Giovanni has been abducted?" asked Bishop Groelsch, one hand clutching Dantón's arm, the other a black umbrella. The media had left and the crowd dispersed, leaving the two to share a quiet moment during the late afternoon.

"His captors will do him no harm, I am sure," Dantón responded.

"That someone would kidnap a man of God!"

"You do not suggest that this young man . . . your own aide . . . renounced his vows and yielded to the temptation of sin and the Devil?"

"God forbid," Groelsch answered. He swung his head slowly as if the hand of an unseen sculptor rotated it deliberately to study its slit-like eyes, hawk-like nose and almost-lipless mouth. "Revolutionaries are desperate men. Violent men. We have had our share in Europe. The Baader-Meinhof Gang in Germany. In Italy, the Red Brigades."

Dantón delicately nudged Groelsch to the left. "A small stroll around the plaza will clear your thoughts and still your apprehension."

They turned up Avenida Catedral to embark on a clockwise circuit of Plaza Azcalatl enveloped by a gentle mist.

Passersby nodded as the two representatives of the Church ambled arm in arm.

"You realize, of course," Groelsch commented, "that the Holy Father's visit is now very much in doubt."

"If this is God's will."

Groelsch halted. "You cannot lightly dismiss . . ."

"You must know," Dantón cut him off, "that many Cristanos express great disappointment in the Church's response to their pursuit of social justice."

"And you, Archbishop?"

"How can I not share the people's concerns?"

"As does our Holy Father. I assure you."

Dantón squeezed Groelsch's arm softly. "How could he not?" Placing a cradling hand on Groelsch's elbow, he urged him forward. "But imagine the message the Holy Father will deliver to the people when he appears at the opening of this . . . this store."

"Mobys?" Groelsch smiled. "We have several in Rome. Many, actually. And the Holy Father appreciates a good espresso, as do we all."

They approached Avenida Plaza Azcalatl, which ran along the up side of the plaza.

Dantón extended his arm eastward. "There. The new Mobys."

Groelsch nodded. "Yes. On the corner. I have walked past it several times."

Dantón stopped and tightened his grip on Groelsch's arm. "That store being built by workers whose wellbeing corporations like Mobys dismiss represents nothing more than yet another monument to capitalism." He leaned even closer. "Do you know that McDonalds and KFC are only two blocks from the Presidential Palace? Right across the street from the American Embassy. Does this tell you anything?"

"Well . . ." Groelsch paused. Many of the faithful ate at these American fast-food places. He likewise but only rarely.

Dantón led Groelsch into the street towards the plaza.

Oncoming traffic reverently screeched to a halt.

Their passage successful, Groelsch unfurled his umbrella against the late-afternoon mist become light rain and lowered his gaze to more safely navigate his way along the plaza's slick cobbles.

Dantón, oblivious of the rain, slowed to match his colleague's cautious pace.

Nearing Bulevar Azcalatl, which ran up two blocks to the Presidential Palace, a voice rose. A bullhorn amplified its anger.

Groelsch looked up.

A crowd waving protest signs of assorted sizes stood in the plaza across the avenue from the new Mobys as the last of the construction workers left for the day. A dozen police wearing riot helmets tapped their palms with metal batons.

"As you can see," Dantón remarked, "not everyone believes that the marketplace is the sole determinant of human wellbeing."

"That is certainly the Holy Father's position," Groelsch responded. The toe of his right shoe caught a cobble. He lurched forward and crumpled as if lowering himself onto a kneeler.

Dantón pulled up on Groelsch's arm to help restore his footing.

The voice from the bullhorn grew louder and more strident.

The crowd took up a rhythmic chant.

Police whistles sounded.

Groelsch's head jerked up.

As if on cue, a small explosion from within the Mobys building propelled breaking glass across the sidewalk and into the street.

The crowd scattered as a delicate pillar of gray smoke floated out from the front of the building and ascended, quivering in the breeze like a cobra summoned from a basket by the music of an enchanted flute.

Groelsch raised a hand to his heart. “I truly fear for our brother in Christ.”

8 | OCHO | 8

BOBBY STOMPED THE COCKROACH before it could scuttle under Suelo's hospital bed. He pressed the buzzer at Suelo's side. No nurse or orderly responded. He pulled the last tissue from a box on the yellow plastic nightstand next to the bed and gathered up the insect's remains. Unable to locate a wastebasket, he took the wad of tissue to the bathroom, dropped it into the toilet and flushed. A trickle of water entered the bowl. He pressed the lever again and held it until the tissue finally disappeared.

"What was that all about?" Suelo whispered, groggy from medication.

"Housekeeping." Bobby set a large, brown envelope on the nightstand.

"And that?" asked Suelo. His head rolled slightly on his pillow.

"A paper I'm writing on U.S. involvement in Afghanistan."

"I better wait before I try to read it."

"And the latest *Playboy*. You can look at the pictures."

Suelo attempted a smile. "Gimme a break. I thought sex with Carolina would loosen my back." The smile dissolved. "You got anything on the priest?"

Bobby shook his head. "It's been three days, and he's still missing. And still big news."

"San Cristo has more to worry about than that. A killing here, a bombing there. And the pace is picking up. That says revolution to *me*."

"My boss isn't too pleased about that little bomb that went off in the new Mobys building," said Bobby. "We had a man out there, didn't we?"

"Someone slips into the building while our guy takes a piss. Or maybe one of the workers brings it in. Stuff like this gets people talking."

Bobby nodded. "Maybe so, Juan, but still it's yesterday's news. Not like a priest who disappears into thin air . . ."

"A fucking *telenovela*," Suelo growled. He grunted in pain. "A soap opera, man." His eyes shifted to the small window to the left of the bed. "This is serious shit, Bobby. Me, I mean. I can hardly walk. The doctors are talking about operating."

"Here?"

"San Cristo's a little short on Mayo Clinics. The generals go to Mexico City or Houston or Miami."

Bobby gently placed his hand on Suelo's shoulder. "It'll all work out. Trust me."

"You talking about me or Father Giovanni?"

"Both. But somebody in *Seguridad* has to take the lead on this with you out of the picture."

Suelo turned back to Bobby. "My boss and our senior people," he whispered. "Almost all political. The district commanders, too. They couldn't find their *pitos* . . . their dicks . . . in the dark. And they don't mind seeing Alonso Quijano embarrassed." He paused to catch his breath. "They figure he's served his purpose. Now they want a president with *cojones*. Big ones."

Footsteps sounded in the hall.

Bobby waited until they passed. "Like a guy who'll send troops into the highlands to massacre a couple thousand *indígenas*."

"That's what I'm talking about, *amigo*."

"Look, I've got to go, Juan. Something I scheduled with María Skavronsky. Take care of the back, huh?"

Suelo grasped Bobby's hand. "Bobby, listen. If you catch a break here in the capital, I can get you a few men you can trust. Beyond that, you may be Mobys' man, but you're on your own. You watch *your* back."

Bobby stood transfixed as María dropped to a crouch and aimed the Glock 9mm provided by the range at the silhouette of a man's upper body printed on a paper target. Quickly but deliberately, she squeezed off three shots.

Suelo had built the pistol range for his *Seguridad* agents, any number of whom were suspected of preferring to deliver a round to the back of the head from a distance of three inches. María Skavronsky, Bobby understood, would enjoy no such advantage in any confrontation. Considering the escalating violence, including the bombing at Mobys—even if the damage was relatively minor—she presented a high-value target to revolutionaries and common criminals alike. Given the increased calls on Bobby's time, she would be on her own more often than not. Having adamantly refused the accompaniment of a bodyguard, the petite and, Bobby could not help noting yet again, very attractive Ms. Skavronsky would be best served by possessing at least basic self-defense skills.

María fired another three rounds. At twenty meters, a kill shot was no easy matter for an amateur firing at a motionless target in a non-hostile environment. Firing live against an attacker demanded major skills and a cool head achieved only through constant training and enhanced by experience in the field where failure was anything but an option. But at least María demonstrated that she could load a weapon and pull the trigger without flinching.

María emptied the magazine.

Bobby drew the target towards them.

"I hope I got this right," said María as if they were out on a date.

Bobby had advanced the target not even halfway when María's shot pattern became unmistakably clear. Closer inspection revealed twelve holes clustered over the silhouette's heart. All had been placed within a three-inch diameter.

9 | NUEVE | 9

THE TIP OF ADELLA'S TONGUE snaked out from between her lips. She spat a small shred of tobacco onto the conference room carpet then withdrew another cigarette from a thin gold case. "You don't mind, do you?"

Garcia-Vega shook his head.

She extended the case.

"Thank you, no," he responded.

Adella adjusted her sunglasses. "I hope San Cristo isn't getting to be like Europe or, God forbid, the States. In California, the cigarette police knock down the door of your hotel room."

Garcia-Vega nodded. "I like a good cigar myself. Cuban, of course."

"A big one, I should think." Adella let a puff of smoke drift slowly out of her nostrils. "I also like a big one every now and then."

Garcia-Vega's eyebrows ascended. The image of Adella Rozen drawing on a cigar intrigued him given the quasi-military correspondent's outfit she wore—khaki pants and shirt resembling the uniform a soldier might have worn on desert duty in the nineteen-sixties yet tailored to display her slim figure and accented with a deep purple scarf matching her purple cloth hair band.

Adella ran her fingers through her hair, still thick and curly, although not as soft as in her youth given the abusive nature of the painter's palette of colorings with which she had long indulged her shifting moods.

Garcia-Vega placed his right palm down lightly on the conference room table and let it glide slowly across the surface. He found a sensual pleasure in finely finished mahogany. "And so, as you have come by yourself, *Señora* . . ."

"*¡Señorita!* Let's get that straight. The three husbands I have had? None do I acknowledge as real men. My lovers? Some were worthy. But I am not now an old woman beyond the desire and ability to take, and give, pleasure."

"*Señorita* Rozen, since you have come here by yourself, I take it you do not wish to interview me for television."

"We will do that soon, I am sure. But not at the moment, *Señor* Garcia-Vega."

"Call me Jesús. Please."

Adella closed her eyes, inhaled deeply, craned her head back and held the smoke in her lungs. Satisfied, she permitted it to wriggle free from between her lips. The smoke undulated towards the ceiling like a neglected wife standing alone before a mirror modeling underwear from Victoria's Secret. "What I wish to talk to you about, Jesús, is more important than a sound bite regarding this foolish young priest."

"Foolish?"

"You don't really think he was kidnapped? I myself saw nothing."

"How am *I* to know, *señorita*?"

"Adella."

"Adella. Yes."

Adella flicked an ash into an abandoned coffee cup. "Let us say kidnapped then. Do I correctly assume that the Pope's visit will not please everyone?"

"Many Cristanos have their differences with the Vatican."

"As clearly do some of their prelates."

Garcia-Vega wondered if he had been wise to send Carlos out of the conference room. But then, Carlos had no political skills and would be useless in a confrontation with an experienced and determined journalist—particularly a woman. If anything, Adella Rozen would cast a spell on him. Women found weakness in Carlos where men could not.

"A kidnapping," said Adella, "makes a good story." She ran her tongue over her lower lip. "But no, what I have come to see you about is a book. A book about the people's revolutionary movement in Latin America. Power to the people, economic equality, ethnic rights. I am, you may know, famously sympathetic."

Garcia-Vega attempted to peer through the dark, purple lenses of the purple-framed sunglasses that hid Adella's eyes. Seeing only his own reflection, he let his gaze drop to her moist, purple lips, her slightly pointed chin, her slender neck beneath the purple scarf and the pale skin that descended into the cleft of her shirt whose top two buttons she had left open.

Adella tossed the remainder of her cigarette into the coffee cup. It hissed. "What the world wants to know . . . what I must first uncover . . . is, who exactly *is* Jesús Garcia-Vega?"

Garcia-Vega threw his shoulders back. If Adella Rozen told his story, he would accumulate major political capital translating into millions of dollars and euros flowing into ANTI's treasury. Of course, writing a book and having it published took time. The election would long be over. But if she liked his story—and why would she not?—she would soon file television and newspaper reports on him. He would be an international figure. Money would flood in.

Adella pushed forward a small digital recorder. "An ordinary journalist might ask, 'Jesús Garcia-Vega, what are you for?' But that is only half the story. What people really care about is . . . what are you *against*?"

Garcia-Vega's eyes shone as if he stood spotlighted on a stage. "What have you got?"

"Perhaps," Adella responded in a commanding tone, "something more specific."

Garcia-Vega looked at the recorder then up. His eyes paused at Adella's breasts, rose to the sunglasses that served as a barrier to her soul—a barrier he would penetrate—then down to those impossibly purple lips. "What am I against? The IMF, the World Bank, the G-8, the G-20 and all other G's, the U.S. Agency for International Development, NAFTA, CAFTA . . . and corporate cafés." Indeed, Jesús Garcia-Vega stood proudly against every form of *capitalismo salvaje*—savage capitalism—that sought to chain the people to the tyranny of the marketplace.

Adella's breathing deepened. She parted her lips. "Yes," she said. "Tell me."

Garcia-Vega ran his tongue along the inside of his mouth. "But first, would you like some wine? I have a very nice Napa Valley Cabernet."

"Perhaps later, Jesús. After." She took off her hair band and shook her purple hair free. "I am so . . . this is all so very exciting."

Garcia-Vega's chest heaved as if he were a sailfish struggling for oxygen on the deck of a boat.

Adella's right thumb and index finger stroked the button beneath the opening of her shirt. "I find strong ideas fascinating. And strong *men*."

Garcia-Vega felt a primal stirring in both his body and soul—a stirring not even a new kitchen with a Viking range could arouse.

The skin on Adella's chest glistened. "You have great vision, Jesús."

Garcia-Vega felt his cheeks grow hot. "We indigenous peoples are the moral reservoir of humanity!"

Adella loosened the button, exposing a bit of her purple brassiere and the pale flesh contained within it. "Bold. So bold."

Garcia-Vega reached for his belt buckle. "The world needs bold men."

Adella let her shirt slip from her pale shoulders. "A strong man . . . a man like you . . . can do anything he wants. *Have* anything he wants."

Garcia-Vega tore at the zipper of his trousers. "Anything?"

Adella loosened her purple belt. "Anything!" Her slacks collapsed to the floor.

"Yes!" Garcia-Vega exclaimed, his breath catching in his throat. "But I must tell you that . . . in an hour . . . when the morning soap operas are over . . . I must call the television and radio stations . . . and all the newspapers."

Adella unfastened her bra.

Garcia-Vega's trousers fell around his ankles. "I have received a telephone call," he wheezed.

Adella hooked her thumbs into the waistband of her purple panties, lowered them over her thighs, knees, calves and ankles then stepped out of them with the fierce footwork of a flamenco dancer.

Garcia-Vega tugged at his shorts. "I have news. It is big. *Very* big."

"Yes," Adella gasped. "I can see that."

María, settled into a corner booth in the bar at the Hotel Azcalatl Grande, cradled a third shot of Pikesville rye in her right hand. A nine-by-twelve brown envelope lay on the table in front of her. "Money talks, bullshit walks," she said.

Bobby cocked his head. "Ms. Skavronsky . . ." He went silent.

"What?" María asked.

"Do you mind my asking if you know anything about your name?"

"Skavronsky? It's Russian. My father's name."

"It was the maiden name of Catherine the First. The wife of Peter the Great."

María's eyes widened.

"She wasn't Russian, actually. But she was pretty much the power behind the throne until Peter died. Then she became empress."

María laughed. "Well, I don't think I'm Russian royalty, do you? Besides, my mother was Cristano. She cleaned houses and worked nights in a supermarket. I can barely remember my father, so no Russian history lessons there."

What little María's mother had told her about her father remained painful, although she attributed to him much of her will to succeed. A civil engineer in Russia, he'd spent several years in a gulag in Siberia, bribed his way to Vladivostok and somehow boarded a ship to San Cristo. He met her mother, an underpaid *indígena* elementary school teacher and daughter of a widow, while working on the construction of a small damn in the highlands. After a rapid courtship, he gallantly elevated her mother's status by marrying her. Just as rapidly, he reinforced his connection with the culture of his adopted Latin home by entering into a series of awkward affairs.

After María's grandmother died, the family sought a new start in the U.S. Less than a year after arriving in San Francisco, her father deserted the family, also leaving behind a distraught mistress and a number of gambling debts.

María's business face reappeared. "You were about to say something relating to current history in San Cristo."

Bobby rubbed his chin. "The thing is that on a *good* day, Colonel Suelo would confront all kinds of obstacles in a matter like this. And this is *not* a good day."

"Colonel Suelo being out of the picture, Colonel Gatling, Mobys is stepping in." She pushed the envelope back across the table. It contained reports Bobby had submitted on what appeared to be two revolutionary attacks—the robbery of a bank in Monte Vista ninety kilometers north of the capital and an attack on a small army convoy returning to the base at Lake Azcalatl. "Major Kennan's job is restoring peace in the highlands. *Yours* is the priest."

Bobby gritted his teeth. He'd known many men and a few women who play-acted at being hard-asses. María Skavronsky, he believed, was the real thing.

"This evening," said María, her voice hushed, "President Quijano is going to announce a twenty-five-thousand-dollar reward for information about Father Giovanni. *Our* money, of course. A small fortune in San Cristo."

Bobby looked into her eyes. "In some circles."

María's jaw jutted forward.

Bobby held his gaze.

María downed the shot.

Bobby shifted his weight. He'd known plenty of women who boasted about drinking men under the table and cheerfully made the effort, only to end up laughing too loudly, sympathizing too much and crying too long—at the bar or in bed. María Skavronsky represented a whole different species. Now he was struggling to stay focused. Her eyes were telling him that she knew she was in his head and totally in control. If his thoughts were shifting from her as a client to her as a woman, she appeared to be signaling, he could back off. She'd call the shots. He coughed into his fist. What was he doing fantasizing like a high school kid? At least, he had the answer to that one. He was just being a man.

"You look . . . I'm not sure, Colonel . . . dubious?"

"We offered twenty-five *million* for Osama bin Laden. It took ten years."

María pushed her glass away, careful not to compromise her nails. "I wouldn't equate a missing priest with the Twin Towers, would you? Besides, that was Washington's money."

"Mr. Scharq's being very generous, ma'am."

"But you think *fifty* thousand would be more effective."

"Possibly."

"Okay, fifty."

"It's your call," said Bobby.

"Okay, we'll sweeten the pot. A *hundred*. Life's all about negotiating, Colonel, and we have a lot at stake here."

"Then again," said Bobby, "getting information isn't always about money. Sometimes bad blood's involved. Someone wants revenge. Or someone's returning a favor or . . . even wants to be a good citizen."

"What are you proposing, Colonel? That we *pass* on offering a reward? Wait for the kidnappers to make another call to Jesús Garcia-Vega?"

"That's hard to say."

"And that's unfortunate, because Whitman Scharq is *not* a happy man. And I think you'll agree that's understandable. Because when you get down to it, what do we *really* know about what's going on here?"

"That's my point, ma'am. We don't."

What *could* they know? Garcia-Vega had appeared on television and radio only hours earlier, although, as they soon learned, Adella Rozen had broken the news in Europe and the States just prior to the announcement in Ciudad San Cristo. And what did they have? Someone telephoned Garcia-Vega that his people held the priest. That and nothing more. No name for the caller or a group. And no demands.

"I won't even ask if the *Seguridad* people can trace the call," said María. "However Colonel Suelo *intends* to extend their capabilities some day won't help us now. But let's assume the priest *was* kidnapped. Why call Garcia-Vega? Why not Archbishop Dantón?"

"The highlands are unsettled. Everyone knows Garcia-Vega supports the native people."

"So does the Archbishop."

"But he still reports to the Vatican. To some extent his hands are tied. And he's not running for president."

María clapped her hands together. "Are we really paying you for *that*?"

Bobby finished his drink and motioned towards María's glass.

"That's enough, thanks. For now at least."

"I'm only saying that maybe this is all about politics."

"*Everything* is about politics, Colonel. And politics when it comes down to it is all about money."

Bobby placed his hands on the table as if to demonstrate that he wasn't concealing anything. "The Pope's visit threatens to pull Garcia-Vega out of the spotlight. Agreed?"

"I won't argue that."

"The kidnappers turn to Garcia-Vega as the only man they can trust. The only man who can take power and effectively promote their cause. The phone call makes him something of a hero and a media star . . . at least for the time being."

"Then you're saying Garcia-Vega is behind this."

"Or an opportunity just dropped into his lap."

A waiter approached.

"*La cuenta, por favor,*" Bobby said.

María opened her purse. "I'll handle it."

The waiter retreated to the bar.

María pulled out her compact and checked her makeup. "So you're suggesting the possibility that Father Giovanni *did* run away. The phone call Garcia-Vega says he received is just a hoax."

Bobby's cell phone chimed. A text message appeared. He wondered if it might be from Bobby, Jr. but discovered that Suelo had texted from his hospital bed.

María freshened her lipstick.

Bobby looked up. "That announcement Garcia-Vega just made? Looks like we have a shot at finding out if it's true."

10 | DIEZ | 10

GIOVANNI, HIS HEAD HOODED, a firm hand clutching his shoulder, shuffled out of the bathroom. This was the procedure whenever he was taken from the small bedroom to which he had been confined. At least earlier that day he had been brought a basin of water, a razor and shaving cream to remove the heavy stubble that made him so uncomfortable.

He needed only seven small steps to reach the bedroom. The hand halted him. He heard another captor unlock the door, and the door squeak open on hinges long neglected. The hand urged him forward. He stepped inside.

Someone removed his hood. The room remained dark as always during the night. It held only one light fixture—in the ceiling—but the bulb had been removed before his arrival. Daytime brought light but no sun—when there was sun. The lone window, nailed shut, remained in shadow, facing a cinder-block wall across an alleyway little more than a meter wide and evidently blocked from entry.

A man in a black ski mask swept the beam of a flashlight towards a small wooden table. Giovanni was grateful that he hadn't shined the light into his eyes, since they'd adapted fairly well to the darkness. The light found a plate on which Giovanni had been served two slices of American-style pizza with pepperoni—hardly comparable to Italian pizza but a welcome dinner nonetheless—and an empty can of Coca-Cola. He had eaten with gusto but carefully to avoid knocking anything over. The man retrieved the plate and the can, left the room and shut the door. The lock clicked shut like a thunderclap.

Giovanni went to the window and held up his watch in hopes that some bit of moonlight or the light from a nearby house might penetrate the alleyway and prove sufficient. His eyes, dry and tired, could not make out the hands with any certainty. He thought it might be nearly midnight, but his failing sense of time limited him only to the primitive recognition of day and night. All he could do was try to sleep—a challenge of major proportions. Given that his body ached with fear and fatigue, he could not yet will his mind to rest.

He placed his hand over his watch. That his captors left it and his ring with him proved heartening. Also to their credit, they hadn't even attempted to find, let alone take, his passport. These men, in spite of the situation, treated him with courtesy. Such kindness served as a testament to their basic humanity. Whoever they were, these were good people at heart. Christ's children. In this he had faith. He would pray for them.

He sat on the narrow bed. Only a few days had passed—whether three or four, he could not be sure—and already, he had stopped seeking a reason for his captivity or a means of escaping from it. All he could do now was wait patiently for God to send a redeemer. Many redeemers would be required, no doubt. He closed his eyes. The neighborhood had grown quiet except for what sounded like a television program playing in a home or apartment nearby. He tried to picture the street beyond the alley. Having had a bag thrown over his head while being pushed into the car that brought him here, he'd never seen it.

He lay down. Sleep, when it came, offered his only experience of freedom. He guided his thoughts to Ostia Antica, ancient Rome's port on the Tiber. He had taken the train there countless outings to put aside his priestly duties and view the world as others saw it. Cast into the lion's den like Daniel, he imagined strolling the familiar Decumanus Maximus—the basalt-cobbled road running the length of the ruins—on a sunlit day. He was not Father Giovanni now but a wealthy merchant going to the baths or the theater or, yes, to a stolen hour with his mistress. Captive in body but not in mind, he would wander along the boulevard savoring the freedom of another place and time—and another self—until sleep overcame him. He might then dream himself back in Rome, visiting his favorite café and observing the city's people—the free-spirited men, the lively children and the beautiful women. Especially the women.

He was picturing himself at the Forum baths, both the pools and floors heated by ingenious Roman engineering, when a sound shattered his reverie. Ostia disappeared as quickly as an image in the cinema with the self-destruction of a projector bulb. Once more he found himself hidden away in Ciudad San Cristo with no idea as to what God intended for him.

And did he hear the door being unlocked again?

Bobby saw determination mixed with fear on the men's faces as they ran towards the house. No one knew what lie behind the door—the lady or the tiger? Whether these men were as competent as Suelo insisted he would soon find out. He'd make no rush to judgment, though. He'd had less than twelve hours to assemble the team, get their weapons and equipment together, and walk them through the plan. Now, given that it was four in the morning, adrenalin would have to overcome the lack of sleep.

Bobby acknowledged his own fear then held it in check. Healthy fear kept a man from taking foolish risks that could jeopardize not only his own life but also those of his team. Of the men he'd served with, only Crazy Greenberg displayed no signs of fear—a trait the Special Forces evaluation process somehow missed. Although he'd earned the nickname for biting off the head of a live snake—he refused to eat it because it wasn't kosher—it was Greenberg's cavalier dismissal of fear that demonstrated how crazy he was. Perhaps it was only karma that in an operation in Bosnia to free a local who'd been providing intelligence to NATO on Serb air defenses, Greenberg was the only man wounded. The last Bobby heard, he had left the Army to teach Krav Maga, a hand-to-hand combat technique developed in Israel, to IDF commandos. Given the situation in the Middle East, maybe being a little oblivious was okay. It wouldn't work in San Cristo. Not now.

His knee aching and sweat rolling down his sides, Bobby signaled the three lead *Seguridad* agents. The first swung a battering ram. It missed both the handle and lock, splintering a hole in the door but failing to open it. Bobby slapped the agent's helmet. He pulled the ram back and swung again. The second blow struck the target head on. The door shot forward with such force that it ricocheted back and hit the other two agents as they charged through the doorway. Struggling under the weight of body armor, the agents retreated a step. Then, responding to the rush of adrenaline, one kicked in the door while the second tossed a flash-bang grenade. The explosion emitted intense light and a concussive sound to daze anyone inside without causing injury or damage.

The entry breached, Bobby followed with two more agents. Others already secured the streets around the house. Bright Lights affixed to M4s illuminated the front room while serving to blind any conscious kidnapper they might find. Bobby had practically begged for night-vision goggles but couldn't get any. For that matter, he would have preferred arming the men with newer SCAR carbines developed for the USofA's Special Operations Command. Big questions had been raised in Afghanistan about the M4's reliability in an extended firefight. But the government of San Cristo lacked the clout to procure them.

Waving his Beretta locked and loaded with a 15-round magazine—two additional magazines peered out from beneath his body armor—Bobby motioned two men towards a hallway to the right.

"*¡Nadie!*" shouted an agent from the end of the hall. No one.

Bobby swept his Bright Light along the wall to the right of the door, found a switch and turned on a bare bulb suspended from the ceiling. The small living room displayed scant furnishings—a sagging sofa covered with a red, yellow and green woolen throw that reminded Bobby of the filling in a fast-food taco, two wooden chairs, a small, glass-topped wrought-iron coffee table, a pair of ceramic lamps painted gold atop mismatched stands and a television set at least twenty years old.

Agents peered into the two bedrooms, closets and lone bathroom.

Only the cry of *nadie* sounded.

Bobby stepped into the small kitchen. He found the light switch and flipped it. The bulb popped. He shined his Bright Light on the sink. It revealed food-encrusted dishes, chipped bowls, cheap metal utensils and plastic glasses along with dozens of scattering roaches.

He shifted the light to the small counter on which stood a stack of pizza boxes. All came from the same restaurant. He'd have one of the men check it out.

They'd also seek out the house's owner, although that task would have to wait until morning when government offices reopened. And then there was no guarantee they'd find out anything of value. If this was a safe house, it would be rented under a false name with the landlord paid in cash by a third party never seen in the neighborhood. *Seguridad* would have its hands full getting anything to work on, and time was not on their side.

An agent knocked on the wall. "*¿Coronel?*"

Bobby turned.

The agent held out a piece of paper.

Bobby studied it and smiled. Unless the late hour was playing tricks on his eyes, he was holding a page torn from an Italian passport.

11 | ONCE | 11

KHAN LAY MOTIONLESS ON HIS BACK, his heart palpitating, his lungs wheezing like a blacksmith's bellows. Gray mid-morning light peeked through the draperies but failed to rouse him. Breakfast held out no allure. His body remained as enervated as his mind was agitated. And he was not thinking about the young lady he had paid the previous evening to perform the act of fellatio. Granted, he had been modestly satisfied. But everything had been so businesslike. Sex offered far more than release engendered by the physical act. One, after all, could pleasure oneself. What truly excited him was the dance of seduction leading to the ultimate conquest.

Rather, a just-received email posed a grave accusation revealing either sheer incompetence or the malice of rank ingratitude. A man boasting of Major I.A. Khan's education and accomplishments did not engage in scientific enquiry without employing a rigorous methodology. Not ever, sir! By what temerity then did a member of the inner circle of his staff dare to suggest that some of I.A. Khan's assumptions regarding caffuel might require further review—and *extensive* review at that? The assumptions of an Oxford man, sir!

Had he erred in accepting this holiday in San Cristo—even if the grand opening offered an opportunity to have his photograph taken with the Pope? Prominently displayed in his office, the photograph would make a grand impression on staff and visitors. A Muslim such as himself—if only by way of youthful upbringing—with the Pope! Extraordinary! But would it not have been wiser had he stayed in Palo Alto? Had he neglected to consider the risk that an ambition-drunk traitor would seek to betray him and climb roughshod over his back to advance his own career?

Khan's breathing reverberated noisily in his ears. He might have been standing on the beach at Hawks Bay in Karachi, listening to the pounding of the relentless, unforgiving surf that each year took the lives of so many careless sightseers.

He reached for his medicine. He was under the impression that he'd taken a pill several hours earlier but could not be sure given his highly anxious state. Considering the extent of his discomfort, increasing the dosage, he rationalized, could not possibly make him feel worse. He coaxed a small, white pill out of its container and placed it in his mouth. Then he reached for the glass of water he kept on his nightstand, drank carefully and swallowed hard. Medical science would relieve his distress as surely as caffuel would purge the lust for oil that spurred the dissolution of the world's economic, political, environmental and moral—yes, moral, sir!—underpinnings. Hadn't he promised that to Whitman Scharq?

Almost immediately, Khan's heart and breathing downshifted to their normal rhythms. Such blessed relief. *Allahu akhbar!* Now he could exercise his copious powers of reason to determine what steps he would next take to prevent an indelicate situation from bollixing his work and, indeed, his entire career.

Certainly, he might return to Palo Alto tomorrow on a commercial airline. But a change in plans might alert Whitman to a potential problem—providing that one or more moles had not already whispered untruths into Whitman's ear.

Therefore no, a strategic retreat would not be in order at this time. Besides, he deserved this respite from the frenzied pace that had taken its toll on his body, not to mention the threatened confrontation with the aggrieved husband who might be stalking him at this very moment. He could just as easily review the data and buttress his case here in San Cristo.

Yet staying in the capital held little appeal. Ciudad San Cristo had proved a dreary place what with María working constantly and Whitman flying out then back then out again to deal with matters of corporate gravitas. But I.A. Khan was nothing if not a resourceful man—a man who calculated his options with precision then acted with purpose. He'd gone online and found—beyond an intriguing new porn site—information extolling the natural beauties of Lago Azcalatl and its namesake village right on the lake in the shadows of the imposing volcano. There he would find a community of carefree American artists and writers, musicians and poets, philosophers and organic gardeners—mostly fellow Californians. If the information proved even reasonably accurate, he would encounter a number of attractive blonde women seeking a wide variety of pleasures devoted to both the spirit and the flesh.

Yes, a stay in Pueblo Azcalatl would be just the thing. Tophole, sir! The lake and the volcano with its rainforest—two jewels of nature caffuel would someday protect—offered more than enough inspiration to undertake an exhaustive review of the data and create a point-by-point refutation of any possible charges against him.

Determined to maintain a reputation fabricated on three continents, I.A. Khan would restrain the limited minds whose imaginations failed to grasp the pressure one faced to provide one's benefactor with eternal fame and adulation in order to assure one's timely payments on a luxury condominium—the additional association fees were exorbitant bordering on the criminal, sir!—along with a Porsche Carrera GT. In addition, one also had to consider gifts sufficient to maintain the affections of several lovely ladies and obligations relating to substantial wagers undertaken with local gaming entrepreneurs.

But the less heartening aspects of reality ought never be dismissed. One's most comprehensive and rationale efforts devoted to explaining the complexities of scientific investigation and its inherent disappointments could fall on deaf ears.

With suddenness reflective of true genius, a thought struck. Khan bolted upright. Archimedes must have felt this way when he entered his tub and discovered how to calculate the volume of irregular objects. "Eureka!" Khan exclaimed. Should his situation grow perilous, he now could defend his position by methods fair or—if required—foul.

"If the priest's within a hundred clicks of the lake," declared Kennan, who'd choppered into the capital from Pueblo Azcalatl, "we'll find him."

María opened the purse on her lap, shuffled several items and found her compact. She'd want to freshen her makeup as soon as she finished with Kennan. He sat across from her in the same corner booth in the Hotel Azcalatl Grande's bar where she'd met with Colonel Gatling prior to the colonel's luckless raid on the house near the airport.

"We own . . . and I mean *own* . . . that fuckin' jungle!" Kennan asserted. "Pardon my French."

"I would hope so, considering what Mobys is paying Crimmins-Idyll Associates."

Kennan pushed away his *Cerveza Azcalatl* and revealed a deck of cards. "Let me show you something about finding what you're looking for."

"Major Kennan, the only thing I'm looking for is a missing priest."

"Yes, ma'am. Some other time." Kennan put the cards away. "Anyway, long story short . . . Recon teams are working the area, talking with the locals. I've met again with General Gomez and all the local police chiefs. Can't say they're happy we're around. Definitely not much help. *Seguridad* . . . they've got this regional commander in Maquepaque." He shook his head.

"Colonel Gatling will remain your liaison to *Seguridad*."

"Bobby can touch base with them all he wants. Just as long as he stays off our turf."

"Let *me* make that decision, Major Kennan."

Kennan flushed. "Yes, ma'am." He stroked the bottle's neck. "Guess I'm a little surprised Bobby's not here."

"Colonel Gatling is following up this morning's activity with *Seguridad* and the local police. And please remember, we have a store to open in a few weeks." María took a sip of mineral water *con gas*. Bubbles bounced off the tip of her nose. She would have preferred something with more kick, but an afternoon alcohol habit put on pounds. Worse, she'd missed her workouts the last two days, which left her feeling bloated. "I asked to meet alone with you, Major Kennan, because I want you to feel you can speak freely. I value your opinion."

"I appreciate that, Ms. Skavronsky. Or should I call you María?"

María smoothed the illustration of the fountain of *las tres señoritas* on the damp paper napkin in front of her. She required no mysterious women's intuition to understand that Kennan sought to step over the line separating her identity as his employer from that of a presumably available woman. She confronted this kind of crap with grating frequency. Years earlier, partners and associates at her law firms in Boston and Silicon Valley hit on her as regularly as they overbilled clients. Not that their behavior surprised her. Her education at Stanford and Harvard Law included fending off the unwanted attentions not only of teaching assistants but professors, a few old enough to be her grandfather. "And you're sure," she asked, "that you can cover all that ground?"

"We've got choppers and an air-assault team good to go twenty-four/seven. The people who took the priest . . . they have to be indigs. They know the terrain. I'll give them that. But if they were all that smart, they'd still *own* it."

"Point taken. But I have two questions. First, do you have enough money?"

"For now. Thing is, María, it's not just about a big-enough reward getting someone to give up the priest's location. Doesn't necessarily work that way. More often than not, what you do is, you pass out a few dollars here and there. Clean an infected hand. Give a kid a candy bar. People talk. Small stuff. A stranger showed up in the village. They saw a vehicle they never saw before. Someone's buying more food or beer than normal. At some point, things add up. What's that old saying? God's in the details. At least, that's what they say in the manual." He stared at María. "Question two?"

"What if they *don't* talk?"

"María, I like the way you think. Really. But no worries. Lots of tools in the old tool kit. And forget the bleeding-heart media. These are Indians. Look at the way they live. How much extra pain are they really gonna suffer?"

María's face displayed only the mask she adopted for such situations. She valued the ability to conceal her emotions. She'd learned that from her mother, who worked two and three jobs, six and seven days a week to provide her with ballet and piano lessons, send her to Catholic school and free her from a part-time job during high school so she could devote all her energy to study, sports and the pursuit of a scholarship from a top university. María had never heard her mother complain during her years at Stanford and didn't even know about her breast cancer, metastasized to her bones and imminently fatal, until spring of her third year at Harvard Law. In tribute, María wore the mask at graduation only one week after her mother died. Pain, like death, her mother taught her, was part of life. The dark-skinned Cristano woman with the improbable name had endured. María, in her way, was also a soldier.

"Bottom line," she said, "you agree they've taken Father Giovanni out of the city?"

"Not to shock you, but he may never have been here. Could've taken him straight to the jungle. The phone call and that page from his passport? Might be playing games to throw us off." Kennan finished his beer. "But if the priest *was* here and Bobby just missed him, he's a long way off now. It's *my* turn."

María brushed a few stray hairs off her forehead. Rainy season could undo the efforts of the most expensive stylist, and what she paid for a cut and a coloring to cover her graying roots could feed a family in the highlands for months. "Agreed."

Kennan leaned forward across the table.

What, María wondered, made men so transparent? Kennan's body language revealed his adolescent thoughts—that she, a woman far from home and obviously lonely, was playing games, sending him signals, asking for what only a man like him could provide. If Kennan thought he could draw her interest, however, he was gravely mistaken. Perhaps someone like Colonel Gatling but not this man.

Kennan leaned closer.

What would come next held no surprise for María. She saw Kennan extend his arm under the table. She felt his hand rest on her thigh just above the hem of her skirt. She saw him smile.

With practiced aplomb, María reached under the table and studied Kennan's face as if she were a stockbroker following the day's indexes in a turbulent market. His mouth turned up in response to the gentle pressure on his crotch. The smile broadened as the pressure increased. Then it retreated. His eyes widened. He seemed to look not at her but through her. Finally, his jaw tensed as he realized that it was not María's hand that had excited him.

"This is business, Major" María said without a hint of anger. "Let's be businesslike."

Kennan rocked back in his seat.

María slid her small but powerful Ruger SP101 back into her purse.

12 | DOCE | 12

"AND HOW DO YOU RESPOND to these charges, *Señor* Garcia-Vega?" asked Adella. She held aloft the day's *La Patria*, aping the American senator Joe McCarthy in the nineteen-fifties, infamous for brandishing supposed lists of communist infiltrators in the U.S. government. "How do you respond to the accusation that you are involved in the kidnapping of a papal representative, of Father Giovanni Sabella?"

Behind Adella and out of camera range, Carlos swallowed. He placed his hand over his mouth to avoid the sound being picked up by the microphone suspended above the journalist before realizing that it was too late—if he had indeed made a noise loud enough to be heard. He glanced at the back of Adella's purple hair. Whatever the *jefe* thought about this woman, he saw in her a *corazón de piedra*—a heart of stone.

One of the two cameramen hired by Adella's local producer zoomed in on Garcia-Vega.

Adella grinned. She had anticipated nothing from San Cristo save drudgery and rain, and here a story had dropped into her lap. Not only San Cristo but also the entire world found itself caught up in Father Giovanni's fate. And who better to scratch, claw and dig beyond the surface to bring the world enlightenment? Adella Rozen uncovered hidden truths that evaded ordinary journalists. Her television and newspaper reports again would enthrall a global audience.

Garcia-Vega's chest puffed out like that of a cock entering a hen house. "Yes, this lie about the priest put forward by the fascists behind our government insults me and the *Asociación Nacional de Tierras Indígenas*. But worse, it insults the people of San Cristo, men and women with bent backs but pure souls."

Adella imprisoned a puff of cigarette smoke deep within her lungs. Jesús would respond long enough, she knew, for her to infuse her bloodstream with a plentiful dose of glorious nicotine. How foolish—how stupid—that a journalist was no longer permitted to smoke on-camera. The famous American journalist, Edward Murrow, always appeared on-camera with a cigarette.

Garcia-Vega's chin edged forward. "Any action taken against San Cristo's puppet government and the powers that pull its strings represents the people's legitimate defense of their rights. If, in response, the Vatican wishes to cancel the Pope's visit, so be it. Let the government be shamed for doing nothing. But I . . . I am only a servant of the people. If the kidnappers believe that Jesús Garcia-Vega can bring this situation to a just conclusion, who am I to refuse?"

Adella lowered the remains of her cigarette, swatted at the smoky haze suspended around her and fired her next question. It was good. *She* was good. This was the old Adella now. And didn't she look alluring in her favorite purple blouse cut low enough to hold the attention of male viewers and drive women to silent fits of jealousy?

Garcia-Vega extracted a cigar from his shirt pocket and lit it. "And let me tell you this . . ." he continued, wagging the cigar for emphasis.

Adella followed the cigar with her eyes as she held herself erect like a runway model in Milan. Or did they slouch? No matter. Her posture reflected the glory of her accomplishment. Adulation would greet her name and image in Rome, Paris, London and New York. The righteous would extol her in Havana and Caracas, Tehran and Gaza, Peshawar and Katmandu. Adella Rozen was as compelling on the screen as ever. If anyone had earned a drink—*deserved* a drink—it was she. How could one drink possibly harm a woman who had consumed alcohol in the volumes she had?

"And another thing," Garcia-Vega sought to add.

Adella nodded. The network would want cut-aways—glimpses of her serious responses to her subject's remarks. The desire for a drink dissolved. A warm flush spread across her cheeks like spilled wine on the page of a treasured book, descended to her neck, chest and belly then crept down further still. After the interview concluded, after the crew praised her and left, she would show Jesús how *she* responded to a man who made history rather than simply reacted to it—a hero who wielded a mighty club against the powers others served in abasement.

She reached for a fresh cigarette. Her face radiated a smile worthy of the Mona Lisa. Here was a man larger than life and the possessor of a manhood whose proportions she could freely describe as more than generous with no risk to her journalistic integrity. If that wasn't better than alcohol, it was at least as good.

Yet the interview left her dissatisfied. That same journalistic integrity—the professional conscience that so often burdened her—refused to be dismissed like a minor functionary in the presence of a king. There was, she firmly believed, something more to this story. All the demons in hell could not keep her from it.

Bobby turned off the television, closed his eyes and let Adella Rozen's interview with Jesús Garcia-Vega replay itself in his head. What had he learned? Garcia-Vega's denials appeared strong and unequivocal. That the kidnappers would contact him was hardly illogical. He could have *Seguridad* pick him up for another conversation—they'd chatted at length after he'd spoken with Carlos Rivera—but Garcia-Vega, if he played to type, would cry persecution, insist that the government was compromising the priest's safety and rouse more support for his campaign. María Skavronsky would not be pleased.

His cell rang. His heart pounded. He took three large strides to his nightstand. It was early enough for Bobby, Jr. finally to get back to him. He'd rehearsed his responses to all the variables that might direct their conversation as if he'd prepared for an operation behind enemy lines. Even so, he'd probably be thrown a curveball. The most detailed plans went south when the first round went off and theory hit the wall of reality. But he'd been trained to think on his feet, and in spite of a couple of drinks, his head remained clear.

No way he'd screw up this time. He wasn't just fighting for his life. He was fighting for his son.

Bobby glanced down at the cell and recognized the number. He let out a long, slow breath. "Hi. I didn't know if you'd be calling."

"A little change of plans," María responded. "Pack your bags."

13 | TRECE | 13

"OHMYGOD, YOU'RE NOT JOKING about saving the world!" exclaimed the woman reclining on the chaise next to Khan's. Her blonde hair set off a George Hamilton tan. The white, cat-eye frames of the sunglasses nestled atop her forehead recalled the 1950s chic of Miami Beach, Las Vegas and Hollywood.

"One does not jest about such matters, madam," Khan responded. Having arrived at the lake the previous day, he had wasted no time getting started on reviewing his data and had left his work only to remain refreshed and attentive.

"Barbara," the woman responded. "Cooper. Just regular American names. Nothing like yours. Is it Arab?"

"Heavens, no, Barbara. I am originally from Pakistan."

"Oh, I hope you don't think that was rude. But shouldn't you be back in your laboratory so you can save the world sooner?"

Khan gently touched the woman's wrist. "Even those of us who labor for the sake of humanity must periodically revitalize body and soul. I am on holiday. With my laptop, of course."

"And you'll be staying here at the lake for a while?"

"A few weeks, although I must go to Ciudad San Cristo in several days for discussions relating to my work. But I shall return."

The woman shifted slightly to capture the full presence of the sun emerging through the afternoon's rain clouds that rapidly scattered like children caught peering into a stranger's window. "I visited India once. A spiritual journey. You don't mind my saying so, do you?"

"Certainly not, madam."

"Barbara, please."

Khan smiled. "And now, Barbara, do you find spiritual contentment here?"

"Kind of. I mean, practically speaking, Pueblo Azcalatl is way cheaper than L.A. Way mellower, too. And the club membership here at the hotel is very reasonable, since I don't have a pool."

Khan let his fingertips linger on her slender wrist. His eyes, hidden by sunglasses at least as expensive and far more contemporary, inspected the appealing flesh peeking out of her aqua bikini top. He surmised Barbara to be in her forties and certainly in magnificent trim. Magnificent, sir!

"You miss Pakistan, I'm sure. Home is always home."

"Pakistan will always retain a place in my heart."

"You sound like you'll never go back."

"Politics, I am afraid. I was a military man. An officer. A major."

"A major? That's very impressive, isn't it?"

"But enough about me for now . . . Barbara. Surely you have lived an equally interesting life, if not one of comparable danger."

Barbara shrugged. Her shoulders rose gently against the back of the chaise, elevating her breasts. "I've traveled. With my husband some of the time."

Khan's stomach tightened. "Husband?"

"Before we divorced. Ted's an attorney in L.A. He had an affair. I found out. He had another. The bastard screwed me out of a lot of money."

Khan shook his head. "But now you have a new life? New . . . friends?"

"A few. Mostly though, I keep to myself. I'm into yoga. I write poetry. I have a lovely garden. Organic. I'm thinking of taking up tarot."

Khan stroked her forearm.

Barbara sat up.

Startled, Khan withdrew his hand.

"Who's that?" she asked, peering at a tall man approaching a table at the patio-bar.

Khan turned. "I believe I know him." His heart fluttered, although he'd taken his medication. A small epiphany struck. Could he be responding to a potential rival? But I.A. Khan was not one to wilt under pressure. Not ever, sir! He shook his head slowly. "A sad story, madam."

Barbara's eyes widened with anticipation.

"Truth be told, you are looking at only *half* a man," he said.

"Half?"

"Perhaps the worst wound a man can suffer." Khan raised his sunglasses, enabling his eyes to exhibit his great sense of empathy. "Quite naturally, a gentleman such as myself would never reveal the details."

Barbara's hand shot to her mouth. "Ohmygod!" She collapsed back on the chaise.

He replaced his hand on her arm

Barbara's collagen-enhanced lips folded in on each other as if she might burst into tears. Composing herself, she released them. "Your work . . . saving the world. I'd like to know more about that."

Khan stroked her arm as he watched her breasts rise and fall, her breathing grow more intense. The game was on, the conclusion foregone. Nonetheless, his curiosity threatened to distract him. What in the world was Colonel Gatling doing here?

The short, wiry attacker thrust the knife towards Bobby's ribcage.

Bobby grabbed the attacker's knife arm at the wrist, raised it upright and slipped his right leg in front of the attacker's right leg. Then dropping to the ground, he threw the attacker onto his back and used his forward momentum to plant his right knee on the attacker's shoulder. The attacker lay helpless as Bobby's right hand reached for his throat.

"¡Muy bueno!" declared General Gomez.

Fifty or sixty soldiers, all *indígenas* except for their senior officer, applauded.

Bobby started to his feet. His right knee buckled. He stumbled and landed on his backside.

Capitán Enrique Hauptmann-Hall leaped forward and extended his right hand.

Bobby enveloped the smaller, soft white hand in his own and shifted his weight to his left leg.

Hauptmann-Hall smiled broadly. "We are honored to see you again, Colonel. Deeply honored."

Bobby took several hesitant steps and retrieved his green windbreaker and the nearly matching green backpack he'd taken with him the night Hauptmann-Hall had been wounded and so many of his men killed. He flexed his right knee gingerly. He'd ice it as soon as he returned to Pueblo Azcalatl.

"You are all right, Colonel?" asked Gomez.

"Fine, sir. Thank you, sir." Bobby did not, however, feel fine at all. He wondered if he would have disarmed his attacker had they been near the same size or gone at it full speed. Besides, combat rarely produced a knife attack anything like the one in the demonstration. An assassin would try to catch his victim unaware. Otherwise, an attacker would flail like a four-armed Shiva, the Hindu destroyer, trading control and precision for a blade slashing repeatedly from multiple directions and angles.

Gomez smiled at Hauptmann-Hall, slapped Bobby on the back and walked off.

Bobby followed along a puddle-strewn gravel path leading to Gomez' office. He listed slightly from side to side like the mast of a sailboat rocked by gentle dockside swells.

Hauptmann-Hall dismissed the men and trailed along like an eager puppy.

Gomez stopped beneath a clump of trees and reached into his breast pocket. "Cigar?"

"*Muchas gracias*," Bobby replied.

Gomez handed a cigar to Bobby and another to Hauptmann-Hall then produced a gold lighter.

Bobby tucked his cigar into his pocket. "Later, *con su permiso*."

"No permission is necessary, Colonel. You are our honored guest." Gomez' lips puckered. He lit the tip of his cigar, drew the flame in then stared at it thoughtfully.

"There's no problem, I hope," said Bobby, "about my being here in the highlands, General."

The general stroked his white mustache, which resembled that of Cesar Romero, the debonair American actor whose movies from the nineteen-thirties he had often enjoyed on television. "The young priest. I understand. But your Major Kennan and his men already are here. He has brought us some bodies. *Indígenas*."

"Revolutionaries?" Bobby asked.

"Perhaps. Perhaps not. This is a nasty and imprecise business."

"There are *other* ways, sir."

"Other ways, Colonel?"

"If I could take some of your men . . . men who know the highlands and the people . . ."

"And if," Hauptmann-Hall interjected, "I could accompany Colonel Gatling. I know I can be of great assistance."

Gomez took a satisfying puff from his cigar. Gray-blue smoke streamed from his mouth like exhaust escaping a leaky muffler. Then deep creases formed in his forehead "Yes, Enrique. Clearly you have become a different man." He took Bobby by the elbow. "Colonel Gatling, you and I want the same thing. And the priest . . ." He placed his hand over his heart and shook his head. "I am Italian on my mother's side."

"Only a small patrol," Bobby urged softly.

Hauptmann-Hall fixed his eyes on Bobby's.

"You are free to work with *Seguridad*," Gomez responded. "They have their own jurisdiction."

"*Seguridad* isn't prepared to operate in the jungle, sir, and we have very little time."

Gomez' cheeks turned crimson. "Colonel, I do not surprise you when I say that the army of San Cristo lacks the resources of the American military . . . or of Mobys Corporation. This is why we agreed, if reluctantly, to let your Major Kennan come here."

Bobby hunched over in a fruitless attempt to lessen his physical dominance. "Your resources, General Gomez, are limited, I know. Your love of San Cristo . . . no limits at all."

Gomez' cheeks returned to their natural pinkish-white. His eyes twinkled. "You and I, Colonel Gatling we are soldiers. I know that you appreciate my predicament. I am forced to think like an accountant. I must consider wear on equipment and potential loss. Expenditures of ammunition. Costs of medical care." He looked at

Hauptmann-Hall. "Burials and what little assistance to families we can provide."

Hauptmann-Hall clenched his jaw.

Gomez clapped Bobby on the back. "But honor has no price. I *will* send men with you to search for the priest and his kidnappers . . ."

Bobby straightened. "Thank you, sir."

Gomez rubbed his thumb and index finger together. "When I have the money."

Giovanni inhaled the damp mountain air then quietly recited the Act of Faith. That his captors removed his hood after leading him into the rainforest compelled him to thank God. Throughout the ride from the capital, the hood had enveloped him like the blackness of the tomb.

How long they had traveled from the capital and to what destination he could not guess. Bound hand and foot on the floor of some kind of truck, he'd attempted to count the seconds and minutes but to no avail. The rain pounding on the roof and the shocks to which the apparently old and worn vehicle subjected his body quickly chased the numbers from his head. He experienced great relief mixed with no little apprehension when they slowed and pulled off the road. Whether they left the vehicle because of mechanical problems or intended to abandon it there, he did not know.

Stumbling forward along the narrow trail, he sought to adapt his senses to a new reality. Neither his eyes nor ears detected any sign of civilization. His three masked captors had given him a warm jacket and revealed only that they would walk until nightfall. Sustenance consisted of a small loaf of bread with a plastic-like crust. He ate half after they removed the hood and placed the rest in his jacket pocket.

An encouraging thought from his childhood emerged. Perhaps, like Hansel and Gretel, he might break off tiny crumbs to mark a path back to the road. His optimism waned almost as soon as the thought exposed itself. His captors surely would see what he was doing. And even if he could avoid detection, the crumbs would be devoured by tiny, unseen creatures or dissolve back into the muddy earth.

Helpless but not forlorn, Giovanni reflected on the past days during which he had been hidden away in the capital. How grateful he was that the faceless men who imprisoned him treated him with courtesy and respect. He had been concerned, naturally, but not simply for himself. How his parents must be suffering although comforted by Christ's love. Yet no matter how difficult their trial, they, like he, must maintain faith. Surely, the police searched for him even now. And the reach of the Vatican extended everywhere, even into the heart of darkness.

The Twenty-third Psalm came to his lips. "Yea, though I walk through the valley of the shadow of death, I will fear no evil, for Thou art with me." What greater comfort could he turn to than Scripture? Yes, faith worked wonders. And yet with every step deeper into the jungle and away from the life he knew, a malevolent question tormented him.

Where were God's rod and staff now?

14 | CATORCE | 14

ADELLA GAZED OUT AT THE RAINFOREST through the white Lexus SUV's windshield pocked with bug-spatter whites, yellows and browns suggestive of a Jackson Pollack painting.

"I bought her practically new," the driver boasted yet again in the functional English he insisted on speaking when he picked her up. "Only eighty thousand miles. Way better than my Corolla, go with God."

Adella took a deep drag from her cigarette like a teething infant suckling at her mother's breast. She was hardly impressed. She'd been chauffeured in limousines as long as buses—even a gold-plated Rolls Royce once—and made love in them. Yet no one could take her for a spoiled member of the privileged class. She'd endured everything from up-armored Humvees under attack in Iraq to tuk tuks weaving like drunks in the sweltering, maddeningly trafficked streets of Bangkok.

"Not so long and we will be back on the highway," said the driver. "This is the old road to Pueblo Azcalatl and Maquepaque. They don't take care of it much now."

Adella shifted her attention to the rough, winding road on which they'd been forced to detour by a mudslide cutting off the highway ascending to Lake Azcalatl. The jungle canopy seemed to smother the two narrow, shoulderless lanes riddled with potholes and littered with small branches blown down by the wind. Not that Adella Rozen was one to complain. She had, after all, bounced her ass on more than one bony mule along the AfPak border.

Adella lowered her window and flicked the remainder of her cigarette into a modest but steady rain. As the window rose, her purple eyelids descended.

A hand nudged her shoulder. "*¡Señorita!*" the driver called softly but with an edge of alarm.

Adella's eyes shot open.

A flare scattered bright crimson sparks up ahead.

The Lexus slowed.

Around a turn sat a police car, its lights flashing. A second vehicle, unmarked, hugged the side of the road.

Adella reached into her handbag for a fresh pack of cigarettes and the ruby-studded lighter presented to her by an icon of the French cinema—never to be identified—after they returned to Paris from a long and exquisitely exhausting ski weekend in Savoie during which neither set foot on the slopes. She let the cigarettes drop and stared at a tall man in a green windbreaker and a uniformed *Seguridad* man shining flashlights into the rear of a battered American-style van wedged between two trees.

"Stop!" Adella commanded the driver as she rolled her window down.

"I do not know if they will allow me, *señorita*."

Another uniformed *Seguridad* man waved them on with the muzzle of his rifle.

"I said *stop*!" Adella shrieked.

The driver braked hesitantly.

Adella stuck her head outside the window.

The *Seguridad* man approached.

"*Yo soy periodista*," she exclaimed. I am a journalist. "Adella Rozen."

The soldier raised the weapon's muzzle to Adella's nose.

The driver nudged the Lexus forward.

"I will have your commander cut off your balls!" Adella screamed in Spanish.

The tall man turned.

Adella opened her door and swung her body forward. "I know you," she called as the tall man receded. "Gatling. Colonel Gatling."

Bobby stared at Adella then turned back to the van.

Another *Seguridad* man advanced to Adella's side of the slowly moving Lexus and pushed the door, forcing her back inside.

"*¡Hijo de puta!*" Adella muttered. Son of a bitch!

The *Seguridad* man clicked off the weapon's safety.

The driver nudged his foot down on the gas pedal.

Adella fell back into her seat.

"*Señorita*, this is very strange, no? It looks like someone has abandoned a perfectly good van. A Dodge. A little rusted maybe, but . . ."

The jungle quickly obscured what she had seen as the road continued to twist and climb. Moments later, the Lexus emerged onto a ridge with a postcard view of the revered cone of Mount Azcalatl. Adella yawned. The volcano made a reasonable impression but would never be confused with Vesuvius. To the left, Pueblo Azcalatl sprawled by the waters of the lake reflecting gunmetal-gray clouds hovering around the volcano's top. But such a town could never hope to rival the beauty of Bellagio or Menaggio on Lake Como.

Adella lit another cigarette and smiled. Even as the sky overhead darkened, her day brightened. She tingled as if she had achieved yet another earth-shattering orgasm. God—if one could give credence to such a superstition—had just confirmed the wisdom of her decision to leave Jesús for several days and come to the highlands. If Colonel Gatling was here and not in the capital, if he was investigating a deserted van on a seldom-used highway, had she not gotten closer to a story with global impact? Questions, of course, remained. A great many questions. Most urgent among them—what did Colonel Gatling know that she did not? Yet no doubt answers soon would be forthcoming. When Adella Rozen marshaled all the forces of her experience and intuition, nothing could be withheld from her. Including a missing priest.

Khan labored to draw a deep breath as he sat in front of his laptop. The numbers on the screen blurred before him. His heart palpitated as if it were a butterfly trapped in a mesh cage. He wiped a bead of sweat from his brow, closed his eyes and pondered taking another pill for his heart. Such was the physical toll imposed by yet another review of the data.

Obdurate in his belief that he could unlock the secret of caffuel—given sufficient funding along with a considerable measure of trust and respect—he required no physician to inform him that his condition reflected his frustration and disappointment. In spite of his superior intellect and scientific acumen, he could manipulate the data only within limitations. Ultimately, continued scrutiny would reveal its inherent flaws.

Conceding the formidable character of the obstacle confronting him, Khan reached for his pills and a glass of water. The situation required the clear thinking only a body free of discomfort could support.

Of course, he had prepared for this eventuality. He recalled the famous line from Dante's Inferno. The inscription on the entrance to Hell read, "Abandon hope all ye who enter here." Rubbish. I.A. Khan—Major I.A. Khan, Ph.D., sir!—would never abandon hope. Like every good military man, he had developed a sound contingency plan. Now, he would take the next step.

María again glanced at the brown travel bag she had placed on the chair to her right. She had no intention of drawing attention to it, but she made no pretense of being immune to the occasional slight impact on her nervous system made by a challenging situation. And if the situation in San Cristo wasn't yet cause for alarm, she could not deny the potential for things going south. That's why Whitman Scharq paid her the big bucks.

"Lovely lady," said Khan, seated across the table on the stone terrace of the Hotel Lago Azcalatl's restaurant. "You must tell me what treasures that bag contains. One would think a pack of thieves was about to snatch it!"

María lowered her head and peered out over the top of her sunglasses.

Khan rocked back in his seat. "Not that I wish to pry. Lovely day it's turning out to be. But I do wish I'd known you were coming up to the lake."

María rested her fork on the edge of the white china plate boasting an elegant presentation of chicken-and-mango salad. She chewed slowly.

A small shadow fell across the table.

Khan pushed his chair back and stood.

María looked up. A woman hovered over her—a woman whose hair, blouse and even shoes all were purple. A cigarette dangled from the woman's purple lips. "Ms. Rozen, I presume."

Adella flipped her purple leather handbag off her shoulder. It fell with a jangling thump onto the patio beside the empty chair at María's left. "Ms. Skavronsky . . . of which I am certain." She sat.

Khan stood at attention. "Major I.A. Khan at your service, madam. *Doctor* Major Khan."

"Of course you are," said Adella.

María raised her glass. "Chardonnay? It's Chilean. Delicious."

Adella bit her lower lip. One more alcoholic binge would abrogate her contract. The pseudo-doctors who ran the countless rehab centers into which she'd been forced—every last quack totally addicted to scolding about addictive behavior—had even forbidden wine. Resigned to yet another day of sobriety, she took a cigarette from her handbag.

Khan fumbled in the chest pocket of his shirt for a lighter.

Adella withdrew her own lighter and ignited her cigarette with the speed and dexterity of a practiced illusionist with a year-round engagement at a Las Vegas resort.

Khan struggled to conceal his disappointment.

María directed her gaze over Adella's right shoulder towards the lake. "Blow it over there."

Adella sent a stream of smoke towards María as if she were smashing a tennis ball at the nose of an opponent caught flat-footed at the net.

The waiter approached.

"*Agua mineral*," Adella instructed. "*Con lima*." She pointed to María's salad, identical to that from which Khan continued to eat heartily. "And one of those."

The waiter smiled graciously. Only his eyes betrayed a hint of whimsical delight. He turned towards the kitchen.

"May I buy your lunch?" Khan asked. "It will only be fitting as Ms. Skavronsky is buying mine."

"Her expense account will provide for the both of us, I am sure."

"You've been to Lago Azcalatl before?" María asked.

"No, this is my first visit to San Cristo."

"You'll find the lake very serene," said María. "Quite spiritual, really."

Adella took another puff and exhaled slowly. The smoke floated towards Khan. "I had a different impression on the drive from the capital. The highway was closed and *Seguridad* was out in force on the old road."

"I know."

"And your man . . . Gatling." Adella studied María's face. "A striking man as far as Americans go." Leaning over the table as if engaged in a conspiracy, she looked intently at María. "I knew a gypsy in Rome. She could see in your eyes if you would submit totally to someone else. Someone who sat at your side or whose photograph you possessed or . . . even someone whose name you simply mentioned. She taught me the secret."

María examined her reflection in her chardonnay.

"You must tell me how one does this, Ms. Rozen," said Khan. "As a man of science, I am well equipped . . ."

"Some secrets may never be revealed," Adella replied. "But that you are well equipped, I am pleased to hear."

The waiter brought a bottle of mineral water and poured it.

Adella raised her glass. "*¡Salud!*"

"*¡Salud!*" responded María and Khan.

Adella sipped. And spat.

"Is something wrong?" asked Khan.

"I was hoping it would taste like vodka, but the power of imagination has its limits."

The waiter brought Adella's salad.

Adella ground her cigarette into a small terra cotta ashtray.

"And what may I ask brings you to the lake, Ms. Rozen?" Khan asked.

"The same reason as Ms. Skavronsky," Adella answered. "We are all concerned about Father Giovanni. Considering the new reward of two-hundred-thousand dollars announced this morning, I suspect our missing priest is even more important to our hostess than to the Vatican."

María glanced at the brown travel bag then turned to Adella. "Really, Ms. Rozen, it's a matter of humanity and common decency."

Adella slid her fork under a piece of mango. "Perhaps that is why I saw your Colonel Gatling with the *Seguridad* men on the old road. I find it difficult, however, to believe that he was there for any reason other than to secure Mobys' business interests. Capitalism has no heart."

María placed her hands in her lap. She took no joy in suffering the leftist venom that threatened the marketplace. Whenever possible, she would counter it through diplomacy and finesse. Other choices naturally remained open.

Adella picked up her handbag and withdrew a pack of cigarettes.

Prepared, Khan lifted the lighter he'd kept on his seat between his legs. "May I join you, Ms. Rozen? Or may I be so forward as to address you as Adella?"

Adella held the pack aloft.

Khan placed his hand over his heart.

"Are you all right, Major?" Adella asked.

Khan smiled. "Your presence, madam. Your very presence." Eyes half-closed in anticipation, he took two cigarettes, placed them between his lips and lit them. He extended one to Adella.

Adella rose.

"I have not offended, I hope," said Khan.

"I saw that in an old movie on TV," María cut in. "I'm sure Ms. Rozen has seen it, too."

Adella accepted the cigarette, circled the table and pulled out the vacant chair. "My view of the lake will be better from here." She reached for the brown travel bag.

"Touch it," said María, "and I'll break your arm."

CULTIVO

| Cultivation |

15 | QUINCE | 15

BOBBY'S KNUCKLES WHITENED as he tightened his grip on the faux-leather handles of the brown travel bag.

General Gomez stood opposite behind the ornate desk in his large office displaying native handicrafts collected by a discerning eye. Lips pursed, he stared at the bag like a child impatient to unwrap a long-anticipated birthday gift but sufficiently disciplined to restrain his urges among adults. "The van you inspected yesterday on the old road," he said. "You see a link to the missing priest?"

"Possibly. I wasn't prepared to take it further."

The *general* nodded.

Bobby held the bag out.

Gomez accepted it. "This should change your situation, no?" He set the bag down gently on his desk and unzipped it. "You do not mind, Colonel?"

"No, sir. Not at all, sir."

Gomez removed a package wrapped in bright-green foil. "Ah, Mobys' Premium Highlands blend." He peered back into the bag. "Six of them. This is very thoughtful. Of course, I am quite fond of Mobys' African blend, as well. I order it online."

"I can have some sent, sir."

Gomez plunged his hand back into the bag and withdrew a rectangular tin of Mobys' signature strawberry-coconut biscotti. "How thoughtful, Colonel. I shall share these with my staff tomorrow morning."

"And the rest, sir?" Bobby asked.

The general peered down into the bag, inserted his hand, took out an envelope, lifted the flap and ran his thumb over a thick bundle of one-hundred-dollar bills secured by a red rubber band. He smiled. "Everything appears to be just as agreed."

Bobby studied Gomez' eyes, vaguely distant in contemplation of what ten thousand dollars might buy. And ten thousand the next week. And ten thousand each week after until Bobby—or Lewis Kennan—found the missing priest. Or the priest's body. Or the priest no longer mattered to anyone but his family.

The general held up a package of coffee. "May I offer you a gift?"

"No thank you, sir," Bobby replied.

"Of course," said Gomez. "Mobys provides all the coffee you wish, I am sure. And in little more than two weeks, San Cristo will be privileged to indulge in the same pleasures. While I am quite often in the capital, I am sorry that certain duties here will prevent me from attending the grand opening and meeting the Holy Father." He turned, opened a small safe set into the wall and placed the money on a shelf.

What, Bobby wondered, would the general do with the cash? Sink it into a new Mercedes? Refurbish his home in the capital? Pay down his children's college tuition in the States? Support his mistress? Ten thousand dollars a week could contribute to one or all. But what did it matter? Bobby'd delivered cash—and lots more than this—to everyone from presidents to village chiefs. "Your tax dollars at work," a CIA contact once reminded him. Was passing on cash from a multinational corporation any different? Of course, Mobys' stockholders would never see this item in an annual report. But as long as their share prices rose and their dividends swelled their bank accounts, would they care? Wasn't it all about return on investment?

Gomez, his back to Bobby, examined the stack of bills as if he were studying a new work of art in his living room.

Bobby cleared his throat. Waiting was the worst part—the demeaning part. Ultimately, he believed he was better than this. And more, that the USofA, which he now represented as a private citizen, was better. But he couldn't help wondering if his tarnished idealism consisted only of an illusion—and one that might ultimately weaken both him and the nation. Idealists, he'd come to believe, posed as many dangers as realists. Often more. To imagine yourself above the world—above human nature, as frail and ugly as it might be—was to risk being destroyed by it. And worse, possibly to lead others to destruction.

Gomez spun about. "Tonight, you will sleep well, Colonel Gatling. Tomorrow, a dozen of my best soldiers, all *indígenas* who know the highlands far better than the unfortunates who accompanied you the last time, will take you wherever you wish to go."

"Thank you, sir. Your generosity is appreciated."

Gomez reached across his desk to return the empy travel bag to Bobby. "Oh, and you will not mind, I hope, if I send along one other man."

Giovanni lowered himself gingerly onto the toilet—worn planking into which had been cut a hole. Outside the small wooden hut stood a masked guard with a rifle. Giovanni again looked for a lock on the door. Again, he found none. That these men did not respect his privacy disappointed him. Worse, it angered him. And anger shamed him. Did not Jesus preach that one should turn the other cheek? Moreover, in their favor, they had supplied him with a new roll of paper.

Giovanni closed his eyes. He had prayed the twenty mysteries of the rosary daily, but the answer to his predicament had yet to reveal itself. Perhaps God was testing him. Perhaps all that had happened signified God's response to his lack of proper faith in Holy Mother Church and Jesus' saving grace. He lowered his chin to his chest. Or perhaps he lacked faith in himself.

He pondered escaping. Surely he could find some way to slip off from his captors and elude them in a jungle so large and difficult to traverse that all the forces of the government of San Cristo had not yet been able to find him. In the cinema, prisoners often escaped from the very worst of confinements. True, they wandered alone and frightened in a strange wilderness for days and even weeks on end, but eventually they found their way to freedom. If only he had a screenplay and a director to guide him. But then, perhaps God intended that *he* should assume those roles.

His spirits brightened with renewed hope. Tomorrow, clear-headed after a good night's sleep, he would plot his escape.

A sharp cry sounded. Giovanni could only imagine a predator having snared its helpless prey in jaws filled with razor-sharp teeth. Dangers unimaginable to civilized Europeans lurked in the jungle only meters away.

Sweat from Giovanni's forehead plummeted to the dirt floor. He shivered. His stomach tightened as if a hand of steel squeezed his entrails. He let loose a cry not unlike the one he had just heard. How long would God leave him abandoned? But he had no time to assess the likelihood of divine assistance as his bowels loosened with an uncontrollable rush.

"You look good, *jefe*," said Carlos to Garcia-Vega, who sat patiently on a black canvas director's chair ten meters from the fountain of *las tres señoritas*. "And ready. The whole country will listen to every word you say."

A crowd of onlookers grew as a young woman with long brown hair and green eyes, her skin an alluring shade between Italian and French, brushed a last dab of powder on Garcia-Vega's nose. The producer from TeleCristo had suggested makeup to enhance his stature as the bearer of important news. To protest would be to quibble. Jesús Garcia-Vega *was* a man of stature.

The young woman removed the small beige cloth protecting Garcia-Vega's freshly starched and ironed uniform jacket then rose from her stool. "You have five minutes. We go on right after the *telenovelas* and game shows finish. And then the commercials, of course."

Garcia-Vega reflected on the probability that the young woman, seemingly not in possession of a single drop of *indígena* blood, was destined for a life of privilege. Today she served as an assistant with a makeup brush and hair spray. Tomorrow, a producer. The next day, an executive. And after that? No doubt she would become one of these new women directors on corporate boards, always seeking, like a miner lusting for gold, to extract every last coin earned by the people through backbreaking toil.

Now, however, she served the purposes of Jesús Garcia-Vega and the very people whose rights and welfare she sought to trample. Not that, if the opportunity arose, he would not wish to teach her the error of her ways and demonstrate how powerful and potent a mostly-native man could be.

"Have you reached *Señorita* Rozen?" he asked Carlos.

"Like you said, *jefe*. She wishes she could be here, but she has much work to do at Lago Azcalatl. She will watch in the hotel bar."

The young woman from the network gestured towards the fountain. "*Por favor, señor.*"

Garcia-Vega rose and walked to a mark on the cobblestones made by crossed pieces of silvery duct tape. Hints of late-afternoon sun trickled down through the clouds. They created a soft, golden glow that would, he hoped, flatter his appearance.

The producer held up the thumb and first finger of his right hand. "*Dos minutos.*"

The young woman checked the miniature microphone attached to Garcia-Vega's jacket and the battery pack at the small of his back.

Carlos shuffled his feet to position himself just out of camera range. "*Jefe*," he whispered, "did you hear about the reward money? It is now *five*-hundred-thousand dollars."

Garcia-Vega remained expressionless and immobile. "The priest could only *wish* he were that important."

"He *is*, *jefe*," Carlos responded. "To *some* people." He leaned in. "I hear that the money all comes from Mobys. And if nothing happens in the next day or two, they will raise the amount again."

Garcia-Vega cleared his throat.

"Maybe even to a *million*. That could loosen lips, huh, *jefe*?"

"No man of honor would ever betray the just cause of the people, even for such a sum."

"God forbid, *jefe*. But a man could buy a lot with that kind of money. They say every man has his price."

"*¡Minuto!*" the producer called out.

Carlos stepped back.

Garcia-Vega took a deep breath and held it. His chest pushed against the buttons of his shirt and jacket.

The crew readied themselves to provide a live feed throughout San Cristo, across Latin America and around the world.

Garcia-Vega exhaled. The sound of air softly parting his lips satisfied him. Indeed, it thrilled him, as did his voice whenever it rang out on behalf of the people. In seconds he would announce that the kidnappers had contacted him with their demands. Father Giovanni could have his freedom—they wished him no harm—for ten million dollars and the transfer of the expanded Azcalatl National Park to the local *indígenas* as their autonomous homeland free of interference from the government and the tyranny of *capitalismo salvaje*.

And just as important—no, even more important in the scheme of things—they would engage in negotiations only with Jesús Garcia-Vega.

16 | DIECISEIS | 16

KHAN NOTED THE CHEMIST'S DISAPPROVING EYES as he examined his purchases on the counter. The pharmacy—to use the American word—was popular with the local community of ex-pat Californians, who found available over the counter many of the products they consumed at home and a good number prohibited save by prescription—if they were legal at all.

"Will there be anything else, *señor*?"

Khan reviewed his selections, including several from what might have been termed an unusual pharmacopeia, along with razor blades and dental floss. He shook his head with satisfaction. "No, my good sir. I believe I have everything."

The chemist placed the items in a plastic bag then accepted Khan's American dollars. "You will please read the instructions on the labels," he advised in a monotone as he counted out Khan's change.

"Most certainly," Khan responded. "If anyone understands the potency particular substances may exhibit, it is a man with a doctorate in biochemistry from Oxford University. Would you not agree?"

The chemist looked away towards a slim woman in shorts and a tank top approaching with a large box of sanitary pads.

Khan snatched the plastic bag off the counter, smiled at the woman and practically skipped out of the store. Emerging on the sidewalk, he stopped suddenly. He had everything well under control to be sure. And yet he couldn't help but believe that he had forgotten something.

* * *

María walked up to the water's edge, turned to Bobby and rose on her toes. "Some things a man and a woman can't do by sat phone," she said.

Bobby studied María in her black spandex shorts, a teal tank top and matching teal running shoes. Whether he'd let his glance linger too long he couldn't be sure. Women, he knew, expected—demanded—attention. The challenge lay in determining just how much attention would prove appropriate. No question, María was well worth looking at. On the other hand, she was his employer. On the other hand, the line between professional and personal was known to blur. Nothing between men and women was simple.

María brought her heels down and thrust her left leg forward to stretch her right calf and hamstring in preparation for a sunset run along the lake before the usual evening rain.

Feeling self-conscious, Bobby looked down over his black t-shirt and mud-stained, dark green cargo pants. Along with his green windbreaker, they'd make up a passable field uniform, given that the quartermaster at the army base had nothing to offer a six-foot-five *Yanqui*. Asking Kennan for assistance—and thus tipping him off—was out of the question. Obviously Bobby hadn't anticipated leaving the capital to spend two days chasing a missing priest through the highlands, but he'd make do. He always had.

María changed her position, thrusting her right leg forward and extending her left straight behind her. "The point is, Colonel, Whitman Scharq insists on important news being delivered face to face. It's corporate policy."

"Regulations. Yes, ma'am." Bobby felt a like he was back in high school wondering if he'd attracted the attention of the prettiest girl on the cheerleading squad. Back then girls had not been a problem. Grown women turned out to be another matter. He shifted his weight. His hiking boots made a crunching noise on the pebbled beach as if he were stepping on bubble wrap. "But the point is, ma'am, there *isn't* any news."

María continued stretching then brought her legs together. "That there's *no* news is *critical* news because no news is *bad* news. And I'd rather hear bad news in the flesh." She raised her right foot and flexed her ankle. "Colonel Gatling . . . It's Bobby, isn't it? Not Robert? Not Bob?"

"It's always been Bobby, ma'am. I've never given it much thought."

"A boy's name." She lowered her right foot and raised her left. "That's ironic, don't you think?"

"How so?"

"I've known a lot of men with, you know, man's-man kinds of names, but in the end, they were really just boys. Overgrown boys." She lowered her foot. "I don't think anyone takes you for a boy, do they, Bobby? You don't mind my calling you Bobby, do you?"

"No, ma'am."

"So the way it is, Bobby . . . We're a long way from the corporate office or Whitman Scharq's penthouse back in the capital. Please. Just call me María."

What's in a name? Bobby thought. A whole lot actually. María would now call him Bobby and not Colonel Gatling. That would suggest a certain level of familiarity. And ignorance. Because she didn't know that Gatling wasn't his name at all. Not originally. The family name had been Gotlinsky before the Holocaust—something he hadn't learned until he turned forty and his father was dying of cancer. How ironic that his father chose an American sounding name for his new life in the USofA not knowing that it was the name of the inventor of the pioneering machine gun that dramatically increased the Union Army's firepower in the Civil War. Blood was hard to escape. And didn't María's last name, Skavronsky, partially mask her real identity as a Latina? Perhaps the two of them had a lot more in common than they realized. And would blood be part of the equation?

"Bobby?" María asked. "You look a little lost."

"No, ma'am. María, I mean. I've been thinking about where we go from here. Time's short. From what Vatican security lets on, it's touch-and-go about the Pope's visit. Trouble is, there's not much I can do until tomorrow."

"Then we'll have to make the best of it. Your full report . . . every last detail about what you've done and what you think we can do . . . can wait until dinner. Eight o'clock?"

Bobby canted his head to the left like a soldier on parade adjusting the stock of his rifle. "Dinner. Yes. That would be nice."

María smiled. "The fact is, Bobby, I'm really a very nice girl when you get down to it."

An unexpected wave of euphoria washed over Giovanni as if he suddenly found himself at Christ's very feet. Here he was a captive, isolated from everything he knew, his life in the hands of others. Yet the loving presence of God, he realized in a flash of profound insight, remained with him because he remained a true, devoted servant of God.

That morning, with little expectation, he had requested a Bible. Much to his surprise and delight, the boy who apparently lived in the house brought him one following lunch. The boy only smiled and said nothing, but Giovanni's heart warmed with gratitude. True, this Bible was printed in Spanish. But placing his hands on a Bible in any language provided enormous comfort. Moreover, his knowledge of Spanish, while limited—he was nothing if not a man of humility—proved sufficient for comprehending most of what he read. He knew the Bible well, naturally. And so he'd begun with "In the beginning," the first verse of the first chapter of Genesis, the Bible's first book.

The story of God's creation enthralled him. How remarkable was the world. And man! And woman! God's banishment of Adam and Eve from the Garden of Eden brought him to tears but joyously so. Although Eve's sin condemned all mankind, every willing soul would be redeemed through Christ Jesus.

Nonetheless, Giovanni wondered if he himself could condemn the parents of humanity. Not that he doubted the teachings of Holy Mother Church. But hadn't Adam and Eve's betrayal of God's command not to eat the apple been impelled by innocence? Could that childlike couple truly understand the gravity of their sin? Could God really hold them accountable?

Giovanni sat on the edge of the bed in the small room in the small house—a cottage, really—to which he was confined in the last of the lingering twilight. How still and peaceful his world had become. The once-shrill cries of the beasts of earth and sky had transformed into reassuring sounds giving testimony to the complex web of life created by God. He now inhabited the very paradise God offered the first humans under the care of hosts—he no longer considered them guards or captors—who remained courteous and solicitous of his wellbeing. He thought of them more as friends he did not yet know well—friends who, along with the family of the house, took great care to meet his simple needs.

Indeed, here in this nameless jungle, life encompassed only the most basic needs and requirements. The sun rose and lit the world. One woke from sleep. One relieved oneself and ate a humble breakfast. Hands toiled in a small garden, cared for animals and perhaps crafted simple objects for daily use. Rain fell in the afternoon. Then darkness descended. One ate another humble meal, satisfied with what the earth provided. Rain returned. One slept. And always, one prayed. No day could be complete without praising the Creator.

He could very well live in such a place as this forever. What did Rome—or Perugia, even with his parents living there—any longer hold for him? He felt like Adam reincarnate, the first man, so close to the earth, the life force and the pure intent of the Word that brought forth the Light that shines in darkness.

Giovanni sighed. He could not yet be in Paradise. Did not Adam require an Eve? Could a man truly be complete without a woman? Most certainly, he had taken a vow of chastity, reflecting Paul's wish that everyone be as chaste as he was. Just as certainly, to break that vow would cast his soul into eternal damnation. But Paul had recognized the frailty of the flesh and also had written that it is better to marry than to burn. And Giovanni knew his own flesh to be frail indeed.

He turned his ring around on his finger, exposing its plain underside while enclosing the engraved cross within his fist. He ran a fingertip over the smooth edge. How much like a wedding band it appeared. He sighed. If he was Adam, who was his Eve? What was she like? When would he meet her?

Darkness enveloped the room. Filled with longing, Giovanni shuddered. Given the nature of his thoughts, would God banish him from this paradise?

Bobby, eyes closed, drifted between sleep and wakefulness. Almost disconnected from his body, he pushed the blanket slowly off his chest. He'd gotten up to pee once during the night. Now, as first light infiltrated through the draperies, he had to go again. But something kept him from rising—a nearby voice soft and muffled.

He opened his eyes and glanced towards María's pillow. It revealed only the depression made by the weight of her head. He touched it. It was still warm. The voice continued. He kicked the blanket from his feet, which dangled over the edge of the mattress, and sat up. Still, the voice buzzed. He searched the room in the early morning half-light. María's skirt and blouse hung neatly over the chair by the window, but he saw no sign of her.

And then Bobby had it. The voice came from the bathroom. María's voice. A series of silences punctuated her words and sentences. She had to be on her cell phone. But who was she speaking with? Whitman Scharq? Lewis Kennan? The Vatican? Her daughter in San Francisco?

He wanted to stand by the door and listen but dismissed the impulse. It was unbecoming of a man like him. Further, what would he learn that she wouldn't tell him? Well, that remained a question. They still were little more than strangers. But why take the risk that she would suddenly open the door and find him eavesdropping? It couldn't be good professionally or personally, as mixed up as the two now were.

No question, he found María captivating. He was feeling . . . *How* was he feeling? He'd never been big on feelings, as his two ex-wives emphatically made clear. Certainly, he wasn't in love—if he actually knew what love was. What he *did* know was that he was way too old for love at first sight or mistaking sex—very good sex—for love. That was fairy-tale stuff or bizarre history like the relationship between Grand Duke Michael, brother of Tsar Nicholas II, and Natasha Wulfert. But when had he last met a woman who could hold her own with him—who could make him feel that whatever he'd done, wherever he'd been, she could match him strength for strength, story for story?

He lay back down.

The bathroom door opened.

María stepped out wearing only teal panties.

Bobby hopped up. "Call of nature."

"Well, go answer *your* call and then you can answer *mine.* I'm not leaving until eight."

"This morning?"

"I have to chopper back to the capital. And for whatever reason, Whit asked me to bring Khan along."

17 | DIECISIETE | 17

KHAN NIBBLED AT HIS MUSHROOM and sausage omelet topped by a tangy salsa of his own recipe. "Gracious of you, Whitman, to let me prepare lunch," he said. "And to meet my request for a little chat on such short notice, seeing as you just flew back to Ciudad San Cristo last evening. So much to do and all."

Scharq took a last forkful of egg and stared intently at his laptop sitting on the coffee table in the penthouse's living room. "I take it you've got something important on your mind. Word is, you're having quite a nice time at the lake."

"A most pleasant holiday, Whitman. Thank you. And I trust your flight was uneventful."

"Just a way to get from here to there. Or from there to *here*, as the case may be." Scharq betrayed a small grimace.

"There's nothing wrong with your omelet, I trust?"

"Very tasty," Scharq answered. "I didn't know you could cook."

"A gentleman alone must know how to care for himself. Self-preservation and all that."

Scharq rested his hand on his stomach.

Khan put his fork down. "Are you all right, Whitman?"

"Too much traveling. The natives are restless."

"Ah," said Khan. "The shareholders again."

Scharq closed his eyes. "So you wanted to discuss something. The caffuel test facility we want to build up in the highlands? The one our pal Al . . ."

"President Quijano, I take it."

"The one our pal Al doesn't seem to support. That's what you want to talk about?"

Khan folded his hands in his lap. "Actually, yes. You are, as always, most perceptive, Whitman."

"You don't think we should wait until María gets back from her meeting?"

"I had rather supposed that we could discuss the matter privately, my concerns being more of a scientific and technological nature."

Scharq leaped from his seat. "Bathroom!"

Khan rose.

The door to the bathroom off the kitchen opened then slammed shut.

Khan smiled. The few drops of the chemical compound he had fashioned at the lake and added to Whitman Scharq's plate had fulfilled their purpose. He had just subjected one of the world's wealthiest men to an extreme but not life threatening intestinal episode. Doubtless, Whitman would be ensconced in the W.C. for some time.

Khan left the table and sat on the sofa in front of Scharq's laptop. He opened Scharq's email and arranged the selection of messages received by name. His heart did not merely flutter but pounded as he found what he sought. A key member of his scientific staff—a man whom he not only hired but also nurtured, sir!—was maintaining regular contact with Whitman. The subject lines alone confirmed his suspicions. The Judas called into question the scientific foundations of caffuel. He turned his head. "Is there a problem, Whitman?" he called out.

The sound of the toilet flushing greeted his question. A loud groan followed.

Khan opened the most recent email. He now fully understood the scurrilous—if not entirely baseless—charges leveled against him. This, however, met only the first of his two objectives. He faced an even more daunting challenge to which he would devote most of the few precious minutes he had made available. Let no man believe that I.A. Khan was anything but clear of mind and staunch in purpose when confronted by adversity. Whitman would quickly enough recover without ill effect, while he would return to the lake and make the most of his holiday.

The toilet flushed again.

"This may take a while," Scharq called.

Khan scanned Scharq's files. He knew what he was looking for—he had long maintained an intelligence gathering operation within the offices of the Mobys Foundation—but what if he couldn't find it? His heartbeat quickened. And then he found it—correspondence with several luminaries in Washington more than hinting at practices none of the parties would wish exposed.

He withdrew a memory stick from a trouser pocket. Should the game come down to one last hand with the chips all in, Major I.A. Khan, Ph.D. would hold the winning cards.

Adella considered letting loose an exultant shriek but instead chose from her arsenal of vocal effects a moan soft enough to avoid letting her intimacy with Jesús escape the bounds of ANTI's new kitchen yet sufficiently throaty and emphatic to lead him to believe that he had brought her to orgasm. And not just any orgasm! Regrettably, he had not, although through no fault of his own.

Adella could not quite shake off her fatigue. Awakened early by a hotel informant who revealed that that corporate *strega*—that witch—María Skavronsky was about to be taken to a nearby helicopter, Adella had cadged a flight back to Ciudad San Cristo. This saved wasting hours on the winding highway—assuming it was open again—then creeping along in the capital's heavy traffic in response to Jesús' call the previous night. He had beckoned her with news. Important news.

"Was it good for you, *amor mío*?" Garcia-Vega whispered in her ear. "Tell me, my love. Tell me how good it was."

"What do *you* think, my darling?" Adella responded. She winced. Her head had not yet recovering from banging against an elegant but unforgiving teak cabinet door. And now the sensitive flesh of her bare ass pressed against the newly installed granite countertop.

Garcia-Vega stepped back slowly, lifted his silk boxer shorts and pulled up his trousers. "Yes, *amor mío*. I think it was *very* good."

Adella had barely raised her panties to her knees when a summoning fist knocked on the door that Garcia-Vega had insisted separate the kitchen from the hallway to avoid his being disturbed while cooking.

"*Jefe*," Carlos called gently, revealing his understanding nature. "*Jefe*, Archbishop Dantón is in the conference room."

"*Momentito, camarada*," Garcia-Vega responded softly.

Carlos' footsteps faded down the hall.

Adella buttoned her blouse. Might the Archbishop, she wondered, detect the scent of their lovemaking? But men were so oblivious. And what would most archbishops know?

Garcia-Vega opened the fridge and removed a tray of crudités. "Wash your hands and take this to the Archbishop, *por favor*."

Adella's eyes narrowed as she zipped her slacks. "Wash *my* hands? And now, I am also to play the little hostess?"

Garcia-Vega shrugged.

Relenting for the sake of the world's hunger for truth, Adella freshened her lipstick, grasped the tray and carried it from the kitchen to the conference room.

Garcia-Vega followed and placed a bottle of Chilean pinot noir on the conference room table just as Carlos set down four sparkling wine glasses.

"News," said Dantón.

The tray of crudités clattered loudly on the polished mahogany.

"Wine?" asked Garcia-Vega.

Dantón stared at the glasses pensively then smiled. "Of course."

Carlos gently extracted the cork and poured.

"Your news?" Adella asked.

Dantón chuckled. "Ever the journalist!"

"A revolution is taking place," said Adella. "From San Cristo will emerge a new world order."

Dantón raised his glass. "*¡Salud!*"

Garcia-Vega and Carlos raised their glasses.

"*L'chaim!*" Adella toasted reflexively. One of the few Yiddish expressions with which she was familiar, it gave her cache in certain circles.

They sipped.

Adella drank. She had earned it. What did the world think she was? A nun?

Dantón set his glass down. "This news is what we have prayed for, although on a personal level it is somewhat disappointing." He paused for effect, as if on stage at the nearby National Theater. "The Vatican has canceled the Holy Father's visit to San Cristo and called Bishop Groelsch back to Rome. Even if Father Giovanni is found today, this decision is final."

Garcia-Vega bit his lip. Was this good news or bad? *Sin duda*, the government—and Alonso Quijano above all—would now look like fools. Surely, the revolutionaries had won this first, crucial stage of the battle.

On the other hand, would Father Giovanni's fate maintain its importance? The media might turn away from the critical role Jesús Garcia-Vega played in this drama.

Yet on the other hand—which obviously was the first hand—the missing priest would remain an accusatory symbol of the government's incompetence. The priest would embody proof, as if any sensible person needed it, that Quijano could not deliver on any of his promises to provide a better life to the people.

Garcia-Vega savored another sip of wine. So be it. The capitalist oppressors from Mobys would open their new store without the papal presence. This was good. Let the rich indulge in their ridiculously expensive lattes and mochas. In time, even they would discover that Mobys was nothing other than a fraud. Only that morning, he had gone online and ordered an espresso machine from Italy—a machine that would make far better coffee than anything an exploiter of the masses like Mobys could ever hope to serve. All things considered, cancellation of the Pope's visit posed no problem at all. Everything was falling into place.

Adella gestured with her glass. "And you, Jesús? You, too, have news."

Dantón leaned forward.

"News of great importance," Garcia-Vega responded. "I have been asked to address the National Assembly the day after tomorrow. The announcement will be made later this afternoon."

Dantón made the sign of the cross. "They gave in! I knew they would!"

Garcia-Vega displayed a smile not unlike that of the Cheshire cat in *Alice in Wonderland.* Thanks to the judicious sharing of ANTI funds, the National Assembly, although dominated by the elite, contained no few allies for the cause. True, the Assembly exercised only limited power. But words spoken in its marble-lined chambers—Jesús Garcia-Vega's words—would echo up Bulevar 8 de Abril, across Plaza Azcalatl and over the fountain of *las tres señoritas*, then continue up Bulevar Azcalatl to shake the very foundations of the Presidential Palace.

"The priest?" asked Adella. "Will you say anything about the priest?"

Garcia-Vega turned towards Carlos then back to Adella. "Say something about the priest? At the National Assembly? No, *amor mío*. Not there. Not then."

Adella's eyes glittered through her purple-tinted contact lenses. "Then somewhere else? Sometime else? Sometime soon?"

Carlos beamed. "Tell them, *jefe*. There is no one here who cannot be trusted. Tell them."

Garcia-Vega peered into his wine glass then raised his eyes. "The revolutionary heroes who have made Father Giovanni their guest have asked me to go to the highlands . . . into the jungle itself . . . to negotiate his release. They trust only Jesús Garcia-Vega."

Dantón raised his glass. "You will bring Father Giovanni out to freedom, just as God brought the faithless Israelites out of Egypt. You will be a hero throughout San Cristo and the world, Jesús."

Adella withdrew her purple cell phone from her purse. "You must tell the world *now*. I will call my crew. You will give me an exclusive interview. Then after your speech at the National Assembly, we will go together to meet the revolutionary heroes."

Carlos placed his hand over Adella's cell and fixed her with all the purpose a one-eyed stare could muster. "We must *record* the announcement about going to the jungle, *señorita*. For the sake of security. Then we will release it forty-eight hours after the *jefe* makes his address to the National Assembly so that no one will know where he is."

Adella lowered her glass as if she'd discovered an insect—large and particularly ugly—lying dead at its bottom. "Record? We are about to witness the biggest story in the history of San Cristo, and you will record it and then wait?"

Garcia-Vega clasped his hands together. "You are certain, Carlos?"

Carlos released his hand from Adella's cell. "*Jefe*, the reward for finding the priest . . . I hear it will be raised to two million dollars. Maybe more. The government is desperate. But the reward will do more than make the priest the most wanted man in San Cristo. If your enemies hear you are going to the highlands, they will watch *you* the way a hawk watches a rabbit. And then . . ." He raised his right hand into the air and smacked it down on his left fist.

"They wouldn't dare!" declared Archbishop Dantón.

"Ah, but the pigs would!" countered Adella.

Carlos nodded. "The highlands are full of *Yanqui* mercenaries hired by Quijano. And the giant American, Gatling, is there with specially selected soldiers."

"Two million dollars," sighed Garcia-Vega. "What man of honor would sell his soul for only two million dollars?"

"Never underestimate the power of money, *jefe*," Carlos advised. "I tell you again, every man has his price."

Garcia-Vega's head shook as if resisting an interrogator trying to force from him information of the highest sensitivity. "Not true, my friend. *You* have no price and *I* have no price."

"We are just two men, *jefe*. Just two."

Garcia-Vega nodded. "You are right, *camarada*." He turned to Adella. "We must maintain secrecy for the good of the cause. I will leave the capital and hide deep in the jungle before the announcement."

Carlos again focused his one eye on Adella. "No one can go with the *jefe* except me, and then I must hide as well."

Adella's forehead purpled along with her cheeks.

"No one!" Carlos repeated.

Garcia-Vega clapped his hands together like a child discovering a much-anticipated birthday cake, candles aglow. "Naturally, I will demand the reward money from the government. Filthy money from Mobys, we all know. And the Vatican's reward also. Every dollar and every euro will go to our brothers and sisters in the name of ANTI to support the new autonomous region of the indigenous peoples of San Cristo."

"But what about me?" carped Adella.

Garcia-Vega grasped Adella by the shoulders. "You must return to Pueblo Azcalatl today and appear as if you are still searching for the priest . . . as if you know nothing." He touched his right index finger to his lips and then to Adella's. "Carlos will get you a copy of my speech to the National Assembly. When I bring the priest to freedom, you will interview him first before he meets the media."

Adella smiled. "An *exclusive* interview. The whole world will see *me* with the priest. And my book," she exclaimed in a hushed voice as reverent as that of prayer. "My book will capture the revolutionary imagination of the entire world. I will be on the New York Times top-ten list. *Sixty Minutes* will feature me. Charley Rose will call me personally for an interview. And Oprah will salute me on her website."

"You see?" said Carlos. "A happy ending for everyone."

Adella's smiled dissolved. "Unless . . ."

"Unless what?" said Garcia-Vega.

"Unless Colonel Gatling gets to the priest before you do. Or someone else does."

The veins in Scharq's neck bulged bluish-purple. They struck a noticeable contrast with the earth tones dominating the walls and furnishings in the penthouse's living room. "And this is all that the money we've put up means to the Vatican?" he bellowed.

"Stay calm, Whit," María responded. "Remember how sick you were at lunch? Besides, we can work around this." Her voice, as always, created an island of calm in the stormy sea of Whitman Scharq's periodic volatility.

Scharq took a breath and let it out with a grunt. "I *am* calm. My stomach's fine. And I'm *still* pissed."

It wasn't about the grand opening. Mobys was bigger than the Pope. Bigger than the Church for that matter. What galled him was the goddam lack of gratitude after everything he'd done for the Holy Father on a visit to San Francisco. That box of peanut-butter-chocolate-chip cookies the Pope took back to Rome? He baked them himself. And how about the specially blended coffee Mobys delivered to the Vatican every week?

María shifted her feet into fifth position, her legs crossed at the knees, her toes pointed out, her arms raised into gentle parentheses framing her head. "Forget about it. It's a done deal. Anyway, we can always dig up an ex-president of the United States or a former British prime minister or some rock star promoting a new world tour. It's only money."

"Tell me about it," Scharq replied.

María simultaneously uncrossed her legs and dropped her arms, then floated onto an oversized leather sofa suggesting an aircraft carrier becalmed on a sea of white marble flooring. "You have something else on your mind, don't you?"

Scharq sucked in another breath, held it as if he'd toked on a joint and released a slow hiss through puffed pink cheeks that betrayed a web of broken blood vessels resembling cracks in a stone-struck windshield. Something else on his mind? Even María didn't comprehend the cross he bore.

In spite of his best efforts to impose order on the marketplace, the price of coffee remained beyond his control. And caffeine freaks the world over, evidencing a cowardly lack of faith in the global economy, were cutting back. Hence his plans to close several hundred underperforming stores—a strategy met by snide comments from analysts and media observers, not to mention a less-than-subtle undertone of unrest among shareholders—all of whom should have applauded him!

Not that he was backing off in any way from his bold vision for the future. The opening of the new store in Ciudad San Cristo was still on target. The company's relentless penetration of its one-hundredth country represented a milestone that would deliver tons of publicity and goodwill worldwide. The ad and PR people were creaming over themselves. No way would he compromise the breadth of Mobys' global presence and the commitment it represented. If the shareholders didn't get it, fuck them.

Scharq dropped his face into his hands. Tomorrow that goddam rabble-rouser, Garcia-Vega, would address the National Assembly. Worse, Alsonso Quijano, that fucking gelding, swore up and down on the heads of the misguided children who read his books that there was nothing he could do about Garcia-Vega's speech. What part did that dickless intellectual not get about Garcia-Vega talking up the revolutionaries? And talking down Mobys? Quijano should have had that would-be Fidel shot long ago. Wasn't he, as president, sworn to protect democracy and free enterprise?

María sprang up and skipped light-footed to the back of Scharq's massive leather chair.

Scharq sat up and lowered his chin to his chest.

María pressed the palms of her hands into his shoulders. Whatever her faults, although she couldn't think of any, she knew what her boss required.

"Goddam, that hurts," Scharq bleated.

"Crybaby," she teased. "Anyway, I have good news. We're getting closer to the priest."

"The little private army we hired? They found something?"

"No."

"Colonel Gatling then? He's got a lead?"

"Bobby hasn't found anything. At least not that you'd want to know about."

Scharq squirmed.

"But I have my sources. The reward we're putting up will do it. Well, maybe we'll need another half-million. Maybe more. *Probably* more. But we're close. And Mobys will be the hero."

Scharq stared down at yet another new pair of fifteen-hundred-dollar Italian alligator slip-ons. After muddying a pair outside Azcalatl National Park only two weeks earlier, he'd scuffed the toe of one of their replacements climbing the steps to his plane for a hurried trip to London and deposited the useless footwear in the bathroom wastebasket of his suite at the Mayfair after checking in. "So let me ask you *this*. What if no one finds the priest? Or the kidnappers kill him? What then?"

María released her hands. "That's a no-brainer. The Quijano government falls by popular demand."

"Exactly. And I'm beginning to think that's not a bad idea."

María patted Scharq on the head. "One way or the other Whit, it'll all work out."

Scharq rubbed his eyes like a sleepy child detained well past his bedtime. Work out? Didn't anyone else understand that nothing simply ever worked out? You *made* things work out. As if preparing to deliver a speech, he cleared his throat.

"Something else, Whit?" María asked.

"This Garcia-Vega. Is he a reasonable man?"

"Is any left-wing revolutionary reasonable?"

Scharq flexed his shoulders. "Let's find out."

18 | DIECIOCHO | 18

EXPECTATION AND FEAR SURGED THROUGH BOBBY. Wrapped in a thin plastic poncho and propped up against a tree, he stared at his laptop, online again thanks to a good hillside satellite connection.

There it was—an email from Bobby, Jr. Yet the more he wanted to read it, the more he hesitated. What had changed in the nearly three weeks since he'd come to San Cristo? What, after all these years, did he really expect to learn from the son he'd basically abandoned?

Maybe the only thing that would prove satisfying was his sense of anticipation. He remembered the days of snail mail when many men in the field carried unopened letters for days. They preferred to fantasize about what their wives or girlfriends had written rather than risk disappointment reading their actual words. Now, as long as he waited, he could hope that the bits and bytes of Bobby, Jr.'s message might rearrange themselves to restore—or at least begin restoring—a failed father-son relationship.

But Bobby Gatling had never succumbed to self-deception. He could no more hide from Bobby, Jr.'s words than run from enemy fire. He clicked.

Dear Dad: A good start. A very good start when you thought about it. Kimberly's in the hospital. Doctor's running tests. Her folks and Mom are . . . Bobby's teeth dug into his lower lip. Not good. Not good at all. And of course, Sandi, his first wife, would be there while Bobby, as always, was elsewhere. But why? What in the wet, mucky highlands of San Cristo was more important than his son, his daughter-in-law and his unborn grandchild? A revolution? A missing priest? Money? A woman he hardly knew but wanted to know very much?

Bobby flicked a small, winged creature off the back of his neck and rubbed where a welt already was rising. It was time to step up. He could be in Sacramento the next night. Who could fault him?

But it wasn't all that simple, was it? If he walked out on Mobys—even for a few days—what then? What would that say about his professionalism? His devotion to duty? His unanticipated fascination with María?

But that was just part of it. If he went to Sacramento, he'd tangle with Sandi again. She'd never let go of the past. Not that he faulted her any longer. And what good would all that tension do his son and the daughter-in-law he'd never met? And the baby he hoped would finally bring them together?

Someone tapped him on the soldier.

Bobby looked up, half relieved to put his thoughts on hold.

"I have received a call on my sat phone, *señor*," said *Capitán* Hauptmann-Hall. His eyes shone with anticipation. "We must go immediately to Maquepaque."

Scharq and María entered the old Sephardi synagogue with two reasons for discomfort. First, and the lesser, was the fact that neither was quite sure how to conduct themselves, although the building was now a museum and not a house of prayer. Scharq had been in a synagogue only once—a big domed building on California Street in San Francisco—for the bar mitzvah of a friend. María had dated several Jewish men, but none of them religious. She'd eaten chicken soup with matzoh balls at a delicatessen once but never entered a synagogue. Supposedly it was much like a church, although she had never found cause to muse over whatever similarities might exist.

Of greater weight was the location—only a block from ANTI headquarters. Scharq wouldn't be caught dead anywhere near the offices of a radical-left organization that drew only whiners and malcontents who had no idea how the world worked. On the other hand, he had been promised a high level of anonymity through the advantage of hiding in plain sight. Who would think to look for Whitman Scharq in this neighborhood below Plaza Azcalatl?

The synagogue itself sat among modest—a euphemism for rundown—offices and apartment buildings, and seldom attracted visitors. Only the nostalgic support of San Cristo's few hundred remaining Jews kept its doors open. Entrenched in business and enjoying the good life, Cristano Jews now attended a modern glass-and-stone synagogue in the norther suburbs. The Mossad, it was common knowledge, had designed the synagogue's electronic security system.

Rather than abandon the old synagogue, built in the early nineteenth century, the local Jewish community kept it open as a link with the past. These were a mixed lot—the descendants of Spanish Jews who had fled to Holland then Brazil then the Caribbean, as well as the *Polacos*—the Eastern Europeans who arrived in the twentieth century. The synagogue's visitors also included American and Canadian ecotourists, Europeans seeking the sun in winter and Israelis looking for a new travel experience. But these people appeared only intermittently. The sign-in book in the entry showed as many days without visitors as with.

The odd visitor certainly was not likely to recognize Whitman Scharq, who wore a bushy black beard purchased by María from a local costume shop. That Scharq somewhat resembled an orthodox Jew, albeit wearing a Panama hat rather than a black fedora, did not occur to either of them.

Scharq might also have declared a third reason for discomfort—a nagging suspicion that in spite of his best efforts, he was not in total control. On the credit side of the ledger, Whitman Scharq understood human nature. While weak men easily fell prey to malicious ideologies, what he had to offer could reverse almost any man's misguided intentions. On the debit side, ideologues by their very nature were irrational. The most logical of arguments—he almost wished he'd brought along a PowerPoint presentation—went over their heads. Nonetheless, he would play the very attractive cards he held. When Whit Scharq smelled blood, he went for it.

Twisting to his right, his knees scraping the pew in front of him, Scharq sought a more comprehensive impression of the environment in which he would bring this rather unpleasant business to a close.

The synagogue's interior hinted at the splendor of its original design—rich, dark, ornately carved woods now water-stained, brass gas lamps unpolished for years, a small balcony overlooking the main floor and pews with red-velvet seat cushions turned threadbare over many years of use.

He glanced at the eastern wall oriented towards the National Assembly. Two mahogany doors carved with Hebrew words enclosed the ark, which formerly contained a handwritten Torah scroll—the Five Books of Moses brought to San Cristo from somewhere in the Caribbean. Above the ark hung a lamp with an electric bulb left burning twenty-four hours a day.

"*Buenos tardes*," a man called.

Scharq turned towards the voice.

The man strode forward from the shadows into the pale light entering almost hesitantly through leaded windows in need of cleaning. "*Bienvenidos a nuestro conversación pequeño*. Ah, but I forget, *Señor* Scharq. You do not speak Spanish as does the lovely *Señora* Skavronsky."

"My language is the language of business," said Scharq. "The language of money. Everyone speaks that."

Garcia-Vega nodded towards a seat next to María. "*¿Con permiso?*"

María nodded in return.

Garcia-Vega fingered his beard—a black, bushy costume piece identical to Scharq's—then adjusted the olive Cuban military cap perched on his head. "I look like Fidel, no?"

Scharq made no reply.

"In his younger years, of course."

Scharq scratched the front of his neck. "Hardly a great honor."

"Obviously," countered Garcia-Vega, "we maintain a difference of opinion."

Scharq shifted his weight. The padding in the cushion, like that of his backside, was virtually nonexistent. "Fidel Castro will go down in history as one of the great political criminals of all time. An enemy of democracy, of freedom . . . of the marketplace."

"*Capitalismo salvaje*, yes. *This* is an international language . . . the language of the oppressor." Garcia-Vega waved both arms with a sweeping gesture worthy of the stage. "The De Leons, the Torreses, the Pedrazas . . . the families whose ancestors built this synagogue . . . they understand. The Strausses and the Rubenzsteins, who came later and own big banks and export companies . . . they understand. The European Catholic families who take the Host each Sunday at the cathedral . . . they also understand."

"It's the wealthy who feed the poor."

"It is the poor who are San Cristo's true wealth."

María held up a hand to each. "Gentlemen, we did not come here to stage a debate."

Scharq leaned in towards Garcia-Vega. "What's to debate? When it comes down to it, you and me . . ." He held up his right hand and rubbed the thumb and forefinger together. "We're just the same."

Garcia-Vega rocked back in his seat. "Bourgeois bullshit." He looked around to see if anyone had entered the otherwise empty sanctuary.

The three of them remained alone.

Scharq stroked his beard. "Think about it. We each want to make people's lives better. We each lead others towards that goal. We each . . . we each want the recognition that comes with doing good." He lifted his hat with his left hand and swept his right over his hair. "And we each like good food, good wine . . ." He looked at María. "And beautiful women."

"I have never been a believer in original sin, *Señor* Scharq. The world was made for men to enjoy."

"My point exactly. There's so *much* to enjoy . . ." Scharq held up his right index finger in point of exclamation. "When you have money."

"Money?"

"Money. *Dinero*. That's the Spanish *I* know."

Garcia-Vega shook his head. "When every man, woman and child has *dinero* in the pocket, then life will be good."

"And what about Jesús Garcia-Vega?" María asked.

"I have a roof over my head, no matter how humble," Garcia-Vega answered. "I eat three meals a day. I am one of the lucky ones."

Scharq leaned in again. "But if you had money. Think what you could do."

"Abandon the struggle? Abandon my people?"

Scharq braced a hand on María's knee and leaned closer. "*Real* money."

Garcia-Vega paused. A man of honor chose his words carefully. A man of honor made sure that he was understood. "Great responsibilities have been placed on my shoulders, and you . . . you suggest that I discard them." He paused and leaned towards Scharq. Their beards touched, seemed almost entangled. "Ten million dollars?" he asked. "*Fifteen* million? *Twenty* million dollars?" He shook his head. "No, twenty million *euros*. What is that to a man like me?"

"Twenty million . . . *euros*?"

Garcia-Vega sat back.

"The hell," Scharq fumed. "The hell I . . ."

Garcia-Vega stood. "Have *you* a price, *Señor* Scharq?" Without waiting for an answer, he turned and walked away.

Scharq slumped against the back of the pew. He sat motionless as if deeply engaged in meditation.

María watched, waiting for Scharq's covered cheeks to turn from the unseen crimson of an undercooked sirloin to the gentle pink of a medium-rare slab of prime rib.

Scharq bolted to his feet, as if cast out by heaven from the higher, mystical world into the base material one he inhabited on earth. "I am not pleased," he said. "I am not pleased at all."

María patted her purse. "Shall we go to Plan B?"

19 | DIECINUEVE | 19

MAJOR RICARDO TORVALDSON'S FOOTSTEPS suggested rapid blows of fists on flesh as he led Bobby and Hauptmann-Hall down a flight of concrete steps to the basement of *Seguridad*'s Maquepaque headquarters. Cool and damp, the air in the stairwell smelled of mold that human hands could never eradicate.

Torvaldson halted at the landing. "What we have, Colonel . . . and Captain . . . is a major suspect in the robbery of Banco Colón."

"Here in Maquepaque," Hauptmann-Hall added.

"We are told this man drove the escape vehicle," said Torvaldson. "Reward money has loosened lips."

"And how reliable is your informant?" asked Bobby.

Torvaldson tugged at the collar of his lemon-yellow sport shirt to better accommodate the ample fold of flesh billowing out from beneath his chin like the sail of a Viking war ship in a North Sea gale. Although a fourth-generation Cristano, his red hair and beard created the appearance of a prosperous Scandinavian banker on a tropical holiday. And a banker he had been before his associates urged that he take his career in a new direction to better protect their mutual interests. Business, whatever role one played, was business. As promised, gratuities from corporations and individuals more than offset his modest government salary while appreciably increasing the income of his various investments. Quite content with his current arrangements, he lived on a nearby estate with stables, a swimming pool and a tennis court.

"How reliable is any informant, Colonel Gatling?" Torvaldson responded.

Hauptmann-Hall shook his head. "But Ricardo, Colonel Gatling and I are not here about the bank robbery."

"Of course," said Torvaldson. "The kidnapped priest."

"Obviously, you think the robbery and the kidnapping are related," said Bobby.

"And you, Colonel, or you would not be here. Whatever they write in *La Patria*, San Cristo now faces a revolution. And revolutionaries, even as primitive as the *indígenas* of the highlands, require money."

"As do informants," said Bobby. "Anything else?"

Torvaldson shrugged. "This man is a known smuggler of automobiles and trucks. Old ones. The guards at our border posts . . . for a few dollars, they let these vehicles pass."

"Like the van I saw on the old road from the capital a few days ago?"

"Exactly."

Torvaldson turned and strode down a narrow hallway defined by unpainted concrete walls. He stopped at a rusted metal door flanked by two uniformed guards, each armed with a .45 pistol and a metal baton.

Bobby felt a chill on the back of his neck.

"Our prisoner," declared Torvaldson, "is *not* a good man. He is an alcoholic like so many of the local people and a . . . how do you say . . . beater of his wife."

"A sinner!" said Hauptmann-Hall. "A violator of the Commandments!"

"And bear in mind," Torvaldson added, "he knows the highlands." He rested his hand familiarly on Hauptmann-Hall's right shoulder—the men's families were closely connected both professionally and socially. "Of great importance, this man worked at *Finca Jiménez* until August, just one month before your unfortunate incident there."

Hauptman-Hall's eyes exposed the transformation in his soul—a look of sadness overlaid by a hint of cunning determination in the righteous pursuit of vengeance.

"Has he said anything?" Bobby asked.

"Not yet," Torvaldson answered. "Like all bad men, he insists on his innocence." He nodded at the guards.

The shorter of the two—his shirt missing a button just above his belt buckle—unlocked the door. The guard waited until all three dignitaries entered and followed them inside.

The lock shut with a sharp crack like the slamming of a rifle bolt.

Bobby examined the room, some four meters square and windowless. A small duct just below the ceiling provided the only ventilation. A single bare bulb emitted a dull glow from a fixture set in the wall at ceiling height to the door's right and in front of the prisoner. Positioned behind his inquisitors, the bulb left them unidentifiable while revealing the prisoner's features.

"It is very cold in here," said Hauptmann-Hall.

"Of course," Torvaldson replied.

The prisoner, small and dark, his longish black hair uncombed and matted, slumped forward on a metal folding chair. His chin lodged against his chest. A plastic tie bound each wrist to one of the chair's front legs. He appeared to be naked, but Bobby made out that his tattered pants closely matched the color of his brown skin. Although the prisoner seemed well into his sixties, Bobby reasoned that he was probably no more than forty or forty-five.

Bobby looked up. Someone stood motionless in the corner behind and to the left of the prisoner—a man of medium height with broad shoulders and large biceps. He wore jeans and a black t-shirt.

Torvaldson took a step forward.

The uniformed guard presented Torvaldson with his baton.

"We speak to the prisoner in Spanish, Colonel Gatling. Captain Hauptmann-Hall can translate for you."

Bobby shook his head. "*No es necesario.*"

Torvaldson placed the tip of the baton beneath the prisoner's chin and gently forced his head up.

The prisoner's eyelids drooped with the heaviness of the sleep-deprived. The left side of his face was swollen and discolored.

"*Dígame,*" Torvaldson ordered in Spanish. "Tell me, my friend, and tell these men who hold your life in their hands, why you robbed the office of Banco Colón here in Maquepaque. And tell me also, my friend, about the priest . . . the Italian father. Where do you have him?"

The prisoner stared blankly.

Torvaldson forced the prisoner's chin higher, exposing his throat. "Tell me."

"I know nothing, *señor*," the prisoner answered. A gurgling sound accompanied his words.

Torvaldson withdrew the baton then tapped it on the prisoner's left ear.

The prisoner recoiled.

"Oh," said Torvaldson, "I think you know a lot. And I think you will tell us." He waggled the tip of the baton in front of the prisoner's eyes. "Because know this . . . I am not your friend, my friend."

"Please," the prisoner whimpered. "I have never robbed a bank. I do not know an Italian priest. I am a God-fearing man. A good Catholic."

Torvaldson raised the baton.

Bobby gripped Torvaldson's hand. "Is this necessary?" He let his own hand drop. In spite of carrying Juan Suelo's authority, he feared he'd overstepped his bounds. "With all due respect."

Torvaldson lowered the baton.

Bobby took a deep breath then released it like smoke from a cigar he was too distracted to enjoy. He had no intention of appearing squeamish. He *wasn't* squeamish. He'd seen a lot worse than what Torvaldson was thinking about. Hell, he'd *done* a lot worse. Early in his career, he'd never considered any interrogation technique too harsh when it came to protecting his buddies, or the men under his command or his country. In spite of what the naysayers preached, getting physical sometimes worked. People who sat behind desks didn't understand what it was like to make the call out in the field with lives at stake. Yet over time he'd come to realize that the USofA didn't need any more Guantánamos—or friends who ran operations like them. Yet the only certainty he could hold to on the issue was that down deep he wasn't certain at all.

"Please," the prisoner whined.

"Tell us then. When did you plan the robbery of Banco Colón?" Torvaldson asked. "Who is your leader?"

"A family man," the prisoner whimpered. "My wallet. Please, *señor*. Permit me to show you my wallet."

Bobby nodded at Torvaldson.

Torvaldson waved the baton.

The man in the black t-shirt stepped forward. He held out a cheap plastic wallet printed with images of Mickey and Minnie Mouse, along with a small flashlight.

Torvaldson took them.

"My hands, *señor*," the prisoner pleaded.

Torvaldson opened the wallet and extracted a lone photo, its edges ragged, its image scratched and worn. He studied it for a moment then handed it and the flashlight to Bobby.

Bobby examined a family portrait taken in the front yard of a wooden shack. A scrawny chicken peered out from among weeds sprouting from an otherwise bare patch of earth. A woman—smaller, just as dark, and bloated by motherhood and premature aging—stood next to him. Her face betrayed no emotion. Two young men and three young women flanked the couple. The sons appeared to be just filling out. The daughters, two of whom might have been the eldest of the siblings, were all attractive. The youngest girl seemed to be first blossoming into womanhood.

Bobby passed the photo and flashlight to Hauptmann-Hall.

"Your family?" asked Torvaldson.

The prisoner raised his eyes. "*Sí, señor.* I told the man who has asked me so many questions already. *Sí*."

Hauptmann-Hall looked up from the photo and smiled. He had not expected to have a role to play, but one had presented itself. He embraced the opportunity. "The girl on the right. She is your youngest?"

The prisoner forced a smile. "*Sí, señor*."

"How is she called?"

"Adelina, *señor*."

"Adelina. A very pretty name for a very pretty girl," said Hauptmann-Hall. He focused the flashlight on the girl's face. "How old is Adelina?"

"Fifteen, *señor*. She was twelve when this photo was taken. Perhaps thirteen. I cannot remember, *señor*."

Hauptmann-Hall smiled. "She must be a beauty by now."

"Oh yes, *señor*. And a *good* girl."

"Adelina," Hauptmann-Hall repeated softly. "She lives with you?"

"With her mother, *señor*. In Nahuapl. Only a few kilometers from here."

"You do not live with your wife?"

"Sometimes, *señor*."

"And your other children?"

Torvaldson tapped Hauptmann-Hall on the shoulder. "We have more serious matters . . ."

Bobby held up his right hand. If Torvaldson played the bad cop, then the Hauptmann-Hall might play the good cop even if Bobby couldn't quite see where the conversation might lead.

"Adelina," Hauptmann-Hall continued. "She goes to school?"

The prisoner shook his head.

"These people," Torvaldson whispered to Bobby.

"She is married? With a child perhaps?"

"God forbid, *señor*. She is still young. Still pure."

"She works somewhere then?"

The prisoner slumped forward.

Torvaldson tapped his chin with the baton.

"*Sí, señor*. At the shirt factory. Here in Maquepaque. Each morning, she walks from the house, although sometimes the bus comes. Some days, they do not have work for her. She stays with her mother then."

Torvaldson bent slightly towards the prisoner. "The shirt factory on Avenida Segundo between the garage and the cabinetmaker? That one?"

"*Sí, señor.* But I do not like her working in the city. A girl like Adelina, she is safer at home with her mother."

Torvaldson turned to Hauptmann-Hall. "We are getting nowhere."

"Let's be patient," Bobby coaxed.

Hauptmann-Hall turned towards Bobby. "Perhaps," he suggested, "we might have an early lunch. Our guest can rest and think about the position he is in. Afterwards, I think, he may wish to confess his sins to us."

Torvaldson looked at Hauptmann-Hall in disbelief then at Bobby. "Colonel?"

"Let's go with it."

Hauptmann-Hall tucked the photo into his shirt pocket. "I myself will buy lunch for the three of us. I know of a very pleasant American-style café nearby."

"Yes, it is very good," Torvaldson affirmed. He glanced at the uniformed guard, who unlocked the door.

"Sandwiches and beer," Hauptmann-Hall continued in the hallway.

The door clanged shut.

"And chocolate-chip cookies. What you call house-made. Delicious! Give me a little time to first attend to some business, and I will bring everything here. After lunch, we will again visit our guest."

Torvaldson studied Hauptmann-Hall's face. "Enrique, I used to think I knew you. Now I am not so sure." He shrugged. "But what if this man will not tell us what we want to know?"

Hauptmann-Hall made a small, stiff bow like a young boy attending his first ballroom dancing class. "Then I will withdraw completely from this matter. But I promise you, this will not be the case."

Hauptmann-Hall grinned as if he had just received a vision revealing the winning side of the national *fútbol* team's next friendly. "I trust everyone enjoyed lunch. And now that our guest has had time to think about his position, I believe he will be very willing to communicate with us."

Bobby took the last bite of a chocolate chip cookie as good as any back home in Virginia Beach.

Torvaldson finished his *Cerveza Azcalatl.*

The men returned to the interrogation room. The same guard took his position inside the door. The muscled man in the black t-shirt leaned against the far wall.

The prisoner raised his head. Although exhausted, his eyes widened in expectation that his captors and their *Yanqui* guest at last understood that he had nothing to tell them.

Hauptmann-Hall stepped in front of the prisoner. An interrogation really was little different from a business negotiation. If one held important information unknown to his adversary, one could dictate the terms of an agreement—or a confession. "Have you had lunch yet?"

The prisoner shook his head.

"I am sure something will be brought to you as soon as you cooperate."

The prisoner stared blankly ahead.

"Cheer up, my friend," said Hauptmann-Hall. "We are almost finished with you . . . except for one thing." He reached into his shirt pocket, withdrew his iPhone and held it up. "You know what this is?"

The prisoner nodded.

Hauptmann-Hall turned the phone on. "What I like is the camera. It is very handy to have a camera in your phone. May I show you a photo, my friend?"

The prisoner sat motionless and silent.

Hauptmann-Hall drew closer until his nose almost touched the prisoner's. "May I . . . show you . . . a photo?"

"*Sí, señor,*" the prisoner whispered.

Hauptmann-Hall backed away and clicked on the photo of a girl of about fifteen—an older version of the girl in the prisoner's family portrait. Her hesitant smile evidenced bewilderment mixed with fear. There could be no mistake, however, that she was a very attractive young woman. A young woman with large eyes and black hair pulled back into a bun. Hair that when released would tumble enticingly down over her shoulders. A young woman with a slim figure not yet betrayed by marriage and childbearing. And *tetas*. A man could easily lose himself in fantasies about such *tetas*!

And there at her shoulder with his arm around her waist stood none other than Enrique Hauptmann-Hall.

20 | VEINTE | 20

"*HE* IS COMING," called a voice from outside the cottage.

Giovanni startled. Over the past several days, he had been certain that God had guided him to this place. Now, he felt overcome with uncertainty. No, worse. A sense of dread—like icy hands tearing at his organs—threatened to eviscerate his very soul. Just what did God want of him?

He cocked his head and heard footsteps retreating. What the men did when they weren't bringing him food or reading matter in addition to his Bible or taking him to the bathroom—indeed, who they were—he still had no idea.

He clasped his hands together. When would all this end? And how? Did God intend that he inhabit a new Eden as a new Adam, producing with his Eve a new and better humanity free of sin? Or did God desire that he be taken back to the capital and reunited with his colleagues in Rome? If that happened, would he welcome a return to everything that was familiar and, to such a sad degree, so corrupt?

"Hail Mary, full of grace. The Lord is with thee," Giovanni muttered. His lips formed words not only soundless but almost devoid of meaning. He closed his eyes. He felt like weeping as Mary Magdalene wept at Christ's tomb. If he did so, he wondered, would winged angels robed in white respond? Would they reveal the answers to this terrible mystery?

He shivered. Who was the "he" the man outside the window had just mentioned? And why was he coming?

The walls of the National Assembly resonated with Garcia-Vega's authoritative voice. "I conclude," he thundered, "that this body must recommend to the president . . . no, *demand* . . . that he immediately withdraw the *Yanqui* invaders from Azcalatl National Park and the entire highlands along with all government forces. *¡Salud, San Cristo!*"

Cheers erupted on the left side of the hall.

Whistles of derision arose on the right.

Garcia-Vega raised his left fist and shook it with triumphal ferocity. *Sín duda*, his prospects for victory in the April election looked good. No, excellent. The reactionaries behind Alonso Quijano, try as they might, could not deflect the course of history any more than they could alter the dynamic geologic forces that periodically shook the very ground upon which the nation stood.

"*¡Magnífico!*" shouted Carlos from just below the rostrum.

Garcia-Vega descended four steps to the main floor.

Carlos took a position at his left shoulder.

Garcia-Vega ambled forward to receive his supporters' acclaim. He would stroll up the hall's central aisle, working the crowd. Men and women would cheer or howled as if he were a *luchador*—a wrestler—exiting an arena overcome with bloodlust.

The assembly's lone *indígena* woman, Magdalena Robles, clawed past several enthused delegates and grasped the right arm of Garcia-Vega's military jacket. He knew Magdalena from his years as minister of housing. Now middle-aged but still fiery in spirit, she remained an attractive woman with still-firm *tetas* and a broad *culo*—an ass—that had long intrigued him.

Carlos' lone eye posed a silent question.

Garcia-Vega's two eyes answered.

Magdalena Robles walked with Garcia-Vega. "Fine words," she said, "but the Assembly still has no balls."

Garcia-Vega glanced down at her large brown eyes then lower. "Come the victory of the revolution and my election, everything will change. The National Assembly will speak with one voice and serve the people's will as we have determined it."

Magdalena Robles squeezed his arm.

Garcia-Vega and Magdalena left the hall as supporters cheered and opponents jeered, emphasizing their displeasure with a variety of indelicate gestures. They emerged on the building's portico flanked by identical bronze azcalatls fifteen feet high.

A carefully assembled crowd surged forward. Many held placards praising Garcia-Vega and damning Quijano.

Carlos stepped in front of Garcia-Vega and waved his right hand.

Half-a-dozen hefty men surrounded the *jefe*, in the process jostling Magdalena and shoving her against Garcia-Vega's side.

Garcia-Vega felt Magdalena's body press against his. She made no attempt to withdraw. Indeed, she could not. And why would he complain of that? Even Whitman Scharq, as rapacious and evil as he was, understood that men—real men—delighted in the scent, the sound, the touch of beautiful women.

Dozens of police in riot gear restrained the media—unlike at the cathedral ten days earlier when Archbishop Dantón had spoken. Shouted questions rose from the pack but melded like streams flowing into a river, their words nothing more than meaningless babble.

Garcia-Vega shuffled forward. The media could wait. Soon they would have the big story they sought. And after, they would dutifully serve the interests of the people.

"*¡Jefe!*" shouted Carlos. He pointed towards a large black Mercedes at the curb. Its driver stood by the open door poised to leap into his seat.

"Yes," returned Garcia-Vega. "I am ready."

"*¡Adelante!*" Carlos commanded.

The burly phalanx pressed forward.

The crowd yielded.

The media sought to break through.

The phalanx dispersed them.

Garcia-Vega, still accompanied by the enticing Magdalena, strode regally towards the Mercedes. Perhaps she would like to accompany him? What was to stop him from whisking her away for a week or so? True, she might have a husband somewhere—he would have to pay more attention to such details in the future—but what of it? What harm could there be in a brief tryst in the jungle while he waited to embrace the heroes who held the Italian priest as their guest? What, in only a few seconds, could he say to encourage her? How might he convince her—if she needed convincing, given the way she clung to him? "Ah, a little breathing room," he uttered.

Something popped. Or banged. Or exploded. And again. And yet one more time.

Carlos wrapped his arm around Garcia-Vega and dragged him towards the Mercedes.

People scattered in every direction. The bigger and stronger among the crowd pushed over those in their way.

Garcia-Vega stumbled.

Carlos held him steady then heaved Garcia-Vega into the Mercedes, leaped in next to him and draped himself over the *jefe*'s recumbent body.

The Mercedes moved forward.

Fleeing remnants of the crowd scattered before it,

"*¡Jefe!*" Carlos roared with a mixture of anger and fear. "*Jefe*, are you all right?"

Garcia-Vega struggled to make sense of what was happening. Had someone shot at him? Tried to silence him?

"*¡Jefe!*" Carlos called again.

Others might lose their heads in such circumstances but not Jesús Garcia-Vega. He now understood everything. Shots *had* been fired. But so what? "I am all right, Carlos," he answered. His voice, calm and sure, reflected the blissful contentment of a willing martyr assaulted by heathens but remaining, by the grace of God, unharmed. Why, after all, should this incident disturb him? He scorned fear. He scorned death. He scorned anyone who sought to prevent his enjoying an intimate interlude with the ripe Magdalena Robles.

"You are sure you are all right?" Carlos asked in disbelief.

"Of course, I am sure."

"But the blood . . ."

Garcia-Vega ran his hands over his uniform. Blood drenched his right arm and side—blood red, wet and warm. Yet he felt no pain. Clearly no assassin's bullet had entered his flesh. He looked up at Carlos. "Where is Magdalena?"

Carlos pressed on Garcia-Vega's shoulders. "You must stay down, *jefe!*"

"And you?" asked Garcia-Vega.

"I give my life for you, *jefe*."

The Mercedes turned south to meet another, humbler vehicle already in place to receive Garcia-Vega and make following him more difficult.

"It is good that you will be hidden in the highlands for a while," said Carlos. "If they come for you once, they will come for you again. And you never know who you can trust."

21 | VEINTIUNO | 21

HAUPTMANN-HALL RUSHED AHEAD like a child at an amusement park too excited to mind the rain then disappeared down the steep trail into the ravine leading to their objective.

Bobby followed, less than pleased that the enthusiastic but undisciplined Hauptmann-Hall could not be restrained. Supposedly, they would find a cottage—a wood and stucco shell with a sagging red-tile roof, an outdoor kitchen and an outhouse—squatting in a clearing a kilometer from a small village containing houses in much the same wretched condition.

Major Torvaldson had apologized profusely. His own people would have undertaken the mission, but other urgent matters required their attention. The budding revolution was sowing unrest throughout the highlands. Besides, with all due respect to Colonel Suelo, they had never been trained for this kind of work. The distinguished American military expert would make short work of the kidnappers and extract the priest. Of that he was sure.

Bobby began his descent of the trail, careful to keep a moderate pace to avoid aggravating his knee. At least Torvaldson had made no mention of Lewis Kennan's presence in the area. Skilled as Kennan was, Bobby doubted that anything good could come of any efforts he made relating to Father Giovanni. Whatever lessons Kennan supposedly absorbed in Iraq and Afghanistan about influencing hearts and minds, he seemed to have no disposition to apply them in San Cristo. But then, Kennan followed rules of engagement established in Alexandria and ignored as a matter of convenience by Washington.

Now, Bobby found himself leading a search mission over terrain as challenging as any in the world. This deep in the jungle, he, Hauptmann-Hall and the patrol were forced to negotiate narrow trails climbing up and down steep hillsides and traversing the tops of ridges that plunged into rushing rivers crossed only occasionally by rickety bridges of wood and rope. Moreover, creepers overgrowing the trails and exposed tree roots threatened to entrap careless feet.

Bobby glanced up. Slate-colored splotches of sky appeared through openings in the triple canopy. An hour of daylight remained. With General Gomez unable to provide night-vision equipment, darkness would make an assault with untrained troops extremely risky. Waiting for first light in the morning made the most sense. They might catch the kidnappers still asleep or at least groggily unprepared. But Bobby had little confidence that the men would keep their nerves under control through a long night of anticipation. He could only choose between the lesser of two evils. They would go for it now with dusk and the rain masking their approach, and the element of surprise in their favor.

Bobby cocked his head, catching the sounds of Hauptmann-Hall returning up the trail before he came into sight. The jangling of the *capitán*'s weapon, ammo magazines and water bottles sounded like the over-enthused rhythm section of a newly formed teen garage band. Bobby held his hand up like a traffic cop. He had no idea how Hauptmann-Hall managed to move so quickly through the dense undergrowth, but the noise he made could get them all killed. The *capitán* might believe that he, like a cat, had nine lives, but Bobby wasn't banking on his or any other human being's sense of quasi-immortality.

Hauptmann-Hall stumbled, righted himself and approached Bobby. "Corporal Chavarría says we are a hundred meters from the clearing where there is the house," he whispered.

"If someone's there, they haven't set out listening posts. Not if we've gotten this close," Bobby responded. "I'll go up to the clearing with Chavarría and take a look."

"I will accompany you, Colonel," said Hauptmann-Hall. "I am not afraid." The tone of his voice suggested a man who meant what he said but feared no one would believe him.

Bobby tapped the *capitán* on the shoulder. "You stay here with the men and make sure they're good to go."

Hauptmann-Hall's shoulders slumped. Then he assumed a position of attention. "*¡Sí, señor!*"

Bobby walked briskly down the trail and found Chavarría. They went on without speaking, stopping just inside the tree line where the undergrowth was less dense but still provided reasonable concealment. The cottage stood twenty-five meters away in the middle of a clearing.

"I have already taken a look, *señor*," said Chavarría. "No people, no voices, no lights inside." He pointed. "The kitchen area is there to the right, but no one is preparing dinner."

Bobby peered out at the cottage. The stillness of the moment left him uneasy. His senses suggested that either the information Hauptmann-Hall had extracted from the prisoner in Maquepaque was false or someone had tipped off the kidnappers about the patrol. His instinct warned that the kidnappers knew they were coming—knew where the patrol was now. If so, they might well have set an ambush hoping to claim a major victory for the revolution. "Wait here," he told Chavarría.

"You are going back for the men, *señor*?"

"Not yet." Bobby stepped off to his right and began circling counterclockwise around the clearing from within the tree line. He moved purposefully while taking care to avoid the possibility of hitting a tripwire attached to a mine or a more primitive booby trap. Primitive, of course, represented an arguable definition of degree since mines—and he'd used them while holding a number of defensive positions—were designed more often than not to maim rather than kill. A plan began taking shape as he considered how many men might be inside the cottage and how heavily armed. The great challenge would not be killing or capturing the kidnappers, who would be pinned down inside, but keeping Father Giovanni alive.

Returning, Bobby instructed Chavarría to continue observing the cottage then headed back up the trail to brief the men.

By the time he returned to Chavarría with the patrol, only the last remnants of daylight remained.

Chavarría held his right index finger to his lips. His eyes betrayed a tension he had not revealed earlier.

Bobby motioned the patrol to get down. "*¿Hay problema?*" he whispered.

"I am not sure," Chavarría answered.

"Did you see something?"

"No, *señor*. I *heard*."

"Heard what?"

"Sounds. A wild pig maybe."

"Or a man?"

Chavarría shrugged.

The patrol waited. Raindrops tumbled from the branches above like soft-edged shrapnel.

Bobby pressed his teeth into his lower lip. If they were going to pull this off, it would have to be now. "*¡Ándale!*"

A sergeant with the belly of a fraternity brother dedicated more to beer than books took one fire team towards the right. They would cover the back of the cottage, which contained no door but two windows, and one side wall with a single window through which the kidnappers might leap to circle behind the assault team or escape into the jungle.

Bobby and the rest of the men, including Chavarría, threaded their way along the tree line to the opposite side of the house. The wall there contained neither windows nor doors, leaving a blind spot to cover the assault on the front door.

Hauptmann-Hall would accompany him. He had no intention of letting the *capitán* out of his sight.

Rivulets of sweat snaked from Bobby's armpits down his sides. His crotch felt as if he were wading a swamp in waist-high water. The plan he'd improvised was workable, but the best of plans often went out the window once the first round was fired. Everyone including Hauptmann-Hall would have to trust Bobby's instructions to keep the patrol from taking casualties and get the priest out alive. If the priest *was* alive. If the priest—or anyone else—was in the house at all.

Bobby, Hauptmann-Hall and their fire team moved forward and got into position. Bobby raised his radio to his lips. "Wait for us to get in the front door," he cautioned the sergeant. "Just wait."

"*Sí, señor,*" came the sergeant's reply.

Bobby raised his hand to signal the dash to the blank wall across the clearing.

Like a greyhound excited by a mechanical rabbit, Hauptmann-Hall sprinted swiftly out of the tree line not to the wall but directly towards the front of the cottage. A cry tore from his throat like that of an Apache warrior attacking a cavalry outpost bent on vengeance and heedless of the prospect of being outgunned.

Bobby attempted to shout but could not release the words. He had seen men engage in acts of incredible bravery but never of such foolishness. And one way or another, Hauptmann-Hall's death would come down heavily on him even if General Gomez had insisted he take Hauptmann-Hall along. Unwilling to abandon the *capitán* to his fate, he took off for the windowless wall.

Chavarría and the rest of the fire team followed.

Hauptmann-Hall easily reached the front door first and released a stream of automatic fire.

The flimsy wooden door splintered open.

Streams of automatic-weapons fire answered from behind and to the other side of the cottage.

Undaunted, his life protected by heaven, Hauptmann-Hall charged over the threshold.

"*¡No tiren!*" Bobby bellowed into his radio. Don't fire!

The firing dwindled then ceased.

Bobby ran along the wall. If Father Giovanni and the kidnappers were in the shack, they undoubtedly had been killed along with Hauptmann-Hall. He turned the corner, approached the doorway and halted.

No sound came from inside.

The surrounding jungle assumed an eerie silence as it had at the *finca*.

His heart pounding, Bobby, followed by Chavarría, hurtled through the open door. As if restrained by a tether, he stopped suddenly. What he saw might have come from a movie employing the theme of magical realism.

Hauptmann-Hall, his back to the doorway, sat on the far edge of a rickety wooden table flanked by two rough benches, both toppled over. Above him, the roof sagged so low his raised hand could have touched it. Water trickled through, leaving small pools on the table's surface.

Bobby sent Chavarría out to form a perimeter along with the sergeant's team. Then he directed his Bright Light to the room's rear wall. The beam lingered on a hole made by a round from the sergeant's fire team then drifted to another and yet another among dozens perforating what remained of the fragile protection the cottage enjoyed from rain, wind and the frequent chill of evening at high altitude.

His breathing calming, Bobby examined the rest of the room. In a corner, two simple wooden chairs lay on their sides. A leg on one appeared broken off as if someone had heaved it against a wall. Broken glass sparkled in random patterns on the floor beneath each window. Shards also glistened atop a pillow and several blankets under which someone appeared to have slept without benefit of a bed. A cardboard box stood overturned. Scattered pieces of a boy's or small man's clothing lay around it.

Hauptmann-Hall spun slowly on his backside. He held his arms out as if he were Christ descending alive from the cross. "Not to worry on my account, Colonel Gatling. Not, as they say, a scratch."

Bobby struggled in vain for words.

"I suspect," said Hauptmann-Hall, his voice reflecting an otherworldly calm, "that Sergeant Nuñez and his men fired when I shot at the door. I had not anticipated that."

"You hadn't anticipated?" Bobby responded.

Hauptmann-Hall's face lit up with the beatific smile of an altar boy lavishly praised for the performance of his duties. "If the kidnappers were here, it is better that I drew their fire than you or any of the men. It is what Our Lord Jesus Christ expects of me."

"Crazy Greenberg," muttered Bobby.

"I do not understand, Colonel."

"Alright now. Let's get focused."

Hauptmann-Hall leaped off the table.

Bobby gently nudged the muzzle of the *capitán*'s M4 down towards the floor.

Hauptmann-Hall followed the muzzle's descent and gazed at his feet. "My apologies, Colonel. This, as you know, is all very new to me."

"No priest," Bobby continued. "No kidnappers. Thank God, no men, no women, no children. Innocent people could have been killed."

"Innocent?" Hauptmann-Hall asked. "You are sure that the natives of these highlands are all innocent? That they do not all collaborate with the revolutionaries?" He lay his weapon down on the table. "No one is born with an innocent soul, Colonel. Except for the Virgin, we are all conceived in sin."

Bobby flicked his Bright Light across the room. A small table with a kerosene lamp that had avoided becoming a casualty stood against the wall to his right. Several magazines littered the floor beneath it. Next to the table stood a door leading into what apparently was the cottage's only other room. He'd taken no notice of it earlier but now understood what had happened. Nonetheless, only a fool took unnecessary chances. He raised his weapon, approached, kicked the door open, paused and went in.

Hauptmann-Hall, weaponless, followed.

A double bed greeted them. Its thin mattress hung halfway off exposing the sagging rope framework that supported it. Two pillows, their cases flung aside, oozed small white feathers. At the right of the bed stood a wooden nightstand, its bright yellow paint chipped along the edges and corners. The sole drawer lay open revealing only a comb and a rosary. Bobby spotted a Bible laying open face down on the floor, picked it up, smoothed several pages and placed it on the nightstand.

Turning, Bobby took a single step towards a small dresser. The top drawer dangled open precariously. It revealed a few shapeless items of women's underwear and an embroidered blouse. He closed it and examined the contents of the drawer below it—a long-sleeve cotton shirt with a large hole in the left elbow, a threadbare pair of pants, an undershirt, a pair of pale blue undershorts and three mismatched socks, all tossed like vegetables in a salad.

"This is strange, no?" asked Hauptmann-Hall.

"Maybe," Bobby answered. "Maybe not."

Hauptmann-Hall picked up a picture frame, the metal discolored and pitted, from the top of the dresser. A crack in the glass ran from the upper right corner to the lower left. The photograph displayed an old man, bent and leaning on a walking stick, a plump woman of seemingly the same age, her hair covered by a red kerchief, and a small boy. He held it out.

Bobby studied the photo. "Probably the people who live here."

"If they went to the village, they must have heard the shooting. I do not think they will return until tomorrow. Or perhaps the day after."

Bobby returned to the main room.

Hauptmann-Hall, still clutching the photo, trailed after him. "It is so quiet in the countryside," the *capitán* remarked. He studied the photo then placed it on the small table near the bedroom door. "You will excuse me for a moment, Colonel. I believe there is a toilet outside." He bent down and picked up a dog-eared National Geographic displaying the Kremlin on its creased cover. "Just in case." He went out, closing the remains of the front door behind him as if it would prevent the damp evening chill from entering.

Bobby flexed his right knee. The sprint across the clearing would cost him in the morning. Then he again surveyed the shambles of the main room. The people who lived here had no electricity, no running water and nothing of value. If the priest had been here, the kidnappers had chosen wisely. The cottage was remote and its inhabitants so poor they had nothing to lose from a revolution—and no reason to betray the men who made one.

The shattered front door burst open behind him.

"Evening, Lewis," he said without looking. "Drop by to make confession?"

Kennan rested his right hand on the Mark 23 at his hip. "Methodists do things differently, you know. You're not a Christian as I remember, are you, Bobby? I mean, in the churchgoing sense."

"Not in any sense. Does it matter?"

"Not to me. But I *do* have a confession. I'm one Methodist with a thing about missing priests."

Bobby turned to face him. "Money *is* a powerful motivator."

"Took a little persuading to get a reward clause in my contract, but business is business." Kennan pulled a deck of cards from the pocket on the left arm of his woodland cammie blouse. "Been workin' on a great new trick."

"Another time."

Kennan tucked the deck back in his pocket. "Quite a show your captain put on. You know there wasn't a lock on the door."

"No harm, no foul."

A low chuckle emerged from so deep in Kennan's throat that he might have been choking on his own bile. "Don't you think you're getting a little old for this shit, Bobby? Figured you'd be more comfortable babysitting the boss lady than humping in the boonies again." He blew a small kiss. "Got a few tricks I know *she'd* appreciate."

Bobby tightened his grip on his M4. Whatever was happening between María and him—or whatever *might* happen given that they'd spent just a single night together—tangling with Kennan would only muddy the waters all around.

Kennan stepped back and held his hands out. "Well, you're in luck here, Bobby. This magnificent home is all yours for the evening. Takin' my guys back down to the village. Hate to disappoint, but I don't think we want to spend the night together."

"Sounds like a plan."

Kennan fingered the ivory skull around his neck. "Tell you *this* . . . If we missed the priest, we're close. And tell you something *else* . . . Fuckin' indigs around here know some shit, if you get my drift."

Footsteps sounded on the threshold.

Kennan whirled around. "The hero of the hour!" He winked at Bobby, brought his hand lazily to his forehead in a mock salute and brushed past Hauptmann-Hall.

The *capitán*, the National Geographic under his arm, watched Kennan gather his men for the return to the village then turned towards Bobby. His eyes seemed double their size as if he finally grasped the potential consequences of his solo assault on the cottage. "There was a rat, Colonel."

"Kennan?"

Hauptmann-Hall stared in confusion then smiled. "No, Colonel. I sat down on the toilet . . . a filthy board with a hole. I heard scratching on the floor. I turned my flashlight on again, and there it was." He crossed himself. "It almost scared me to death."

"I find that difficult to believe, Captain."

Hauptmann-Hall's eyes returned to normal. "But of course, Colonel. This is just an expression, no? A man like me no longer fears death, it is true." He shined his flashlight around the room. "Have you learned anything, Colonel?"

"I'm not sure."

Hauptmann-Hall let the magazine drop to the floor. "*I* have learned something."

"Which is?"

"*Indígenas* can be civilized. I found toilet paper . . . not one roll but two . . . on a little ledge."

"Good to know," said Bobby.

Hauptmann-Hall stepped closer. "And the rat . . . Do you know what he was doing?"

Bobby shook his head.

"He was in a corner pushing something. I kicked at him. Do you know what he did then?"

"I suspect you're going to tell me."

"He ran away."

"Rats do that. If you're lucky." Bobby reached for his water bottle. "Tell the men we'll spend the night here."

"But there is more, Colonel. The thing he was pushing . . . He abandoned it." Hauptmann-Hall held out his left hand.

Bobby spotlighted the tightly drawn fist with his Bright Light.

As if impersonating Lewis Kennan teasing an expectant audience, Hauptmann-Hall slowly unclenched his fingers. On his palm sat a man's gold ring. The outside of the ring displayed an engraved cross. The inside revealed the initials GS.

22 | VEINTIDOS | 22

KHAN RAISED A PLUMP STRAWBERRY so red it might have been Photoshopped, held it to his quivering lips then paused. The fruit gleamed. Its sweet scent almost blunted that of the perfumed oils from Mendocino with which the blonde goddess Barbara had anointed herself.

"Major Khan," Adella called from behind his back as if she had stalked him and now prepared to pounce.

Khan stood. "Ms. Rozen, I did not expect . . ."

Adella stepped forward. A purple cover-up, matching sun hat and purple beach bag suggested an idle by the pool during a brief interlude of sun.

"Not off on one of your investigations, I take it," said Khan.

Adella glanced at Barbara then back to Khan. "Even Adella Rozen must restore her energies now and then. And I have a hair appointment later this afternoon."

"Then you must join us," Khan offered. A gentleman could not simply dismiss a lady even in the presence of another—even if he enjoyed an intimate relationship with both.

Adella, who knew when a woman was fucking a man she was fucking, stared at Barbara.

"Yes," Barbara said, attempting to rid herself of negative chakras. "Please."

Adella sat at the table, reached into her beach bag and withdrew a book with a purple jacket. The title, in Italian, was printed in gold. "Blood and Honor: A Manifesto for Peace Through Violence," she translated into English. "My first book. I am rereading it."

Khan turned to Barbara. "May I introduce you to Adella . . ."

Barbara's face brightened, her chakras suddenly all aligned. "Oh, yes." She picked up the last remaining dolma from her Middle Eastern sampler. "The TV star."

Adella smiled. "Well, *signora* . . . I presume it is *signora* . . . hardly a star. I do not *make* the news . . . most of the time."

"I saw you on television . . . about the kidnapping," Barbara returned. "The priest. So sad. I'm not into organized religion, but I *am* very spiritual." She leaned forward. "Do you think the kidnappers will meet with . . . you know. He was on TV before we came out to the patio for lunch?"

"Garcia-Vega," said Adella. "Jesús Garcia-Vega."

"Yes. Exactly."

"I am quite sure *Señor* Garcia-Vega will bring Father Giovanni to freedom."

"This Garcia-Vega chap," Khan offered. "He will play the hero. Not good for the government. Not good for Mobys either as I take it."

Barbara's eyes displayed a look of puzzlement. "But it's good for the *priest*."

A waiter approached.

Adella waved him off.

Barbara licked her lips. "Did you know that Major Khan is going to save the world?"

Khan cleared his throat.

"After the new Mobys store opens next week," said Barbara. "That's pretty important, too. There's a Mobys on Rodeo Drive in Beverly Hills. Two, I think. I used to go there all the time."

Adella studied Barbara. What made California women—even women her age—so childlike and oblivious yet so alluring? This woman seemed to defy time with her flowing blonde hair, blue eyes and a melanoma-threatening tan Adella could never hope to match given the ghostly skin dictated by the dominant Ashkenazi strain of her genetic code. And those impossible tits like grapefruits—tits that invited eyes to stare and hands to caress.

Nonetheless, this ripened California beach goddess would have to hunt for pleasure elsewhere. I.A. Khan was Adella's—at least when

Adella needed a man here at the lake. Jesús Garcia-Vega served her well in the capital, but he was off in the jungle, incommunicado and useless. What Khan did with this woman when Adella occupied herself with Jesús was of no concern. But this was Adella's time. As for Barbara with the unnaturally flat belly and those long legs almost free of cellulite . . .

Barbara's eyes shifted to Adella. She placed the surviving dolma between her lips and held it there.

"Well, it's a pleasant day, isn't it?" asked Khan.

Adella's almost-purple tongue darted out and moved slowly across her mouth.

Barbara let the dolma linger between her lips, unhurriedly released it and flipped her blond hair off her forehead.

Khan noted subtle changes in his California lady. Barbara's cheeks hinted at flushing. Her chest rose and fell as if she were short of breath. And if he wasn't merely imagining it, her nipples had hardened.

Barbara gazed at Adella.

Khan swiveled to witness a pronounced flush spread across Adella's cheeks and down her neck.

"How long will you be here, Ms. Rozen?" Barbara asked.

"Several days. I cannot be sure." Adella's shoulders twitched. "Until the priest . . . Until . . ."

"I hope," said Barbara, "we'll be able to share your company. Major Kahn and me."

"Share," Adella repeated. "Share."

Khan's chest heaved. His lungs ached. But why? He remembered taking his medicine. And now he felt—what? Something hard. Something hard touching him, stroking him, pressing against his manhood. A foot. From the angle of approach, given the laws of geometry and the inherent precision of higher mathematics, it could only be Barbara's. And then—a second foot. Not Barbara's but Adella's—the women stimulating him in tandem. And what was this? Adella and Barbara rubbing their feet against each other?

Yet the more they sought to arouse him, the more his thoughts turned not to the intriguing possibilities of rumpy pumpy *a trois* but to caffuel, the future of the world and, more important, *his* future. Naturally, he remained the master of his fate and captain of his soul. Hadn't he worked well past midnight the previous three evenings contemplating new data models that might advance faith in caffuel's efficacy?

Barbara looked at Adella then turned to Khan. "I left room for dessert."

As if his very thoughts mocked him, Khan felt his entire body slacken. His burnished South Asian skin seemed to melt down his cheeks. He felt a suddenly pronounced wattle forming beneath his chin. His legs threatened to fail in any attempt to rise from the table. How cruelly misfortune had struck! Here he was invited to enter paradise in what already was paradise, and he simply could not work up a stiffy. An unwilling casualty of hormonal or emotional treachery—or both—he remained soft. Limp. As ductile and yielding as a length of rope—a bloody short and useless length of rope.

And what—or who—had brought him to this sorry state? At least he confronted no conundrum here. Quite clearly, Whitman Scharq stood ready to sever the bonds of loyalty that I.A. Khan had so assiduously woven over the years.

But Major I.A. Khan, Ph.D. consisted of sterner stuff. He had already secured revealing information that would enable him to defend his position. Now, he entertained a new thought even more appealing than that of the delicious opportunity that was about to pass him by. His hopes, if not his organ, shot up.

"*¿Revolucionarios, señor?*" The short, stout woman's response mixed impassiveness with disdain. "*¡Nunca!*" Never had revolutionaries come to the village.

"*¿Extraños?*" Bobby asked. Had strangers arrived in the last week? He was retracing ground on which Kennan's heavy footsteps had already fallen, but a too-blatant denial or a slip of the tongue might provide the opportunity to pick up Father Giovanni's trail.

"*Yanquis*," the woman replied. "They came yesterday and left this morning. They said *you* would come, too."

"And a priest?" Hauptmann-Hall asked. "Have you seen a priest? A foreign man. An Italian."

The woman laughed, revealing the stumps of brown, tobacco-stained teeth. "*You* are a foreign man, although you speak Spanish."

"A priest," Bobby repeated.

"To see a priest, *señor*, we must go to church in San Tomás. It is a walk of one hour. No priest comes to such a village as this except when someone is dying . . . and only if the priest has nothing better to do."

Now, as the sun passed through thickening clouds slightly to the west over Mount Azcalatl, little else remained to be done. The woman had offered no more hint of Father Giovanni's whereabouts than the two-dozen other women and dozens of children—none seemingly older than nine or ten—doing laundry at the village trough or tending their gardens while looking after dozing pigs and scrawny chickens picking at insects. As to men, only a few of the very old remained in the village.

The woman gazed silently down at her toes painted a brilliant ruby red.

"*Muchas gracias, señora,*" said Bobby.

The woman took two steps back, wheeled around and trudged off.

"You cannot trust these people," said Hauptmann-Hall. "They are heathens, no matter what they say. They know where the priest has been taken. In this, I believe Major Kennan is correct."

Something appeared in Bobby's peripheral vision and vanished. He jerked his head to the right and stared at a small house.

"What do you see, Colonel?" asked Hauptmann-Hall.

Bobby motioned with his M4 towards the house. "I'll go that way." He checked to see that Hauptmann-Hall's safety was on then removed the magazine and placed it in the *capitán's* hand. "You go around the other way."

"There is a round remaining in the chamber, is there not, Colonel?"

"Keep it there."

Hauptmann-Hall moved off to the right.

Bobby circled to the left.

Reaching the back of the house at the same time, they observed a young man—the only young man evidently left in the village—slumped against the wall of cracked stucco. His right hand, fingers splayed, covered his stomach. Seeing Bobby and Hauptmann-Hall approach, he crumpled into a crouch, his back braced against the wall.

Bobby and Hauptmann-Hall drew nearer.

The sour stench of loosened bowels greeted them.

Hauptmann-Hall raised his hand to his nose and took two steps back.

The young man, dressed in a faded blue t-shirt, its collar stretched and shapeless, and muddy khaki pants with holes in the knees, stared down between his sandaled feet.

"I do not remember seeing this one," said Hauptmann-Hall. "Or smelling him."

"*¡Levántese!*" Bobby said, less a command than an invitation.

The young man stood uncertainly. He appeared to be fourteen or fifteen with smooth cheeks and an upper lip sprouting sparse, black fuzz. His left eye was swollen shut. A purple and yellowish bruise surrounded it.

"*¿Quién es usted?*" Hauptmann-Hall barked. Who are you?

The young man pressed his shoulder blades against the wall. His open eye reflected fear.

Something about the young man struck Bobby. He shouldered his M4 and held his hands up, palms out. "*Somos amigos,*" he said. We're friends. He wished he'd brought chocolate bars, but he'd taken only two from Pueblo Azcalatl and eaten them both. He had, of course, other options. He took off his backpack and pulled out a red flip-top box of Boots filters—popular Mexican cigarettes he'd picked up in Maquepaque along with several cigars, only one of which was left. The Boots were cheap and didn't carry the cachet of an American brand, but they served their purpose at times like this. He opened the top and held the box out.

The young man's head wobbled from side to side.

Bobby thrust the pack forward. "*Está bien.*" It's okay.

The young man again shook his head, still without vigor, as if even that small amount of exertion taxed his strength.

"Me, neither," Bobby said in Spanish. "I have not smoked a cigarette in many years." He examined the young man's face, imagining what it looked like without the bruise. "Not since I was in Moscow. Do you know where Moscow is?"

The boy nodded feebly.

Bobby smiled. "Russians smoke too much. Smoking is very bad for you." He tossed the cigarettes into his backpack.

The young man stared blankly ahead.

"Now I only smoke cigars," Bobby said with a chuckle. "Cuban, preferably."

Bobby detected a slight yielding in the young man's open eye, a willingness to believe that perhaps the giant *Yanqui* and the army officer with the yellow hair might not harm him.

Ignoring the boy's stench, Bobby leaned closer.

The young man pressed harder against the wall having no route by which to escape or the vigor with which to make an attempt.

Bobby held out his right hand.

The young man turned the bruised left side of his face towards the wall.

Bobby placed his fingertips on the underside of the young man's chin and gently brought his full face into view. The bruise and the swelling appeared consistent with the contact of a fist or a rifle butt. He continued his inspection.

Hauptmann-Hall took another step back.

Bobby tapped his own chest. "I am Roberto. They call me Bobby. What do they call you?"

The young man looked up into Bobby's eyes. "Pablo," he answered softly.

Bobby patted the young man's shoulder then squatted. Towering over the young man would only increase his fear. "Does your head hurt, Pablo?"

The young man nodded.

Bobby grabbed the first-aid kit he had thrown together in Maquepaque. He extracted a small bottle and shook two tablets into his palm. "Put these in your mouth."

The young man made no response.

"Aspirin. Good medicine." Bobby held up one of his water bottles. "Put the aspirin in your mouth and drink them down."

The young man took the aspirin, drank and held the bottle out towards Bobby.

Bobby shook his head, took out another small container and withdrew two tablets. "When was the last time you ate, Pablo?"

The young man looked down.

"You can tell me, Pablo. When did you eat last?"

"Yesterday, *señor*. In the morning. I tried."

"Have one of the men cook him up some rice," Bobby instructed Hauptmann-Hall without turning. "Maybe we can find some bananas."

"And a bath. He must have a bath and clean clothes," said Hauptmann-Hall. "After he has told us what he knows."

Bobby held the tablets out. "Listen, Pablo. You take these, also. For the diarrhea. Chew them. In an hour you can eat. And I'll give you more of these and tell you when to take them."

The young man put the tablets in his mouth.

Bobby motioned to the water bottle. "Chew the tablets first then drink slowly. And keep the bottle."

The young man followed Bobby's instructions then placed the bottle on the bare earth between his feet.

Bobby grinned. He'd made a connection. But more than that, he'd figured out what about the young man had puzzled him. He looked into the young man's good eye. "The *Yanquis*, they know who you are, right?"

"*¿Señor?*" the young man responded so softly that a rustling in the trees almost concealed his voice.

Hauptmann-Hall glanced from the young man to Bobby and back.

"Pablo, do you know the house . . . the little house at the end of the ravine?" He pointed in the direction of the house Hauptmann-Hall had attacked—where he'd found Father Giovanni's ring. "A kilometer that way?"

The young man dropped his gaze to the water bottle nestled between his dilapidated sandals.

Bobby again lifted the young man's chin. "Pablo. In that house, we saw a photograph."

"*¡Dios mío!*" Hauptmann-Hall shot out.

The young man startled.

"Pablo," Bobby continued. "In the photograph I saw an old couple. And a small boy. Younger than you are now."

The young man, his head motionless, looked away.

"*¿Sus abuelos?*" Bobby asked. Your grandparents?

The young man nodded.

"The *Yanquis* knew that—or *thought* they knew?"

The young man's head bobbed up and down.

"But you didn't tell them anything."

The young man's head shifted left then right then left again.

"And your parents . . . they are here in the village?"

The young man's chest heaved then slowly collapsed. "No, *señor*. My mother died when I was born. My father sent me to live with my grandparents. I never saw him again. I do not remember him very well."

"I understand," said Bobby. "I am sorry. But tell me . . . the men of the village . . . they are working somewhere else?"

"*Sí, señor.*"

Bobby turned towards the jungle then back. "But some have fields here. They are hiding."

The young man made no effort to refute him.

"They are hiding because they are afraid of the *Yanquis*. And of us."

The young man nodded.

Bobby scratched a small bite on the underside of his neck. "Your grandparents . . . they are hiding, too?"

The young man betrayed no more response than a stone carving of an ancient god.

"Or maybe they have gone somewhere."

The young man's shoulders heaved. Tears streamed from his open eye and oozed from the other.

"They went with the priest?"

The young man wiped his nose with his arm. The wet glistened on his dark skin.

Bobby clenched his teeth. His knee hurt.

"*El cíclope* took them," the young man answered. "He wanted *me*, too, but I ran away and hid in the jungle. I was cold all the night. And sick. The *Yanquis* found me. They threatened to take me with them, but . . ."

Bobby stared into the young man's good eye. "*¿El cíclope?*" Did he know Homer and The Odyssey? "*El cíclope* is a character in a story."

The boy reached for the water bottle, raised it to his lips, tilted his head back and drank deeply. His open eye brighter, he replaced the water bottle between his feet. "In school, our teacher reads the myths of the Greeks to us. They are different from ours, but I like them."

"And *el cíclope*?"

"*El cíclope* also is *real*."

Bobby felt something gnawing at him. It would be easy to dismiss the young man's words as a delusion springing from his weakened condition or emerging from the porous boundary that existed between myth and reality in the highlands as it did in other remote areas of the world. But he could no more let go of those words than he could make sense of them.

The boy bowed his head. His hands held fast to the empty water bottle. "*El cíclope* took my grandfather and grandmother so they would not say anything."

"And the priest? The Italian?"

"*El cíclope* took Father Giovanni, also."

23 | VEINTITRES | 23

GARCIA-VEGA CRIMPED THE EDGES OF THE DOUGH to seal in the spicy pork filling then flattened the yielding ball between his palms. He had already completed half a dozen, as well as more filled only with cheese. The inside of his mouth moistened with anticipation. He dropped the first pupusa onto the lightly oiled griddle. It sizzled. He softly hummed a childhood melody.

He had offered to cook for the men who guarded him, and why not? These were the men for whose liberty he had pledged his life. Men who risked their own lives for him and would follow with all their hearts the path of freedom and justice he laid out for them.

A dozen more stuffed dough cakes filled the griddle to be accompanied by his signature, fiery coleslaw. He regretted only that he lacked access to the very finest masa flour and cheese, not to mention first-rate cumin and cilantro. These were available in Pueblo Azcalatl, but Carlos had warned against sending anyone into the town with a shopping list reflecting the *jefe*'s uncompromising standards. Security triumphed over even the *jefe*'s will.

Garcia-Vega nonetheless acknowledged his satisfaction. If the quality of the pork left something to be desired—the pig certainly was no prizewinner—still, the local people had raised it and then slaughtered it in his honor. Furthermore, his guards had stocked the small kitchen shed with the best of what was available from the well-watered earth of their corner of the highlands.

He lacked only a proper beer. A Bohemian Pilsner might serve as an interesting choice. Or perhaps a Kronenbourg from France. But he would settle for *Cerveza Azcalatl* kept chilled in a battered plastic cooler placed into a shaded hole in the ground.

Contented and at peace, Garcia-Vega eyed the sizzling pupusas. True, a pachamanca with fish, chicken or lamb tempted his palate more at the moment. But several ingredients understandably were not available, and a pachamanca prepared without integrity insulted both the people of Peru, whose national dish it was, and the culinary arts. Jesús Garcia-Vega shamed no one. Pupusas and a reasonable if mundane domestic beer would suffice.

If he had one regret, it was the lack of a woman. One had been offered—a widow only several years older than he and dedicated to the revolution. He had politely refused. His stay, after all, would end in just two or three, or perhaps four, if not five, more days. Surely, the liberator of his people stood above taking a woman for his own pleasure as if she was nothing more than chattel. Such harlotry represented the vices of capitalism rather than revolutionary enlightenment.

Besides, he'd caught a glimpse of the village's offering. How desperate did they think he was? How could they believe that this woman with her bovine countenance and expansive body bearing fold after fold of dark brown, sweat-soaked flesh could possibly compare to the pale, red-haired, worldly Adella Rozen? But of course, only Carlos—the one man he could trust without question—knew about Adella.

Wielding a gently warped spatula, Garcia-Vega turned over several of the pupusas. His humming grew louder. He felt useful again. He had not considered preparing meals before his arrival, but time hung on his hands as heavily as sacks of coffee beans on the backs of exploited workers. Isolated, his only stimulation consisted of honing the speech he would present to the media along with the priest and pondering, of course, his remarks upon signing the papers officially declaring his candidacy for president.

Alas, his guards—his security, he corrected himself—all noble men of the highland soil, offered nothing in the way of meaningful conversation. Carlos had left after delivering him to their custody in order to contact the kidnappers and see to the security of their meeting. Such irony! He was as much a prisoner as the priest.

He'd brought books, naturally, but a rereading of Herbert Marcuse went only so far. *Goldfinger*, the old James Bond thriller he had begun before leaving the capital, struck him as decadent in this environment. He certainly did not wish to be seen with a copy of *Gourmet* or *Bon Appétit*—magazines to which he subscribed under a *nom de guerre*.

Eyes closed in a state of semi-meditation, Garcia-Vega let the scent of the frying pupusas invigorate him. Everything was unfolding according to plan. His political acumen had brought him to the brink of success. The government would suffer a major embarrassment, its brutal incompetence revealed.

Almost ready to call the men to dinner, Garcia-Vega began placing the pupusas in a hand-made reed basket. Then, as he lifted one of the treats off the griddle, his legs began to give way. Above him, the shed's metal roof vibrated as if shaken by prankish children. The pupusa dropped to the griddle. A splash of hot oil leaped up and struck the underside of his right wrist. He cried out in pain. The still-vivid memory of the shots fired at him outside the National Assembly days earlier threatened to overwhelm him with a sense of terror he had not experienced then.

Garcia-Vega's left hand gripped the table onto which he'd placed the basket and a half-emptied bottle of beer. His breath caught in his throat. Surely the earth must come to rest.

Five, ten, perhaps twenty seconds passed. Time proved too difficult to calculate when a *terremoto* threatened all that seemed fixed and sure.

Then the roof quieted. The ground firmed beneath his feet.

He filled his lungs with air. His head cleared. What was there to fear other than the lack of an appropriate ointment for the burn that seared his delicate skin? Doubtless the men would make or procure an effective folk remedy—the kind his mother had tendered in his youth.

Undaunted, Garcia-Vega removed the remaining pupusas from the griddle. Voices rose around him. The sounds of the jungle again sang in his ears. Life continued, leaving men a little wiser. The forces of nature—as of history—had again demonstrated the relentless power that would always overwhelm the petty and perverted ambitions of puny human beings. The volcano—the mighty Azcalatl—had revealed its supremacy over the earth and all its inhabitants. *Sín duda*, the gods—Garcia-Vega identified with the *indígena* pantheon rather than with the Father, Son and Holy Ghost imposed on an enslaved people—had made known their dissatisfaction with Alonso Quijano and the capitalist criminals who supported him.

Just as surely, Azcalatl, the volcano god, had sent him a personal message. Change was inevitable. Jesús Garcia-Vega would ascend to the very pinnacle of power.

His lungs satiated, his nerves calmed, his spirits elevated, he would wait patiently for Carlos' return, the journey to the priest and his triumphal appearance in Pueblo Azcalatl to mesmerize the awaiting media. So what if he spent another few days—even weeks—in this hellhole from which he had escaped so many years before? As president of San Cristo, he would make it a paradise, a phoenix alighting from the ashes of the old, corrupt society destroyed utterly and completely in order to save it.

A guard, his barrel chest heaving, ran into the shed. "Are you all right, *jefe*?"

"All right? All right?" Garcia-Vega glanced down at the basket full of savory pupusas. "I can taste victory as surely as you will taste the most delicious pupusas you have ever eaten. Gather the men for dinner."

The guard closed his eyes, sniffed and walked off reassured.

Garcia-Vega lifted a pupusa to his lips. No meal would ever please more than this one eaten with Azcalatl's blessing.

A small, sharp jolt sent Garcia-Vega stumbling backwards.

The pupusa plummeted from his fingers to the earthen floor.

He regained his balance and stood erect, defiant. Renewed confidence suffused his entire being. Let the soulless rulers in the capital tremble. Azcalatl had sent yet another omen by keeping him from being thrown against the hot griddle. The god surely favored Jesús Garcia-Vega.

Yet Garcia-Vega also understood that he commanded the respect and devotion of the people not only through his courageous idealism but his hardheaded realism as well. Quickly, he stepped out of the shed lest the earth shift again. Blind trust and disaster went hand in hand.

The gods, as everyone knew, could be fickle.

Khan picked up a wooden carving painted in brilliant red, blue, yellow and green. Standing somewhat disinterestedly in the center of the native-crafts marketplace, he had witnessed it topple from a table adjacent to the one at which Adella examined woven, multi-hued handbags. His curiosity suddenly piqued, he studied an artisan's interpretation of the mythic azcalatl—half bird and half phallus—shielding *las tres señoritas* beneath its wings. Despite its fall to the cracked concrete beneath his feet, it seemed no less worse for wear.

"Interesting piece, this," he commented.

Adella looked up. Was the monstrosity Khan held an offering to placate her for the sudden loss of Barbara? The two women had shared a highly satisfying sexual experience while Khan helplessly looked on. The next day, Barbara telephoned that a friend's cat unexpectedly had passed on to a tenth life. She would have to spend the next week "sitting *shiva*," a term which seemed to Adella tantalizingly familiar yet still alien. Might it be a Hindu rite? Loyal and supportive, Barbara would have time only to engage in a series of mourning rituals involving hardboiled eggs, incense burnings and long periods of immersion in a hot tub.

With Garcia-Vega still hidden away, Adella had promised to consider Khan's offer of lunch at a vegetarian restaurant run by a couple from Oakland followed by an afternoon stroll through the marketplace.

Khan also had offered drinks, if Adella was so inclined.

Adella was.

"I rather thought," said Khan, "you might allow me the honor of purchasing this for you."

Adella surveyed the bird-phallus' length and girth. Its ample dimensions suggested those of a gold smuggler she had interviewed in Tunis. Or was it the rug seller in Tehran? "Are you insane?"

Khan placed his hand over his heart then reached into his jacket pocket. Responding solely to the comforting presence of his medication, his heartbeat regained its normal pattern.

Adella held her hand to her forehead. "I have a headache. Get a taxi."

Khan smiled wanly and led Adella to a taxi stand where drivers smoked and chatted in front of a dozen vehicles of assorted makes and vintages, all boasting a variety of rusting dents and scrapes.

A fellow in a cream-colored shirt opened the curbside door for Adella.

Khan stepped briskly around to the street side and entered the taxi. "Hotel Lago Azcalatl, *por favor.*"

"Five dollars," said the driver in English. "Unless you want a tour. I can take you up the mountain and around the lake."

"Yes," Khan replied. "The five dollars, that is." The ride from the hotel into town had been four dollars, but he lacked the energy with which to thwart the driver's attempted larceny.

"No tour?" asked the driver with a hint of despondence.

"Another time, perhaps," Khan answered.

Adella, her seatbelt left unbuckled, fidgeted. She wished she'd brought her knitting. She lit a cigarette. She wished she'd brought a flask. She inhaled deeply.

The taxi moved in fits and starts up Avenida del Lago, the pueblo's main thoroughfare. After crawling all of a block, the driver turned left, racing ahead of an oncoming bus. The elaborate cross, assembled from translucent beads, that dangled from the rearview mirror gave off what Khan suspected might be a death rattle.

The bus squealed to a halt.

The driver took notice of his passengers' discomfort—or, to be more exact, Khan's discomfort. He slowed his navigation of the old town's narrow side streets similarly choked with trucks, taxis, autos, scooters holding three and four passengers balanced like circus clowns, and pedestrians. The latter seemed to dismiss any distinction between street and sidewalk—although little existed to suggest a sidewalk.

Khan found his heart pounding and his cheeks growing warm. This was not the way to the hotel. Was it possible? Had they fallen victim to a revolutionary? Were they being kidnapped? Would they be held for ransom? Would they be killed if Whitman Scharq or the chairman of the media conglomerate for whom Adella worked declined to pay?

"You don't mind?" asked the driver.

"Mind?" Khan asked in return, his voice cracking as if he had returned to the awkward depths of adolescence.

"I must stop at the shop of my brother-in-law," the driver stated. "He repairs televisions, radios, computers, electric fans. My wife has a small TV for the bedroom. It will take only a moment. No extra charge."

Adella detected a piece of tobacco affixed to her upper teeth, worked it loose with the tip of her tongue and spat out the window.

Khan's cheeks cooled. "Certainly, my good man. We will be delighted to see more of Pueblo Azcalatl."

"Oh yes," returned the driver. "Tourists do not come to this neighborhood. Sometimes, the Americans who live up in the hills in their big houses, they come. But not often."

Khan eased back in his seat.

As if a switch had been turned off, the sunshine faded. A heavy mist began to accumulate on the windshield. The driver ignored his wipers. The street beyond resembled the work of a pointillist with a vision problem.

"*Momentito, señor*," the driver advised. "Then I will bring you and your wife back to your hotel."

Adella, her right elbow propped on the window still open in spite of the sudden mist, her chin nestled in her palm, rolled her eyes and flicked an ash into the street.

For all the carefully cultivated amusement-park charm of Pueblo Azcalatl's tourist areas, the bulk of the city still endured life in the Third World. Exhaust fumes choked streets marred by potholes and trash. Small children in shorts hawked lottery tickets. Beneath large umbrellas, men hovered over smoking grills, poking at sausages whose ingredients no European health department could account for in good conscience. Women stood placidly on street corners straddling baskets of bananas and beans for sale. Couples of every age peered leisurely into grime-covered shop windows.

What right, Adella pondered, had any government to claim legitimacy when it let its people live in squalor while its leaders enjoyed unimaginable luxury? Pangs of pity squirmed in her heart. Only a vigorous massage, cocktails by the pool—or on the covered section of the patio should rain fall yet again—and dinner with a good wine could even begin to extricate the sorrow from her soul.

The taxi halted.

Khan sighed.

The taxi crept forward.

The mist became a shower.

Adella shifted her attention to a small café with a bright red awning, the front torn and flapping rhythmically in the breeze sweeping off the lake. Her thoughts drifted to the special dishes the chef at the hotel might add to that evening's menu.

The café's door opened.

The taxi slowly moved forward.

Adella turned her head and stared. Who was that man coming out of the doorway—the man with the black pirate's patch? Could that be Carlos? She watched the man reach his hand out and open the curbside door of a battered car partly obscured by traffic. But no, he could not be Carlos—he appeared to be without an iPod. But yes. Yes, she could see now that he might be Carlos after all. She leaned out the window. Yes. It *was* Carlos.

Her gaze fixed, Adella reached for the door handle. And damn if the driver didn't press down on the accelerator like a drag racer just as a woman, a plastic rain hat concealing her face, slipped into the passenger seat.

COSECHA

| Harvest |

24 | VEINTICUATRO | 24

"O HOLY ST. ANTHONY," MUMBLED GIOVANNI, his mind numbed by fatigue and doubt. "Be our protector and defender. Ask God to surround us with the Holy Angels, so that we may emerge from every danger in the fullness of health and wellbeing. Guide our life journey, so we will always walk safely together with you, in God's friendship. Amen."

What that journey would be Giovanni had no idea. The sure and holy path he had chosen for himself—at the urging of his mother and with the blessing of his father—had disappeared. The way forward lay concealed. Slumping in a chair with his head hanging heavily, his eyelids half-closed and a fever alternately burning and chilling him, he felt like a castaway in a novel, a Robinson Crusoe without the companionship of a man Friday to comfort him.

He had prayed the entire day and into the early evening. If God intended deliverance for him, he accepted his rescue by the authorities and a return to his duties with all his heart. If God desired that he assume a new life here in these remote highlands then God's will be done. He wished, he yearned, he prayed only that God never abandon him, that God . . .

Voices sounded outside the door.

Giovanni struggled to raise his head.

The voices grew louder.

His shallow breathing transformed itself into short gasps.

The door opened.

He blinked, attempting to clear his vision in the near darkness. What was that he saw? Could it be? He blinked again. Was that Mother Mary come to redeem him? Would she lead him on the path homeward? Or . . . was it Eve? Had his Eve come at last to claim the Adam with whom she would create a new world?

He watched her come closer, stand by his side and gently raise her hand.

"Father Giovanni," she said softly. "You will find peace now."

A cloud of oily gray smoke darkened the sky as Bobby painfully jogged towards Nahuapl. Thick stands of twenty-five-foot-high ilama trees—their spiky, fibrous-centered fruit recently harvested—circled the town like sentries who had abandoned their posts upon hearing the first shots of battle and then returned afterward to pretend they could prevent a second assault.

Bobby pulled even with Hauptmann-Hall and slowed him to a walk. The rest of the patrol caught up. Weapons locked and loaded, they approached an outlying *colonia*—a small neighborhood where the charred skeletons of several small houses clustered together on wet but blackened earth. Walls leaned at odd angles like drunks attempting to support each other destined to fall.

Above, Bobby detected the whir of rotor blades.

Then from within the *colonia*, an unseen woman released a slow, piercing wail in counterpoint to the helicopter.

A small, brown dog of no particular breeding approached, barked tentatively then fled.

From behind a nearby house, its walls unmarked by flames but its windows shattered, two heavily armed men—significantly taller than indigenous Cristanos—stepped forward. They pointed the muzzles of their weapons at Bobby.

A gust of air rushed past as if a violent storm had come up.

Bobby spun around.

A UH-60 Black Hawk helicopter lowered itself on the edge of a cornfield adjacent to the *colonia*. It bore the familiar red, blue and gold logo of Crimmins-Idyll.

A second helicopter caught Bobby's eye. A Super Cobra gunship armed with Hellfire missiles descended to an altitude of some three hundred feet and hovered.

Bobby lowered his eyes and watched the Black Hawk's rotor blades slow.

A big man in woodland cammies emerged from the Black Hawk followed by eight heavily armed troopers, all in matching body armor and custom-cammie berets.

A previously unseen trooper ran towards the chopper. He carried an XM25, which fired shells that could be programmed to burst in the air—and thus render walls and barriers ineffective—at a distance of over two thousand feet.

The big man gave a thumb's up.

The Black Hawk's engine went silent.

The big man strode towards Bobby.

The troopers in front of the house lowered their weapons.

"Goddam, you're worse than a cyst on the ass," Kennan barked. The ivory skull on its gold chain hung over his neck protector. "And don't think Alexandria doesn't know it."

"You mean," said Bobby, "you've been laying all kinds of shit on Allen Crimmins."

"This is no fuckin' game, Bobby."

Bobby glanced at the burnt houses then at the troopers behind Kennan. Each carried a new SCAR MK-17 assault rifle. And each wore his game face—eyes narrowed, lips tightened. Despite masks of carefully applied green, brown and black paint, he recognized two of them. "Well, Lewis," he replied, "I don't suppose it is."

"Ronnie," Kennan instructed one of the troopers, "take the guys and see what you can find. And check those fuckin' trees, huh?"

"Yes, *sir*!" answered Ronnie. Bobby knew the man to have been to be a former Air Commando.

Kennan reached out for a broad-shouldered, heavyset trooper who might once have been a defensive end on a college football team. "Simmons, you stay with me."

Hauptmann-Hall stepped forward, the color drawn from his face. "*Señor*, what has happened?"

"If I didn't know better," said Kennan, "I'd figure *you* attacked those houses over there. The way you staged that assault the other day? You're a fuckin' one-man army, *Capitán*."

Hauptmann-Hall swallowed hard.

"Somehow," Bobby retorted, "I'm thinking that you *do* know better, Lewis." He turned to Hauptmann-Hall. "Take the patrol and look around."

Kennan grabbed Hauptmann-Hall's shoulder. "Stay the fuck right here."

Hauptmann-Hall swept Kennan's hand away.

Bobby stepped in front of Kennan. "It *is* his country, Lewis."

Hauptmann-Hall and the rest of the patrol slipped off.

Kennan shrugged. "Might as well learn what war looks like." He turned to the trooper who had run out to greet him. "Carlos, have a couple of the guys stay with those clowns."

Carlos saluted.

"Discipline," said Kennan. "Just because we're private . . ."

"Lewis," Bobby cut him off. "Were you here when this . . . when whatever happened, happened?"

"Sorry to break this to you, Bobby, but you don't outrank me here. And you're not in command."

Bobby peered over Kennan's left shoulder as two Crimmins-Idyll troopers carried a stretcher with a filled body bag towards the Black Hawk.

Kennan turned to watch their progress then faced Bobby. "Del Valle. Wife and two kids in Phoenix. Have to pay a call when we get back."

"So you *were* here?" Bobby asked.

Kennan stroked the ivory skull. "Wish I *had* been."

Bobby grimaced.

"But here's the story," said Kennan, "since the lovely Ms. Skavronsky'll want your report as well as mine." He pointed to the cornfield. "We put a small team down there." He turned. "Our guys get within fifty meters of the house over there, and they take fire. Rick Walters . . ."

Bobby rubbed the back of his neck. "Walters? We were in Bosnia."

"Walters takes a round through the fuckin' throat. Hammonds and Del Valle bring him to the chopper to get him to Pueblo Azcalatl. Hospital in Maquepaque isn't worth shit, but they've got a decent place over by the lake to take care of all those old-time California hippies."

"He all right?"

"He'll live, yeah. Won't be singing *The Star Spangled Banner* before any ballgames though."

"And you let your guys call in the Cobra?"

Kennan rocked back as if he'd discovered Bobby was contagious. "Jesus fuckin' Christ. That's why we brought it in country."

"You don't think it was a little overkill? We're here to *defend* these people."

Kennan pointed to the thick black smoke still ascending over the smoldering houses. "That's not exactly a mushroom cloud, is it? Tell you what it *is*, though. Fuckin' restraint. *Our* guys were the ones takin' fire. We could have vaporized the whole fuckin' neighborhood."

"Colonel Gatling!" rang Hauptmann-Hall's voice from the muddied front yard of a surviving house. He charged forward like a *fútbol* player outrunning defenders to the ball to go one-on-one with the opposing goalie. "Colonel Gatling!" he shouted.

Bobby drank from his water bottle.

Hauptmann-Hall slowed, glanced at Kennan and stopped ten feet away. "Colonel Gatling!" he called again, his voice as loud as if he still stood at a great distance.

Bobby wondered if he had a cigar left and whether it would be sacrilegious to smoke it. A shot of Pikesville—or two or three—struck him as more appropriate. He put the water bottle away.

Hauptmann-Hall drew nearer, his eyes red-rimmed, his breathing rapid and shallow. He pointed to the houses from which he had come. "You cannot believe, Colonel. You cannot believe."

Kennan looked at Hauptmann-Hall, shook his head and poked his right index finger into Bobby's chest. "Believe *this*. Del Valle was just fine after the Cobra turned the houses where the fuckin' bad guys had holed up into kindling."

Hauptmann-Hall tugged at Bobby's jacket.

Kennan brushed Hauptmann-Hall's hand away. "Nothing you haven't seen before," he said to Bobby.

Hauptmann-Hall grabbed Bobby's arm and pulled him forward.

Simmons pressed the butt of his weapon against Hauptmann-Hall's chest.

Bobby stared into Simmons' eyes and pushed the weapon away.

Hauptmann-Hall again tugged at Bobby. The *capitán*'s unexpected strength caused Bobby to lurch forward. He regained his balance and followed Hauptmann-Hall into the muddy street that split the *colonia*.

Kennan and Simmons followed.

Hauptmann-Hall suddenly sprinted towards a gap between two houses.

Bobby followed at a jog. A shock coursed through his knee each time his right foot landed on the wet ground.

In a small open space, two of Kennan's troopers stood over the badly burned bodies of three small men.

Just beyond, Bobby spotted a dozen blood-drenched bodies, arms and legs twisted at what seemed anatomically impossible angles. They gave the impression of dolls tossed into a pile by a child indulging in a temper tantrum.

Several meters away, a small girl in a torn pink dress sat rocking back and forth in a pool of water. The tiny fingers of her left hand filled her mouth.

A trooper saw Hauptmann-Hall approach and slide-stepped to intercept him.

Kennan, the toes of his boots almost brushing Bobby's heels, waved him off.

"Why?" cried Hauptmann-Hall. He squatted over the body of an old man with a large hole in the sole of his left sandal. He made the sign of the cross over the man's forehead then shifted his attention to a woman with mud-splattered tufts of long gray hair.

A small yellow dog licked at the half of the woman's jaw that remained intact.

"Del Valle," Kennan whispered.

Bobby let his gaze linger over each body then looked at Kennan.

"My guys rounded up everyone over five they could find."

"And Del Valle?" asked Bobby.

"Could've been Haditha or Fallujah all over again. What the fuck, pick any village in Vietnam back in the day. Del Valle, Gutierrez and Bilheimer are searching the indigs for weapons. Old woman pulls out an AK from under a blanket or whatever she's wearing. Gutierrez sees her, but she fires first. One round. And it jams. No shit! You ever heard of a fuckin' AK jamming? I can see an M4 failing after firing a couple hundred rounds, sure. But *nobody's* ever heard of a fuckin' AK jamming this way. Russians designed 'em for fuckin' illiterate peasants like these who can't keep a weapon any cleaner than their assholes. Single fuckin' round goes through Del Valle's right eye. He's dead before he hits the ground. But we got Jesus on our side. Fuckin' AK doesn't jam, I lose Gutierrez and Bilheimer, too."

"And these people?"

"You don't know who else has a weapon or maybe even some kind of explosive belt."

Bobby stood mute.

"You're a fuckin' bleeding heart, you know that? These people don't give a fuck about American lives."

A sharp cry suggesting a desperate appeal to heaven cut them off. "Colonel Gatling!" Hauptmann-Hall sobbed.

Bobby stepped around the body of a young woman folded on her side like a fetus, her mouth agape as if she'd modeled for Edvard Munch's painting of The Scream.

"*¡Dios mío!*" whimpered Hauptmann-Hall.

Bobby crouched beside him.

Kennan and Simmons stood several paces behind.

Hauptmann-Hall brushed the fingertips of his right hand on his jacket then gently attempted to wipe away a smear of dried blood along the right cheek of what now appeared to be a girl no older than her mid-teens. Unruly strands of blood-clotted black hair covered the girl's forehead. Her large, death-blank black eyes suggested a gentleness of soul—a fairy-tale princess fallen victim to an evil spell placed with all the malevolence a wicked witch could summon.

Bobby flashed on the image of Anastasia Nikolaevna, the youngest daughter of Tsar Nicholas II.

Hauptmann-Hall's shoulders heaved then stilled. "You know this girl," he whispered.

Bobby shook his head.

Hauptmann-Hall's eyes widened with disbelief. "But surely . . ." He reached into his jacket, withdrew his iPhone and called up the photo of himself and the girl taken in Maquepaque.

"The prisoner's daughter," Bobby whispered.

Hauptmann-Hall looked up. His eyes locked on the ivory skull dangling from Kennan's neck. He shot to his feet. An angry howl flew from his throat. He hurtled forward. The stock of his weapon flew in an awkward loop towards Kennan's chin.

Kennan stepped to his left, grasped Hauptmann-Hall's right arm with his right hand and yanked him down.

Hauptmann-Hall collapsed onto his backside.

A single round burst out of the *capitán*'s M4. Another round followed.

Bobby reflexively assumed a crouch and raised his weapon.

Then the world—and time—exploded.

Hauptmann-Hall found himself puzzled. Was the deafening roar in his ears an echo of the round shot from his weapon or the cry that rushed from his exhausted lungs with all the fury of the missiles that had struck the *colonia*? Then came the answer like a flash of lightning illuminating secrets kept concealed by the dark of night. He had heard the discharge of the weapon of *another* man—the man who had stood at Major Kennan's side. Yet while the burst from the other man's weapon had stopped up his ears, it had opened his eyes. Although he could see nothing of *this* world, he now possessed a vision of the next.

Hauptmann-Hall saw himself ascending to heaven to sit with Jesús at the right hand of God. And then he was falling to earth. Only a priest could raise him up. Did a priest live in the *colonia*?

Was the priest they sought—Father Giovanni—nearby? Would death take him before he could receive extreme unction?

Then with a suddenness that filled him with awe, his uncertainty dissipated. Bridging the gap between realities, the *capitán* understood with all the purity of his faith that his soul indeed had been cleansed. Through the gift of his wounds, he was emerging from life into death and, fully chastened, into everlasting life.

His soul staggering towards the gates of heaven, he took comfort in belief. He had believed as a child. He believed now. He believed that the Azcalatls would win an upcoming friendly with Mexico. He believed, moreover, that some day these heroes would win the World Cup to be acclaimed by every patriotic Cristano and have the most beautiful women in the nation bare their *tetas* for them. Yes, *tetas*! What sin could be associated with such an attraction? Did not God torment Adam with Eve's treasures? Was that not part of his plan for humanity? Did not the Holy Mother have *tetas*? But of course, she did. He had once seen a copy of a painting—*La virgen de la leche*. The artist had bared one of the Holy Mother's breasts. Which one he could not remember. Most surely she had revealed them to Joseph. Would she now reveal them to him? And would the Holy Mother with her holy *tetas* weep for him? Would his wife weep for him? Was that she who leaned over him? Or was it the azcalatl—not a blasphemous heathen fable at all but so very real—assuming the Holy Mother's form? Or was it Jesús? Had Jesús come for him at last? Did Jesús have short, graying hair and a mouth that silently repeated, "*Está bien*"? Surely Jesús had come because all that Enrique Hauptmann-Hall had endured had served God's purpose. Just as surely, he would see the heavenly throne and hear the angels singing God's praises because God had planned this for him. God had a plan for everyone.

Hauptmann-Hall's body trembled as if mighty Azcalatl again shook the earth. Then as he sensed his last breath escaping from the corrupt flesh that imprisoned his soul, one final question seized him like the icy hot grip of the hand of *el Diablo*.

What if God had no plan for him all?

25 | VEINTICINCO | 25

KNUCKLES RAPPED URGENTLY ON THE DOOR, but Jesús Garcia-Vega was in no mood to be roused from his bed. Not at this hour of the morning.

"I am sleeping!" he shouted before pulling his thin pillow over his head.

"An important message, *señor*," rang out the now-familiar voice of one of his hosts.

"What is it?" asked Garcia-Vega's bedmate, expressing both fatigue and alarm.

Garcia-Vega lifted the pillow and examined the contour of the woman his hosts had finally found to keep him company through another lonely night in the jungle—a young woman of tolerable appearance with hair that flowed down her back and more-than-acceptable *tetas*. He rested his hand on her hip then let it fall to caress her backside. "Go back to sleep, *amor mío*."

A fist pounded on the door with even more force.

"*¡Señor!*"

Garcia-Vega cleared his throat. "*Momentito*." He swung his legs over the side of the small bed and pulled on his shorts. Then he put on a shirt and trousers. A man in his position had to keep up appearances.

Barefoot, he went to the door and opened it.

"*Señor*, we must leave immediately."

Garcia-Vega took two deep breaths. "Leave? You are taking me to see the priest?" He turned to go back inside and find his socks and shoes.

"No, *señor*."

Garcia-Vega halted. "Then what? What can be so important at this hour?"

The man shifted his weight from one foot to another. "We have, *señor*, a change in plans."

Whitman Scharq inhaled deeply and smiled. Nothing proved more comforting, more reassuring than the aroma of a proprietary-blend-demi-super-low-fat-yes-whipped-cream-Mocha-Almond-Cinnamon-Mediterraneo. The training team brought in from San Francisco had prepared the treat and rushed two to the penthouse along with two signature apple-hazelnut-chocolate muffins.

Alonso Quijano sat on the largest of the living room sofas, an identical espresso perched on the glass-topped coffee table in front of him. The recyclable cup displayed the universally recognizable Mobys logo—the silhouette of spouting sperm whale leaping with unrestrained joy out of a steaming mug of coffee.

Scharq sipped then opened his eyes. "Now *that's* why people engaged with the twenty-first century anywhere in the world pledge their allegiance to the Mobys brand."

Quijano stared at his own cup, its contents untouched. His muffin sat beside it unwrapped.

"So?" Scharq asked.

Quijano grasped the cup, raised it to his lips and sipped. "It is very good, *Señor* Scharq. But I must tell you . . ."

Scharq sighed. "I've gotta tell *you*, Al, that you don't look primed for the Mobys experience. And you haven't touched your muffin. It's *super* food, you know." He pointed towards one of the penthouse suites expansive windows. The calories in that baby could feed one of your villages out there for a day."

"Oh, I am . . . primed. It is just . . . The reason I asked to see you, *Señor* Scharq . . ."

"Whit," Scharq urged. "We've been through this before, Al." He took a bite of muffin then threw his head back and drained his espresso in one long gulp.

Quijano drew a breath and held it like a man approaching a fork in a road, his choice made, but the way forward uncertain and potentially dangerous. "What I wish to tell you, *Señor* . . .

Whitman . . . is that Crimmins-Idyll must withdraw Major Kennan and his men immediately."

Scharq licked his lips.

Quijano bit his. "Perhaps I have not made myself clear."

Scharq crushed the empty cup in his hand then cleared his throat. "Al, let's get this straight. Kennan and his people are here because you have a budding revolution on your hands. People have been killed."

"Yes! That is exactly my point. People have been killed."

"So there you go, Al. Kennan and his crew are just doing the job we're paying them to do. Doing it for *you*. And let's not leave anything on the table. They don't come cheap."

Quijano's lips pressed together then parted. "Major Kennan and his people have massacred innocent citizens of San Cristo in the town of Nahuapl."

"The way I hear, Kennan's boys defended themselves against terrorists."

"The matter is not that simple."

Scharq tossed his crumpled cup in the direction of the kitchen. "I rest my case." He pointed to Quijano's espresso. "You gonna finish that, Al?"

Quijano pushed his cup across the coffee table.

Scharq stretched his arms over his head. He'd spent too much time on the corporate jet these past few weeks. Put out too many fires. And now this. What did a writer of children's books know about the dynamics of the global economy? How could he hope to understand the measures required to smite revolutionaries who wanted to force their workers paradise on everyone and make it hell for the people who paid the bills?

Quijano clasped his hands together. "If Major Kennan and his people do not leave San Cristo within forty-eight hours . . . I will be forced to order the Ministry of Justice to have them arrested."

Scharq scowled. "Arrested? As in put them on trial?" Almost instantaneously, his eyes lit up. "Oh, shit, that's good, Al!" He chuckled. "You really had me going."

Quijano's expression remained unchanged. His eyes may not have revealed the heart of a warrior, but neither did they display their usual passivity.

Scharq shot to his feet. "Kennan and his people are American citizens. They're here on behalf of Mobys, which means they're here on behalf of the United States of America. Whatever Washington says about encouraging democracy and human rights, no court in San Cristo has or ever will have jurisdiction over those guys."

"They have committed a terrible crime, *Señor* Scharq."

"Killing a bunch of Indians? And please, don't bore me with details." He tore off a piece of his muffin and held it up. "These guys are doing the dirty work so the Mobys Foundation can give your country . . . *your* country . . . a huge chunk of valuable land to enlarge *your* precious national park and strengthen *your* economy while we protect *your* environment. And what are you doing for *us*?"

"If these men stay, Jesús Garcia-Vega will win the election in April."

Scharq gobbled the piece of muffin then sipped from Quijano's now-lukewarm espresso. "And if that left-wing-commie-radical-son-of-a-bitch brings the priest out of the jungle alive, you're toast. Even before your fill-in term is up."

Quijano's shoulders slumped then recovered. "But if he does *not*?"

"*You* can't find the priest."

"Kennan and your Colonel Gatling . . . *they* can not, either."

Scharq shrugged. "Toast."

Quijano thrust his jaw forward.

Scharq sat, leaned back and clasped his hands behind his head. "You know what I'm thinking, Al? I'm thinking you're not the man I thought you were."

Quijano stood. True, he was not one to raise his voice or threaten. But Alonso Quijano, acclaimed the greatest Cristano literary figure of his generation, bore in his breast no less pride in his person and in his country than any other man. "All your money, *Señor* Scharq. It has gained you nothing."

Scharq glanced at his watch. "I wouldn't be too sure about that, Al. We open in a week."

"Of this I *am* sure," Quijano exclaimed, his voice full, its timbre rich and sonorous. "Justice will prevail. I will complete my term and win another."

Scharq's lips vibrated noisily as he blew out a Bronx cheer. "Toast."

Bobby drained the last of his beer and contemplated going back down the hall for a piece of chocolate cake. Major Torvaldson had provided the cake along with lunch for his men and several local officials following a few words praising the courage of the late Enrique Hauptmann-Hall, expressions of concern for his family, and a series of toasts culminating in fealty to the Azcalatls in their quest for *futból* glory. The evening before, Lewis Kennan had flown the body back to the army base at Pueblo Azcalatl from where General Gomez would send it to the capital for a period of official mourning and political free-for-all.

Now, with Gomez having withdrawn the patrol from the field, all Bobby could do was finish his report to María in an office near Torvaldson's and wait for her instructions. Whether Mobys would offer the general even more cash to renew the search for Father Giovanni, he didn't know. Certainly he and Hauptmann-Hall had come close. But close, as the saying went, meant no cigar. The thing was, the priest could be right under their noses, and they'd never know. Torvaldson had no new intelligence. They'd all have to start from scratch.

Bobby felt badly about the *capitán*, of course. Yet the day ultimately had proved quite pleasant. He'd slept in a bed. He'd also found time to dig into his pack for Pushkin's epic poem *Poltava,* commissioned by Tsar Nicholas I as a propaganda vehicle to build Russian national identity. Juan Suelo had undergone a successful operation in Houston paid for by Mobys. Even better, Bobby, Jr. had emailed. Kimberly wasn't out of the woods entirely, but she and the baby had stabilized. Best of all, they'd asked him to call that evening.

Bobby unfolded from his chair and rubbed his right knee. Given all the ground he'd covered over the preceding days and the way experiencing death made you want to indulge in life, he'd earned a piece of chocolate cake—and another beer, as well.

His cell phone startled him.

"How's it going?" María chirped. In spite of the disaster at Nahuapl, she sounded upbeat, seemingly enveloped in a woman's afterglow as if they'd left each other just an hour before.

"Okay. You?"

"I'm still thinking about the other night."

Bobby couldn't come up with anything to say. Women had this compulsion to go over everything that occurred in their lives as if they were required to continually file after-action reports, but chatting on the phone was not a component of his skill set.

"That doesn't embarrass you, does it?" María asked.

He felt like a high school freshman flustered by the voice of a girl he'd called after working up his courage for months. "No, no," he replied. "I was thinking about *you*." He'd score points with that one.

"So here's the thing," María said, her voice segueing from romantic to pragmatic. "President Quijano's office received a tip . . ."

"A tip?

"Late last night. About Father Giovanni."

"They didn't call Torvaldson. *You* didn't call *me*."

"I just got word. And no one else knows."

"Where?"

"Outside Pueblo Azcalatl."

"Pueblo . . . we were heading in the wrong direction. I can go with Torvaldson and his people. I'll coordinate with Lewis Kennan."

"It's over, Bobby. Quijano sent a *Seguridad* team from the capital. They've already gone in."

"Then we're fucked."

"You're not listening to me. They brought Father Giovanni back to the capital early this morning."

Bobby tossed his book into his backpack. "One of Torvaldson's people can drive me to Ciudad San Cristo. Better, Kennan's Black Hawk can fly me down."

María laughed. Her voice sounded light again, even girlish. "Slow down. Father Giovanni's not there anymore."

"Where'd they take him? I should be in on the debriefing."

"Sorry about that. The body's on a plane to Rome."

26 | VEINTISEIS | 26

GARCIA-VEGA PONDERED CARLOS' ABSENCE as he took a seat in the largest of the meeting rooms at the Hotel Lago Azcalatl. Microphones covered the linen-draped table before him.

Terrible questions raced through his mind. With the priest dead—his constitution undoubtedly unable to abide the food or water or tiny organisms that passed from one person to the next in the jungle—had the kidnappers panicked? Had they murdered Carlos and hidden his body? Or were they holding Carlos as a bargaining chip in regard to yet-unknown demands they would make of ANTI and personally of him? And if Carlos *had* been kidnapped, what could they seek from Jesús Garcia-Vega that he would not willingly give them with all his heart? Furthermore, how could they betray the man who championed their cause, submitting himself to such grave personal risk that he had endured a vicious attempt on his life?

"Jesús!" asked Adella. "Can you do this?"

Garcia-Vega tilted his head back and squeezed two drops of moistener in each eye.

"You *must* do this," she continued. "You *will* do this." Her voice suggested a mother steeling her child to overcome his natural trepidations and set off for his first day of school."

Garcia-Vega put the small bottle in his pocket and nodded.

Adella stepped away and took her place just to his left. The media conference had been called at her urging—she naturally would serve as moderator—so that Garcia-Vega could reply to all of the wild accusations and speculations spinning out of the capital, as well as Pueblo Azcalatl and Maquepaque. Quite appropriately, she had arrived early to provide her camera crew, who had driven up the previous evening, with the best possible sight lines.

Glancing around the room, she saw an even larger-than-usual horde of Cristano media along with television crews from Sao Paulo to London to Tokyo, along with her own production team.

Garcia-Vega held up his hands. "Ladies and gentlemen, you all know the rules of this interview." He looked over at Adella, resplendent in a knee-length purple jacket. "*Señorita* Rozen will conduct the questioning."

A disaffected murmur ascended.

"When we are finished," Garcia-Vega continued, "I will take questions from the rest of you."

Adella wasted no time and jumped in. "*Señor* Garcia-Vega, as regards the latest developments with Father Giovanni Sabella . . ."

"I weep for him," Garcia-Vega answered. "A tragedy of cosmic proportions."

"But you have not seen the body," said Adella.

A louder murmur rose from the media.

"I was informed only of Father Giovanni's death and nothing more."

Adella tilted her chin upward to make certain that her face was fully lit and free from unattractive shadows beneath her eyebrows and nose. "*Señor* Garcia-Vega, you promised to bring Father Giovanni out of the jungle. Alive. What must the people of San Cristo think of you now?"

Garcia-Vega heard the question but could not comprehend. What was Adella insinuating? Her question struck him as strategically unsound. It potentially cast him in a bad light. More than that, it wounded him deeply. How could anyone believe he had done anything wrong in this matter? "Traitors," he stammered. "Traitors."

"*¡Señor!*" called out the reporter from *Dar Voces*.

"*¡Silencio!*" Adella shot back.

The reporter lowered his eyes.

"Your expectations," Adella continued. "Did you set them too high? Did the kidnappers *really* trust you?"

"Did they . . . of course! No one supports . . ."

"But now, how can the people believe you? Without a body, how can they even believe that Father Giovanni has died? And how can they believe that Jesús Garcia-Vega commands the respect of the men and women *really* leading the revolution . . . the men and women in these highlands beneath the very shadow of Azcalatl shedding blood and sacrificing their own?"

"They can . . . I am . . ."

Adella stepped closer to fill the frame of every video and still camera. She held aloft a small, white pad on which she had prepared a number of questions. "Do you know? Do . . . you . . . know?"

Garcia-Vega leaned away. In spite of Adella's scent, lights glinting on her hair, spittle glistening on her purple lips—in spite of his overwhelming desire to have her here and now in a fit of matchlessly passionate sex—she physically repelled him. "Know what?"

A merciless glint appeared in her eyes. She leaned forward even further. Her hair, artfully sweeping across her forehead as the result of several hours in the hotel salon, brushed Garcia-Vega's cheek. "Who killed the priest?"

Garcia-Vega blinked. "Killed?" he responded. "Do you suggest . . . ?" What had come over Adella? What was she trying to do to him? They were allies. Kindred spirits. Lovers.

"I ask you again, *Señor* Garcia-Vega. Who killed Father Giovanni Sabella?"

Garcia-Vega sat motionless as if he'd been slapped. Not one of his hosts had mentioned—or even hinted at—such an awkward outcome. Alive, Father Giovanni meant everything to the cause. Death rendered him useless.

Adella eased back. Now she could unload her bombshell. A well-placed source in Rome had for a price—there was always a price—provided her with critically important information. Father Giovanni's body had been taken directly from the plane that had landed at Fiumicino Airport the previous day—even as his parents were being notified—to a police laboratory. And she knew the results of the autopsy.

"*Señorita* Rozen," Garcia-Vega sputtered. "Father Giovanni's death brings shame to *Seguridad Nacional* and all the organs of a corrupt and inept government."

"You are avoiding the question, *Señor* Garcia-Vega," countered Adella. She turned squarely towards the cameras and paused, waiting for her crew to frame her in a dramatic close-up—but not so close as to reveal the lines and wrinkles that plagued her in spite of the make-up she had so artfully applied. "I have it on good authority that Father Giovanni was killed by shots fired from a handgun. A *small* handgun."

27 | VEINTISIETE | 27

KHAN SLOWLY ROTATED HIS CIGAR above the wooden match to develop an even ash along the outer edge of the wrapper. To his right, seated with legs sprawled in the penthouse living room, Whitman Scharq and Gusher Wells did likewise.

María set down a tray with five glasses and a bottle of Australian Shiraz.

"Quite the little hostess," Wells remarked.

Scharq held his cigar aloft. "Sure you won't join us, Colonel?"

"No thank you, sir," Bobby replied from his seat at the far end of one of the sofas. Not that he would have minded lighting up a Salazar Torpedo, perhaps his favorite cigar. But he was on duty—whatever that meant at the moment. Employees got too close with their employers at their own risk, although he'd gotten a whole lot closer with María than a cigar or a glass of wine.

María sat.

Wells blew a stream of smoke towards the ceiling. His piercing eyes followed its hypnotic ascent then flashed to Scharq. "I gotta say, Whit, it's mighty considerate of you to fly me back from Rio on one of your jets. And the suite is beautiful. Everything you folks at Mobys do is first class."

"Business is business," said Scharq.

"And that's just what we're gonna do," Wells continued. He looked at María. "Your young lady here, she . . ." He coughed into his fist. "She . . ."

Scharq settled back in his seat. "She took care of those pictures of you and a few young friends . . . pictures I know you'd rather Mrs. Wells or anybody else not see."

Wells glanced at Khan then Bobby. "There's no need to get into details . . ."

Scharq waved his hand. "Just a bunch of guys on the beach working on their tans. Let's leave it at that. Because I believe *you* have something for *me*."

"I'm grateful, Whit. To you and to Mobys. I want y'all to know that. Hell, *everyone's* grateful. That's why I'm seein' to it that the United States of America takes care of *you* for a change."

Scharq set his cigar gently into a crystal ashtray. "I'm all ears."

"What the House is gonna do," said Wells, "is add a rider to a bill revising standards for school lunches for inner-city kids fed on Uncle Sam's dime."

"How sweet," María remarked.

"Waste of money. Handouts are un-American."

"And?" Scharq asked.

"In a word, Uncle Sam's gonna pay y'all some mighty impressive subsidies to *not* grow any more coffee beans than you can turn into actual, drinkable coffee. That covers what *y'all* don't grow and what y'all's friends around the world don't grow."

An ash fell from Khan's cigar. He slapped at his thigh.

"You okay there, Major Doctor?" Wells asked.

A small hole, its edges brown and ragged, appeared in Khan's slacks. "I am unharmed, sir."

"The beauty part is," said Wells, "all y'all have to do is tell the government how much coffee you're *not* growing, and the more y'all report, the more money y'all get."

"That's damn generous of you, Gusher. You and your colleagues in Congress and our friends in the right-thinking media who appreciate Mobys' contribution to America's gross domestic product, not to mention the wellbeing of their stock portfolios."

Khan rocked forward. "A question, if you don't mind, Congressman." He turned towards Scharq. "And I know, Whitman, that you are thinking the very same thing." He faced Wells again. "If coffee production is limited to beans for human consumption, what about caffuel?"

"What about it?"

"Sir, we are on the brink of an energy revolution."

Wells flicked an ash. It fell on the coffee table.

"Maid'll get it," said Scharq.

"See, Major Doctor," answered Wells, "it's like this." He held his cigar aloft with his right index finger raised as if he were about to fire a six-shooter into the air. "From what I heard from Whit the other day, caffuel's not just a little further off than expected. It's deader'n an armadillo lyin' under the wheel of a semi."

"A scurrilous accusation, sir," said Khan. "You defame Mr. Scharq."

Wells turned to Scharq. "Looks like the Major Doctor figures he'll be left suckin' hind tit."

Scharq ran a sip of Shiraz over his tongue. "I.A., there's big money involved here. And the best part is, it's big money for doing nothing. And as far as you futzing with the data, which would absolutely ruin your reputation in the scientific community, well . . . as a businessman, I get it. We won't change the world, that's true. But you've turned lead into gold.

Khan stood and pointed a finger at Wells. "And *you*, sir! You will again buy your seat in the United States House of Representatives."

Wells' blue eyes iced over like a Panhandle highway on a January midnight. "That's what I do, Major Doctor. Gettin' reelected's my job."

Khan turned to Scharq. "And *you*, Whitman . . . You will allow this? I concede that our research on caffuel may exhibit a few temporary flaws . . ."

"Give it a rest, I.A.," said Scharq. "You're liable to upset Colonel Gatling."

Khan glanced at Bobby. "And what would you have Colonel Gatling do? Kill me?"

Bobby looked fleetingly at María. Did Whitman Scharq—did *she*—think of him as nothing more than a gunman, the kind you ran into in third-world countries where the strong made their own laws and enforced them with private armies?

Khan's breathing grew labored. He raised a hand to his chest. He had become gravely agitated, he knew. But only a common man—a man of limited imagination and vision—would fail to respond to such beastly news without a healthy measure of agitation. Major

I.A. Khan, Ph.D. would not take such injustice, such humiliation, sitting on his bum. Regardless of the consequences, he would defend himself.

"Be warned, Whitman," Khan said. "I have it in my power to bring down you and the entire Mobys organization."

"You're way off base here," said Scharq.

"I have long been privy to secrets but kept my peace in consideration of your generosity. Now, I fear . . ."

María placed her purse in her lap. "I.A., really. Whatever this is about, we can come to an accommodation."

Bobby glanced at María then at Khan. Whatever dirty laundry Khan threatened to air, it was no business of his.

"I am beyond accommodation," Khan retorted. "I insist that my research on caffuel move forward as planned. Unless, of course . . ." He gasped, doubled over and pressed his fingertips to the coffee table to steady himself. Catching his breath, he rose, stood erect and locked his eyes on Scharq's. "Unless, I am awarded expanded research opportunities in other areas, a doubling of my annual salary and compensation for past services rendered. Something in the range of seven figures would suffice."

Scharq shook his head.

"I have files, Whitman," Khan spluttered. "Documents from your own laptop detailing the flow of money from Mobys Foundation to various of your friends in Washington . . ."

Wells clenched his teeth. They severed the tip of his cigar.

". . . and into your *own* pocket."

"Bullshit!" countered Scharq. He took a breath to calm himself. "And more to the point, I.A., you don't have the balls."

Khan thrust his chest out in a display of doggedness befitting a man who prized honor above all. "I must caution you that seizing my laptop will do you no good. I have secured the data beyond your grasp. No one can access it but me. Absolutely no one."

Scharq flashed a small grin. "Let me get this straight. No one but you can access these files under any circumstances?"

"Not anyone. Under *any* circumstances, sir!"

Scharq shrugged. "You might have given that one a little more thought."

María opened her purse.

Khan searched Scharq's face for a hint of acquiescence but found none. So be it, he resolved. Let the chips, as the saying went, fall where they may. He had reached critical mass, arrived at the point of no return. "Rest assured then, Whitman . . ." He froze in place unable to form the words that would force Scharq into a change of heart.

"Glass of water?" asked María.

Hands trembling, Khan reached into his pocket and withdrew his medication. He urged the cap off the bottle and turned it over. Nothing descended into his waiting palm. He held the bottle up only to discover it empty. His mouth fell open. A sense of disbelief swept over him no less intense than if he'd learned that Pakistan had turned Hindu. How could he, a distinguished man of science, have forgotten to renew his prescription? Weakened but undaunted, he forced the words from his mouth through sheer willpower. "Mobys . . . is doomed!"

María reached into her purse, withdrew her Ruger SP101 and placed it on the coffee table.

Khan's eyes widened. An unseen hand clenched at his throat. "You . . . wouldn't dare . . ."

Like a child artfully swiping a forbidden candy with her mother's back turned, María snatched the small pistol away just before Khan toppled forward.

Wine glasses tumbled. Ashtrays scattered. The table's thick glass cracked then cleaved in two beneath his weight.

Bobby reached out and pressed his fingertips to Khan's neck.

Wells looked down at the toes of his boots. "Sumbitch!" he muttered. "That wine better not stain."

Scharq stood. "María, please get Congressman Wells some napkins."

Bobby withdrew his hand and shook his head.

"And make the appropriate arrangements."

"There's no family," María said. "At least not in the States. And we have no contact information for Pakistan. If we did, I'm not sure anyone would step up given that I.A. seemed to have made a few enemies in his day."

"Then no complications," Scharq declared.

Bobby looked at María.

María held up her lipstick. "No matter how a woman organizes her purse, it's always so hard to find anything. You didn't really think . . . ?"

Scharq perused Khan's prostrate body. "Sorry about this, Colonel. I assume, however, that a man of your background finds this all in a day's work. I say this because I have to fly back to San Francisco this evening. While I'm gone, I want you to accompany María on an urgent piece of business. And I expect it to be completed before I return."

28 | VEINTIOCHO | 28

GARCIA-VEGA EXTENDED HIS ARMS towards the fifteen-foot-high, sugar-white marble Christ frozen in agony on a cross covered with coffee beans behind the altar of the National Cathedral. "He truly was a man of the people," he said. "In his own way, of course." His voice filled the nave and found its way through the transept into the sanctuary. If it reflected the buoyant confidence of a magnanimous victor, what could be more logical? *Sín duda*, María Skavronsky's request for a meeting—despite Carlos' mysterious disappearance—changed everything. Mobys wished to concede. "And the people," he continued, "has emerged victorious."

Even as the words flew from his lips a crease furrowed across Garcia-Vega's forehead. Why had this woman brought the *Yanqui* giant with her? Did she believe that Jesús Garcia-Vega could be intimidated even while she surrendered? The man who had ventured into the dangerous highlands of his own free will and emerged unscathed, even if treachery had left him empty-handed? Could this most hardened of capitalist running dogs be that naïve?

"So let's get down to business," said María.

Bobby, seated at her side, made no effort to engage in the conversation. His presence was sufficient. And although in a church, he considered that the anniversary of his father's death was approaching. He would need to attend a synagogue service with a *minyan*—ten adult Jews—to say *Kaddish* in his memory.

Garcia-Vega lowered his arms. "Always business," he replied. "Very well then. The matter is simple. You have withdrawn your support for Alonso Quijano and left the presidency to me. In return you seek favors."

"Not exactly," said María.

"Let us be honest, *señora*. You are in no position to do anything else. Clearly, the massacre at Nahuapl and the murder of the priest have demonstrated to the people what they already knew. Quijano is a capitalist tool not fit to lead the sacred nation of San Cristo."

"An unfortunate incident, Nahuapl," María responded. She dabbed at the corner of her right eye with her index finger. "And Father Giovanni. I can tell you as a mother, my heart breaks. The truth is, all this *does* leave *Señor* Quijano's candidacy untenable."

Garcia-Vega cast an expectant eye at Bobby. "And you will be leaving San Cristo along with your Major Kennan and his criminal gang, Colonel Gatling?"

Bobby rested his hands on the pew in front of him. "The matter of Major Kennan and his group remains undecided, sir. It's out of my hands. But yes, sir, I anticipate leaving San Cristo following the grand opening of the new Mobys store at the end of the week."

The corners of Garcia-Vega's mouth turned up with unrestrained joy. "Well, let me inform you, Colonel, that my first official act shall be to forbid private American security forces from ever again soiling the dignity of our beloved homeland."

María clasped her hands together as if in prayerful supplication. "*Señor* Garcia-Vega, let's not be coy. We'd like to make a deal."

Garcia-Vega warded off a grin and rose on the balls of his feet. The capitalists had surrendered. Now they asked for terms. "As you wish, *señora*. But let us not, as you say, be coy. You must tell me how Mobys believes it will . . . believes it *can* . . . enter into a new relationship with the People's Republic of San Cristo."

María's freshly plucked eyebrows arched upward. "The what?"

Garcia-Vega searched María's eyes. Perhaps she was not as astute as he thought her to be. He looked at Bobby. "Colonel Gatling, do I not make myself clear?"

"I believe you do, sir."

María placed her hand on her purse. "*Señor* Garcia-Vega, you are way off base."

Garcia-Vega lowered his head as if peering over reading glasses at an unexpected distraction.

"We've chosen a replacement for President Quijano," María continued. "And he *will* be elected. As to *your* candidacy . . . There's a phrase for it back in the States. Maybe you've heard it? Chopped liver."

Garcia-Vega swayed like a pious Jew praying at the Western Wall. He grasped the top of the pew in front of him to steady himself. What was this woman saying? If the Americans were determined to do all in their power to prevent him from winning the presidency, why had they asked to meet with him?

"A deal, you said. What kind of deal?" he asked. Then as if Carlos was whispering in his ear, the woman's intentions became clear. "You think you can buy me off. You think every man has a price. But what is twenty million . . . twenty-*five* million to a man like me?"

María turned to Bobby. "What do you think, Colonel? Does *Señor* Garcia-Vega have a sense of his own worth?"

"*Thirty* million," said Garcia-Vega, leaving no doubt he was a man of principle.

Bobby examined María's eyes.

María opened her purse and withdrew a black iPod.

Garcia-Vega squinted.

"You recognize this?" María asked.

Garcia-Vega made no reply.

"Remind you of someone, maybe?"

"What have you done, *Señora*?" Garcia-Vega asked sotto voce. "Where is Carlos?"

María held the iPod, earbuds attached, aloft. "*This* is Carlos. At least, what remains of the Carlos you once knew."

Garcia-Vega stood as motionless as the crucified Christ in the apse behind him.

"It's all cued up," said María.

Garcia-Vega slipped the earbuds into his ears.

María pressed PLAY.

Garcia-Vega stood rigid and attentive. Then, as if he'd taken a knee in his groin, he collapsed into the pew in front of María and Bobby. The iPod—Carlos' iPod—played the conversation he had held with Carlos and Archbishop Dantón the day before the priest had flown into San Cristo with Bishop Groelsch and Adella. He heard his own voice comment that with Mobys' official presence in San Cristo only weeks away and the Pope's personal blessing imminent, Alonso Quijano would gain strength even in the face of the burgeoning revolution. He noted the archbishop's response, imagining the people's reaction—and the Vatican's—should something happen to the Holy Father's emissaries from Rome and the government prove unable to respond. He contemplated Carlos' resolute assurance that should an incident occur, the *jefe* would save the day as always. The results could only be to their advantage. And he listened to his own proposal that they kidnap the priest—a proposal uttered almost frivolously but then detailed so logically and coherently that it assumed a life of its own.

María held her hand out.

Garcia-Vega hesitantly offered the earbuds to María like a little boy presenting his report card to his mother, his failing grades already revealed.

"Or would you like to keep it?" María asked. "We have copies."

"You blackmailed Carlos," said Garcia-Vega. He looked at Bobby. "You threatened his family. You forced him . . ."

"No, sir," Bobby replied. "That would be unethical and illegal."

"You *murdered* Carlos!"

María shook her head. Her dark, lustrous hair reflected a sudden burst of sunlight streaming in through the cathedral's windows. "Nothing to be gained there. It was all a matter of reaching a mutually satisfactory outcome. A win-win situation."

As if he'd been slapped from behind, Garcia-Vega's head fell forward, his lips slightly parted, his eyes without focus.

"Carlos approached *us*. Us being *me*," said María. "Months ago. We just kind of kept in touch." She held the iPod aloft. "And then *this*."

Garcia-Vega took a deep breath. "Impossible!" he blustered. "Not Carlos!"

María peered into his eyes. "Carlos knew we would offer a reward in response to the kidnapping. He figured the price point, too."

"Price point?" Garcia-Vega asked.

"After the kidnapping, Carlos strung us along until the reward was high enough and the chance of his getting caught was a little too great thanks to Colonel Gatling and Major Kennan. A classic example of risk and reward. And then . . . well . . . we closed the deal."

Garcia-Vega turned and stared at the marble Christ. Suddenly a sense of clarity befell him no less breathtaking than a starry sky viewed from atop Mount Azcalatl during dry season. He pointed his right index finger at María. "It was *you*!" He flexed the finger as if pulling a trigger. "*You* tried to kill me after I spoke at the National Assembly. *You* killed Magdalena Robles."

Bobby jerked his head towards María.

"Honestly, *Señor* Garcia-Vega," María countered, "if I wanted you dead, you'd be dead."

A dull ache worked itself through Bobby's right knee. He attempted to stretch his leg beneath the pew, but the close quarters constrained him.

"In all candor," María cautioned, "It might be more helpful for everyone concerned if you simply acknowledged that someone, identity unknown, tried to send you a message."

Bobby again studied María's eyes. Had she been fooling him? Or had he been fooling himself?

"Regarding the woman who was with you," said María, "a terrible shame. An accident, I'm sure."

"And the priest?" asked Garcia-Vega.

María placed the iPod back in her purse and brushed a wisp of hair away from her face. "So do we have an understanding then?"

Bobby gazed at the marble image of the suffering Jesus who, as everyone knew, had been betrayed by one of those closest to him. Was trust in another human being always destined to be misplaced?

"Fine then," María continued. "We were discussing a price. *Your* price."

Garcia-Vega's nostrils flared with contempt. As always, the capitalists placed a price on everything. Jesús Garcia-Vega was the most important man in San Cristo. *Was*, that was. With the evidence against him securely in the hands of such unprincipled opponents, he held no hope of winning the election. And what would happen to the financial and moral support offered by compatriots like Lenny Birnbaum back in the States? Even revolutionaries in Berkeley—or at least some—were capable of embarrassment. Garcia-Vega's eyes bored into María's. "What is thirty million euros . . ."

"*Three* million. *Dollars*. In an offshore account. Plus a one-bedroom condo in a building Mobys owns in Miami. There's a Mobys store in the lobby. And another by the pool. Take it or leave it."

"This is what you offered Carlos?"

"*Four* bedrooms. Different building. Nicer but not all that much. More cash." She shrugged. "The man *does* have a family. And, oh," added María, "a new iPod."

Garcia-Vega leaped to his feet. "A Viking range top," he declared, his voice forceful and commanding. "Professional series . . . with a grill."

"Already installed. It's a kitchen to die for. And you'll find a bottle of Dom Pérignon in the fridge."

Garcia-Vega bowed his head as if in prayer then raised it. "A provision to protect my investment income from inflation. Perhaps in the form of a small gift deposited to my account each Christmas."

"Done," said María. She reached into her purse and lifted out the iPod, her wallet and her Ruger. "Here," she said, extracting an email printout. "Your boarding pass. It took a little doing, but we were able to make the reservation for you. And it's business class. You leave tonight. Our people will accompany you until Colonel Gatling takes you to the airport. Unless you'd like to attend Mobys' grand opening on Saturday."

Garcia-Vega eyed the doors leading out to Plaza Azcalatl and tugged on his jacket. A man—a serious man—had always to make an impression on those he might encounter as he strolled to his humble apartment or, better, to the bar at the Hotel Azcalatl Grande for drinks and lunch before packing. "Thank you for your invitation, but it will not be necessary."

His footsteps firm and purposeful, Jesús Garcia-Vega strode forward towards a new life and a kitchen filled with possibilities.

María reached back into her purse. "Damn, I forgot," she called out. Her voice echoed throughout the cathedral.

Garcia-Vega halted.

She held up her hand. "Here's a twenty-five dollar gift card. It's good at any Mobys anywhere in the world."

29 | VEINTINUEVE | 29

SOMETHING HARD PRESSED AGAINST Bobby's left cheek. He ran a hand over his pillow and discovered a small square object wrapped in stiff paper. He opened his right eye then his left. A dim stream of light filtering through the not-quite-closed drapes suggested that morning had not progressed much past sunrise. He held the square up and squinted.

"Happy Halloween!" María sang out in a soft, lilting voice in keeping with the early-morning stillness. "It's chocolate from San Francisco. Scharffen Berger. From Berkeley, actually. Well, they make it in Illinois now. I asked Whit to bring some when he flew back yesterday." She leaned over and brushed her lips across his right cheek. "Someone needs a shave," she cooed. "Especially today."

Bobby checked the digital clock on his nightstand. "You going for a run?"

"The gym. Yoga. Maybe the elliptical."

Bobby turned on his lamp, cast an appreciative glance at the chocolate and placed it on the nightstand. Looking up, he examined María in black tights and a pink sleeveless t-shirt bearing the words, DANCERS ARE ON THEIR TOES.

"Join me?" she asked.

"Maybe when the grand opening's done later I'll get some weight work in."

"Well, don't sleep too late. I'll have breakfast sent up when I get back. Whit expects us in the lobby at ten sharp."

Bobby rubbed his eyes.

"You got up last night," said María. "Twice."

"Sorry. Didn't mean to wake you." He scratched the whiskers under his chin.

María sat at the edge of the bed. "You've been thinking about things."

Bobby sensed that María wanted to engage in a heart-to-heart. Unfortunately, he'd never been much good with talks. "Things?"

"Things. As in men always hold things in. They hold things in and get quieter and quieter until they explode. It's not healthy."

Bobby flexed his ankles.

"*Two* things," María said. "Number one . . . us."

"Us?"

María stood, held her arms out parallel to the floor and rolled them in tight circles. "You visiting me in San Francisco after seeing your son. You still want to, don't you?"

Bobby clutched at the blanket as if it were a life ring buoy. "You bet. I'll be there."

Those, of course, were words. Not that he didn't mean them. But still, he felt like maybe they were pushing things. He and María had spent a few great days and nights together—the nights in particular—since returning to Ciudad San Cristo. Tonight they'd all fly to San Francisco. Tomorrow he'd drive up to Sacramento to see Bobby, Jr. and Kimberly, and start mending fences. It would be awkward to some extent, but he'd committed himself.

On the other hand, he wasn't at all certain that staying with María in San Francisco was such a smart idea. Fate—if there was such a thing—had thrown them together. People away from home and under stress reached out to each other. Call it the life force if you wanted. But if he spent even a few days with María in her home—and her daughter—both living their regular lives, would everything be different? Not just a little but radically? Was María capable of having a man in her life?

And more honestly, was he capable of a relationship with María—or any woman for that matter? All the years he'd spent alone had defined home as little more than a place to pass evenings attempting to write an article he might actually sell or cocooned in an alcoholic haze until the next assignment came through. And anyway, what exactly *was* a relationship? What did she expect? And if things seemed to be working out with María, what would happen when he went back to Virginia Beach? And then when the next call came from Alexandria? Unless he turned his life in a different direction—devoted all his energy to writing or maybe entered a doctoral program so he could teach—he'd go back to leaving any traditional sense of home and anyone important to him far behind.

María closed her eyes and rotated her head. "So there's no problem. Unless it's number two."

Bobby released the blanket and ran his hands down his cheeks. There was no running from issue number two—by far the tougher one. After thirty years of helping to protect the USofA from its many and varied enemies, he'd gladly accepted the generous pay and benefits offered by Crimmins-Idyll. But he'd come to understand that while the company called its employees contractors, they really were just mercenaries—soldiers of fortune. No matter that Crimmins-Idyll operated under a variety of legal umbrellas. He, like Kennan and all the rest, pocketed what to a lesser or greater degree was blood money. At least in that regard, Bobby Gatling was an open book. What gnawed at him was that María was all secrets—Salomé removing one of her seven veils to draw him in while remaining in hiding beneath the other six.

As if she was a fortune-teller reading his thoughts, María leaned closer. "You really think I put those two rounds behind Father Giovanni's left ear, don't you?"

Bobby bolted upright. "How do you know that? The location of the kill shots? And the number?"

María, her expression unchanged, placed her index finger on Bobby's lips. "Knowing things is what Whitman Scharq pays me for. Just as I know that you're wondering whether I killed Father Giovanni to embarrass Alonso Quijano so Cristano politics would get rid of him for us and leave our hands clean."

"Should I ask?"

"Jesús Garcia-Vega and every leftist from here to the highlands had all the motivation in the world to kill the priest. He turned into a political target the moment he was kidnapped." She withdrew her finger. "But Bobby, even if I *did* kill Father Giovanni, why should that change anything between us?"

Bobby placed his right palm gently on María's cheek. He'd have to figure out whether he and María saw things too differently. *Were* too different. But if he was really going to be honest, he'd have to ask himself what María could have done that was any worse than some of the things he'd done? And more than that—much more—he'd have to admit that he wasn't at all concerned that he and María were too different. What worried him was that they were all too much alike.

Bobby stepped outside the Hotel Azcalatl Grande just ahead of Whitman Scharq and María. Two Crimmins-Idyll men in loose-fitting white shirts followed. The mid-morning sun shone brilliantly, creating a sky of intense blue untainted by the faintest suggestion of clouds. According to the television, this would be the first October thirty-first in the recorded history of Ciudad San Cristo without a trace of precipitation.

"Even the weather loves Mobys," Scharq sang out. "Nature knows when it's met its match."

"Mocha, this is Latte," Bobby called into his radio headset. "Espresso's being poured."

"Should go down smooth, *amigo*," responded Juan Suelo, returned to duty, if still experiencing a degree of discomfort and seated in a command post in a corner office atop the Banco Colón building. The vantage point enabled him to observe armed riot police and casually dressed undercover men along the short route Whitman Scharq would stroll to the new Mobys. If required, *Seguridad* and police would quickly roust the small knot of protestors led by Archbishop Dantón parading with large signs near the front of the store.

Scharq took María by the arm and clapped Bobby on the back.

Bobby kept his attention on the pedestrians swarming past the luxury shops and smart cafés on Avenida Londres. He wondered how many would follow shortly to be able to say that they were there on the day Mobys made history in San Cristo. Bobby knew that a vast crowd already had gathered to glimpse the dignitaries attending the grand opening ceremonies, including a Cristano actress who made movies in Mexico City. If all went as planned, the event would begin in another twenty-eight minutes.

The walk itself, if uninterrupted, would get them to the store early enough for Scharq to spend sufficient time playing the jovial host. At precisely ten-thirty, he would extend a brief welcome to the American Ambassador and present him with a four-foot-high Mobys mug made of lightweight plastic foam. Then the candidate chosen to replace Alonso Quijano—whose own invitation had been withdrawn—would assist Scharq in cutting a three-foot-wide red ribbon and tighten the knot securing San Cristo, Mobys and the United States to each other.

"Whit, what time did you say we're flying out?" María asked.

"Eight," Scharq answered as he strode like a victorious Caesar making his way through the Forum to accept the well-earned adulation of Rome. "We'll have dinner onboard."

Bobby's eyes swept the sidewalk and street ahead. He'd planned to have a squad of *Seguridad* men lead the way, but Scharq had rejected the idea. Why provide the revolutionaries with any sign of fear? If the recovering Colonel Suelo did his job, the local people would duly note the obvious yet restrained presence of security personnel. Heavy-handed displays of force, Scharq maintained, never won over hearts, minds or taste buds—as long as they could be avoided. Besides, a video or photo of Scharq behind a massive team of armed men could make him look foolish. He remembered the way John McCain came across after visiting a market in Baghdad with a huge military escort and telling the media how much security in Iraq had improved. No, everything was under control. The grand opening would go off as smooth as a baby's butt.

"Might just get a run in later," María chirped.

Arriving at the corner, Bobby peered left then right along Avenida Plaza Azcalatl. Two blocks away, the new Mobys store occupied the lower floors of its newly completed four-story building looking down on the plaza. Mobys would house its San Cristo offices on the third floor and lease the fourth.

His attention shifted halfway down the block towards the intersection at Avenida Colón. His gaze stopped on a woman in a purple blouse and purple mini skirt, her left hand clamped down on a purple sunhat, galloping towards them.

Bobby stepped in front of Scharq and reached for the handle of his Beretta.

The woman drew closer.

As if part of a circus act, two men in civilian clothes emerged from the crowd and hoisted her by her armpits. The woman's legs churned furiously as she floated above the sidewalk.

"*¡Hijos de puta*!" Adella bellowed. Sons of bitches! "Mr. Scharq! Mr. Scharq!" she called.

"It's the Italian reporter," María informed Bobby.

Bobby removed his hand from his weapon and signaled to the men.

Adella glowered at María, cast a lingering glance at Bobby then grabbed Scharq's free arm. "Mr. Scharq . . ."

"Adella Rozen," María whispered in Scharq's ear. "The Italian . . ."

"Got it," Scharq replied. He looked pensively at Adella. Perhaps they might have a drink before his plane left. Perhaps the plane might depart a little late. It was *his* jet.

"Where," asked Adella as they walked slowly, "is Major Khan?"

Scharq waggled his head from side to side to loosen the persistent tightness in his neck and shoulders. "Major Khan has gone back to California."

"Really?" asked Adella. She shrugged. Khan had failed to inform her he was leaving but so be it. She sought to unravel a bigger mystery. Where was Jesús Garcia-Vega? And where was Carlos? Why had he not returned to the capital?

The light at Avenida Colón turned red.

Three uniformed officers halted traffic and waved Scharq across.

Scharq stopped on the far corner. "Listen, Ms. Rozen. Our new store is just down at the end of the block. Let's make this quick. Maybe I can buy you an espresso a little later and tell you about the history of coffee. It's fascinating."

Adella glowered. An American had the gall to preach to an Italian about coffee? "*Mazel tov!*" she muttered.

Scharq turned to María. "Do you have a gift card for Ms. Rozen?"

Bobby stepped closer. "Ms. Rozen, we have a tight schedule."

Adella positioned her purse primly in front of her skirt and raised her chin. "Then shoot me, Colonel Gatling. As perhaps you shot the sainted Father Giovanni. I give my life gladly as a martyr in the name of justice."

Scharq walked on.

Adella caught up.

Scharq halted.

A nearby dog barked loudly. Another joined in.

María squeezed Adella's arm. "I think, Ms. Rozen, that will be all."

"You are hurting me!" cried Adella.

María smiled. "Then we understand each other."

A low rumble sounded up and down the street.

Scharq cocked his head.

Bobby, María and Adella did likewise.

The rumble grew into a grinding sound like that of hundreds then thousands of feet stomping rhythmically on the pavement.

Scharq grabbed a lamppost.

Adella ran to the curb.

The rumble grew louder still.

Traffic lights swung from their mountings.

Brakes squealed.

Plate-glass windows flexed, distorting the reflections they cast like mirrors in a carnival fun house.

Men and women, elbows flying, tumbled out of shops.

Bobby pried Scharq off the lamppost and out into the street.

The sidewalk undulated beneath their feet.

"You remember the Loma Prieta quake in '89?" María called out.

Half a block ahead, the crowd in front of Mobys stumbled towards the open space of Plaza Azcalatl. Men and women gawked as the tops of office towers swayed like metronomes. Others stared at the plaza's center where the fountain of *las tres señoritas* threatened to topple.

The rumbling softened.

The ground firmed.

The buildings became inert.

The fountain stilled.

An unearthly silence engulfed Ciudad San Cristo as if the city was an old phonograph that had played a record at the wrong speed until an unseen hand pulled the plug.

Adella approached Scharq. "Did the earth move for you, too?"

"The store!" Scharq bellowed.

María sprinted ahead.

Bobby trotted forward with Scharq, his knee assaulted by the unyielding concrete.

Adella followed. The brim of her sunhat flapped rhythmically like the wings of the mythical azcalatl.

María stopped in front of the store and raised her hand to her mouth.

Scharq halted fifty feet away. His chest heaved. The air entering and escaping his lungs sounded like the discordant music of a broken accordion. He bent over, braced his hands on his thighs and shook his head.

Only a rubble-filled shell remained of the Mobys building.

Ignoring the risk of aftershocks, a dozen *Seguridad* agents and a matching number of bystanders tugged at chunks of concrete.

Sirens wailed.

Adella thrust her micro recorder into the face of one of the police.

Scharq collapsed to his knees.

María gripped the arm of a middle-aged barista attempting to comfort two teen-age employees among a knot of uniformed Mobys personnel filling the street. "*¿Quién está en el edificio?*" she barked. Who is in the building?

The barista made no response.

An ambulance arrived.

A fire truck followed.

A chorus of sirens signaled that additional help was on the way.

Archbishop Dantón, refusing to be led away by one of the protestors, repeatedly made the sign of the cross as if he were both cursing the fallen building and blessing those who perished within it.

Bobby hoisted Scharq to his feet. He would have preferred to join the would-be rescuers, but that would leave Scharq vulnerable in the confusion. His job was to stay with the man who paid him.

"Jesus!" Scharq sputtered.

Bobby swiveled his head.

On every side of the plaza, buildings stood virtually undamaged. The Banco Colón building to his left. The National Cathedral to his right. The soaring Banco Azcalatl tower across the street from the Presidential Palace. The earthquake had spared them all. In the center of Plaza Azcalatl, the waters of the fountain of *las tres señoritas* glistened in the sunlight as they continued their playful splashing.

María seized Scharq's right elbow. "Whit, it'll take hours before we can figure out how many of our people are in there. Maybe days."

"Send flowers. Money, too. Enough but not too much. And call our lawyers in San Francisco. We're gonna sue the architects, the engineers, the contractor . . . anyone we can think of . . . up the ass. I want everyone's insurance company writing checks."

"Let's get you back to the hotel," María coaxed. "Bobby will take you. I'll wait here."

"I'm fine," Scharq responded. He brushed his hands across his slacks. Small puffs of grit burst into the air.

Adella approached at a run, her recorder raised like the sword of a centurion leading his legionnaires against the barbarian hoard.

Scharq tightened the knot in his tie and ran a hand over his suit coat. "It's just a little setback. We'll rebuild. Nothing can stop progress."

"Whit," María urged. "We really have to get you back."

Scharq checked his watch. It was ten-thirty on the dot. "I'm starving. Should have eaten breakfast. Too excited. Like a kid. I could go for . . . I don't know . . . pancakes and eggs. Maybe a steak with that. Definitely a steak. I could whip something up, but I can't wait. We'll call ahead for room service."

Adella spotted her camera crew and ran off, her steps quick and light. The day held untold promise.

María took Bobby's hand. "It's essential that Whit flies back tonight as planned. You, too. Our local people here can handle things, but I'll stay a few days. Show the flag."

"Right," Bobby said. "You should."

"Could be a week. Think you might be in Sacramento that long?"

"I'm not sure how long Bobby, Jr. and Kimberly'll want me around. She's kept the baby, but she needs a lot of rest. And my ex . . ."

"No need to tell me about mothers wanting to be around their kids when there's a problem."

Bobby squeezed María's hand. Seeing again how tenuous life was, it was nice to think that she'd be waiting for him in San Francisco. Sure, there were risks involved. But how many shots at happiness did you get in life? How many shots did he have left? Maybe their hands stayed clasped because they both had blood on them. Maybe happiness—real, lasting happiness—came with a price.

María squeezed his hand, slipped hers away and rose on her toes.

Bobby bent over.

Their lips touched, lingered then separated.

María drew away. "Work to do."

Bobby watched her trot off to the rescue effort.

"So what do you say to a big ol' American breakfast, Colonel?" Scharq asked. "Goddam, I'm hungry!"

Bobby slipped his hand into his pocket and withdrew the chocolate María had given him. "Here you go, sir."

Scharq took the gift, tore apart the wrapper and crammed the chocolate into his mouth.

Bobby studied Scharq's face. He saw not the visage of a powerful man but that of an anxious boy whistling in the dark.

Scharq clapped his hands together and held his palms in a position of prayer. "Man to man, Colonel, what do you think?"

Bobby surveyed the pile of rubble marked by a roiling cloud of dust and teeming with would-be rescuers. The phrase from the Psalm came to him: "Yea, though I walk through the valley of the shadow of death . . ." How often he had walked that valley. And yet the weeks to come offered so many possibilities to renew life. How was he—how was anyone—expected to make sense of it all? He turned back to Scharq. "I guess this gives a whole new meaning to 'trick or treat.'"